A HEMLOCK LATTE

Copyright © 2024 Muller Davis

All rights reserved.

No part of this publication may be reproduced or transmitted in any form or by any means electronic or mechanical, including photocopy, recording, or any information storage and retrieval system now known or invented, without permission in writing from the publisher, except by a reviewer who wishes to quote brief passages in connection with a review written for inclusion in a magazine, newspaper, or broadcast.

Print ISBN: 978-1-73362-701-6
eBook ISBN: 978-1-73362-702-3

First Printing, 2024

www.monkeymonkeylove.com
muller@monkeymonkeylove.com

Printed in the United States of America

For all those who don't fit
And for my brother too

Freshman English

STUDENTS		1st WEEK	2nd WEEK	3rd WEEK	4th WEEK
		M T W T F	M T W T F	M T W T F	M T W T F
Jesus Garcia — Out of Gas ~~IIII~~ II		✓✓✓ ✓	✓✓✓✓	✓✓ ✓	✓✓ ✓
Nathan Garcia — "I hate you" Class leader?		✓✓✓✓	✓✓ ✓	✓ ✓	✓ ✓
George (Jorge) Gutierrez — Ears / gang signs		✓✓✓✓	✓✓✓✓	✓ ✓	✓ ✓
Robertson Sandoval — gloves-burns? Couch surfing?		✓ ✓ ✓ ✓	✓ ✓ ✓ ✓	✓ ✓	✓ ✓
Clarissa Sosa — Tomboy		✓✓✓✓	✓✓✓✓	✓ ✓✓	✓ ✓
Carl Stevens — Red → true danger? Black?		✓✓✓✓	✓✓✓✓	✓✓✓	✓✓✓
Lissa Trevino		✓✓✓✓	✓ ✓✓	✓✓✓	✓✓✓
Amanda Vernet		✓✓✓✓	✓ ✓✓	✓✓✓	✓✓✓
Alex Rudolph → The Mouth			✓✓✓ ✓✓✓	✓✓✓	
Archie Gordon — Parole Officer 505-234-7691					✓✓✓

The Poets

Isabel Vasquez
Lori Perez
Perry Serrano
Sammy Anderson — shouting another poem!
Tiffany Rodriguez
Drew Gonzales
Ned Loeb — Cool-as-ice
Peter Wallace — Creeping Ghost

Mr. Gabriel Abrams

A steady edge of sunlight pierced through the wide window. On the first day of school a breeze slipped in but couldn't sweep away the aroma of detergent that had been used to scrub the classroom clean. The students stared at their new teacher—this oddity—with his untucked shirt and messy black hair pointing skyward. He stood perched at the front of the room ready to say something, yet saying nothing.

New to the teaching profession, the teacher swallowed a mouthful of saliva that barely forged its way down his throat. He inhaled the chemical detergent aroma that burned in his nose, sunk down into his stomach, and burned there too. This was how he imagined teaching would be: a classroom filled with young students poised to ingest his every syllable—he just never imagined freezing up.

He had planned on what to say. For at least a year, he knew exactly what he would say on that first day. No introductions. No meet and greet. Just down to the foundation of what the students needed to know now.

He swallowed his twisted gob down his resistant throat, and a word dribbled out:

"Be ..."

Someone giggled.

"Be," the teacher repeated, this time raising his palms with his fingers outstretched. "Be happy with who you are."

More giggles. But the teacher had gained momentum.

"Be happy with who you are because you can be nobody else. You are yourself, you can't trade yourself in. You can't make yourself vanish."

He prowled around the room and the students twisted in their seats to watch him.

"I don't know what I can teach you, what you can learn, but this truth you can't make go away. Be happy with who you are, be ecstatic with who you are, be inspired and do amazing things with what you were given on the day you were born."

Words spiraled out of his mouth. His nervousness melted away in a lubricated flow of the exact ideas of his life articulated. He could spin no bad phrase, he burned with perfection. And this without a script, with only a desire to be a fire-breathing perfect picture of what a teacher could be—*should be*. In that moment he was the embodiment. He was Adam. He was Aristotle. He was Dionysus. Beowulf. Alexander the Great. Bruce Lee.

Satisfied, he stood in the back corner of the classroom, his energy settling into dramatic waves around him. His voice grew as soft as a cloud, and the students leaned in closer.

"This is it, this is your life. It has begun."

The teacher's head drifted down, his chin almost touching his chest.

This was the moment when the applause should burst up off the audience.

But the teacher smelt smoke. He looked over and saw a student with a Bic lighter clandestinely setting fire to another student's shoelace.

When the New Mexico State Highway Patrol called, I was watching TV, flicking through five hundred channels of nothing. The state trooper claimed they had found my brother's car abandoned in the lava tubes parking lot in Grants, New Mexico. My brother might be dead, the trooper suggested, though there were tell-all signs of an intentional vehicular abandonment. No perishables in the car. No regular stuff like a knife or a sunglass case or coins. No water. Little gas. The car seemed cleaned out, zipped up, intentionally forsaken. In the lava tubes, they don't send out search parties for missing hikers without permits, he said, because these caves, made a million years ago from retreating lava that are hundreds of miles long, tend to collapse in on themselves and no one ever knows. In one of the uncharted underground passageways, a ceiling falls and it affects not one soul; no one ever notices. It happens all the time. This fact makes the lava tubes a perfect place for fleeing individuals to ditch their vehicles, which might not be noticed for several days, and the authorities figure they were lost in a collapsed cave. No search. No record. No body.

"Do you know how many people used 9-11 as an opportunity to fake their own deaths?" The full voice on the other end of the phone commanded authority. "Did your brother have any reason to flee his life—a bad marriage, a thing for exotic lands, criminal activity, trouble at work? It says here he was a teacher."

I could see my brother shirking all responsibility in a desperate attempt to cling to his past shreds of freedom, to his glory days as a finely tuned and tanned man/child skittering the globe in search of adventure. Gabriel had finally settled down with a real job. And as a teacher! Our mother's endless hole of worry in regards to Gabriel's well-being had begun to dissipate. But no more. Here you go mom—open wide, here comes more stress. Gabriel's off again. And this time he's leaving in the lurch a classroom crammed with eager students. Maybe he'll call, maybe he won't. Maybe he'll drop us one of his cryptic postcards, maybe we won't hear from him for a year. Or two. Or five. I can see him lounging on a beach in southern Thailand, sipping a banana lassi, smoking a local dubber, chattering up the young hotties as if he were the king of the expats—going by some nickname like Saddhu or Slate or Pineapple or by nothing at all. Just dude. Mystery dude.

Asshole.

Typical Gabriel.

Maybe rummaging for adventure he's dropped himself in the middle of some South American rainforest in order to fight his way out. Maybe without a dime he flew to Buenos Aires. So often I've heard his diatribe about how one of the worst aspects of our isolated society is our lack of need to learn another language. In India, he's said, even the illiterate speak three languages as opposed to an American with a PhD who knows only English and an *hola* or two.

Twenty-seven years old, knowing only English, teaching at a school where many of the families came from Spanish backgrounds and some spoke only Spanish, Gabriel felt ill-equipped. Los Pinos High School had few Spanish-speaking teachers, and the administration encouraged none of their teachers to learn Spanish; in fact, when Gabriel was hired, they didn't even ask if he spoke Spanish.

Lacking the gift of a second (or third) language, Gabriel felt the best way he could learn another language—the only way, he feared—was to be dumped somewhere where he had no friends, no money, where no one spoke English, and from where he could not escape. Learn to communicate or starve.

If Gabriel split town—leaving his first real job incomplete, leaving his students with a string of disconnected substitutes—I don't know where he would go. Maybe back to India, not just to blow his mind on so different a culture, but to blow his spirit in some desperate attempt to lose himself, his culture, his family, his friends, his brother.

"Write a motto for your life," Gabriel said to his class on the second day of school.

When Gabriel discovered himself as a teacher, all his arrogance gained purpose and weight. He had thought he had found his calling before, but when he started teaching he knew—he knew like the bright sun in the morning can promise a perfect day. The warmth filled in where he hadn't known he was cold, and when it hit it elevated him.

"Write a motto for your life," he repeated, pointing to the dry erase board where he had written the same.

No one was writing. Nothing but bulking bags—book bags and backpacks and purses—sat on the desktops.

Gabriel glared at a girl in the front. "Take your purse off your desk."

And she did.

"Take your packs off your desks."

And they did.

"Now take out your notebooks, take out your pencils, take out your pens."

"I don't have a notebook."

"I don't have a pen."

The chorus rose up like a swell.

"I don't have a pencil."

"I don't have a notebook."

"Borrow one, borrow some, tear sheets in half." Gabriel pranced around the room. "Use a pen, use each other's pens, use your blood. Write a motto for your life and write it from your soul—"

"What's a motto?"

Gabriel stopped. He glanced at the girl who was staring up over her round glasses.

"A motto," Gabriel began, now pausing, thinking. In his belly the butterflies fluttered anew. What *is* a motto? He glanced around at the anxious faces. He swallowed. His second day as a teacher and he stumbled.

"A motto is something ... a motto is—let's look it up."

Gabriel went for the red Webster's Dictionary. He flicked it open and landed on the right page.

"'Motto: a short saying that expresses a rule to live by.' Perfect."

"I don't get it."

"What don't you get?"

"We have to make one up?"

"That's right."

"I don't understand."

"It's a saying that defines you, that you live by, that, that—"

"What's yours?" the girl with the round glasses asked.

Butterflies like nettles in his belly. In preparing Gabriel had concerned himself with what to ask the students, never imagining that they wouldn't know what a motto was and never considering being asked to give his own.

No worries though, for Gabriel had spent years doing improvisational theater, where a funny, made-up line of dialog would skip his head and drop right onto his tongue. So Gabriel paused, waiting. His lips were perched, ready to deliver a few words that would ease together into a poetic, thoughtful motto. But nothing appeared. Only dread. The class was silent, staring. In his head a horrible image glistened. He saw himself as the worst teacher ever, he saw himself as Mr. Bloodwell, his greasy-haired high school chemistry teacher. Gabriel shuddered at the thought. He wanted to be nothing like Mr. Bloodwell, yet in that moment he imagined himself as Mr. Bloodwell. Gabriel craved experiences—good ones as well as awful ones. Every emotion, every adventure, every disappointment was part of that big mess of Gabriel's life—and he wanted to feel it all, he wanted to experience it all. It inspired him. And there it was—

"Experience," Gabriel said, which sounded great, but he needed a few more words, for this was a model for his students, and from them he wanted more than a single word.

He stepped forward, head back, eyes squinting—"Experience life as an adventure."

And there it was—his motto—spinning out in the open. Gabriel felt the words weaving around the room like a curl of smoke. There was silence and Gabriel accepted it as if it were a hovering bubble of awe.

"That's a motto?" a boy in the back asked.

"Yes, that's a motto."

"I don't get it."

"Using ten words or less describe your life, telling what is most important to you, what code you live by."

"I don't get it."

"Me neither."

"Live like an eagle soaring, sow like mad, preach from a stage to change the world, fall into a hole and find myself." Gabriel sprang around the room coaxing and cajoling and encouraging. "What do you do—what do you want to do—what can you not live without? Come on, what is it? Think it, believe it, live it! Now write it."

"I don't get it."

"Me neither."

"This is stupid."

Undeterred, Gabriel leapt around the room—"Who are you? What are you? Why are you? What's the most important thing to you?"

With fiery eyes, Gabriel dropped to a knee in front of a student who sat gnawing her fingers, and his whirlwind came to a halt.

He breathed, "If you didn't have to be here, what would you be doing?"

The student looked at Gabriel. She smiled, glanced down, and started to write.

Gabriel had planned twelve minutes for the mottos, but when the bell rang ending class they still hadn't finished. Sweating Gabriel felt as if he had run a marathon yet he had most of the rest of the day to go.

In his second period class—

"I don't get it."

"Me neither."

"This is stupid."

In all of Gabriel's freshmen classes, this seemed to be the default mode.

Third period—

"I don't get it."

"Me neither."

"This is stupid."

The students remained rough; it was Gabriel who grew smooth. After he stumbled when asked what his motto was in his first period, Gabriel, in his subsequent classes, would pause when asked as if thinking up a motto on the spot, and, while wholly manufactured—"Experience life as an adventure!"—it was no less convincing.

But still—

"I don't get it."

"Me neither."

"This is stupid."

Some of Gabriel's students did try and that in itself was an achievement, yet Gabriel was unaware of the victory, for he had grand ambitions. 'Coach bags rule' and 'Bitch on my tip' seemed like failed mottos. Maybe Gabriel had hoped for them all to have written 'Save the world'.

"Live like a sand dog," a tall girl in the back of Gabriel's third period said smiling.

"Okay, good. Next."

"I don't know," the student said.

"At least give it a try," Gabriel said.

"No, 'I don't know'—that's my motto."

"Oh, okay, good."

The next boy shrugged.

Gabriel asked, "Did you write something?"

The boy shrugged again, and when he did his enormous ears twitched.

Gabriel glanced down at his empty notebook. "No? Nothing? What's your name?"

Like a turtle struggling to raise his head the student shrugged again.

Gabriel shuttled to the podium where he glanced at his class list and found a name that might be his.

"George," Gabriel said, moving back towards the boy.

"It's Jorge." Jorge pronounced his name in Spanish with a soft 'J' and a soft 'G'.

"Okay Jorge, what's your motto?"

Jorge shrugged again—almost too cool, probably nervous in front of the class.

"Come on, what's your motto."

"I don't have one," Jorge said.

"What do you live by?"

"I don't know."

"Why don't you know?"

"'Cause I don't."

"Why?"

"'Cause I don't."

"Give it a try."

"I don't have to do nothing."

"Well that's certainly something."

Jorge crossed his arms, swallowing down a smile.

*A*loud to his freshmen Language Arts students in his first, second, and third periods, Gabriel chose to read a Hermann Hesse short story, "The Poet," because the protagonist gives up everything for what he believes.

Before deciding to become a teacher, Gabriel had been sure he was destined to be famous. He had figured when he became a movie star he would then go about saving the world with all the royal power that accompanies that position. He had moved to Hollywood and after a solid month of auditions he realized thinking about saving the world wasn't enough. He needed to actualize it on a daily basis and with the bulk of his energy, and going from one demoralizing audition to another wasn't helping anyone. Even though his whole life he had dreamed of being a celebrated actor,

Gabriel, just like that, let go. He wouldn't need his face to grace silver screens and billboards and be plastered across social media; he wouldn't need to be noticed and exalted in every coffee depot on the planet. It wasn't so much him giving up his cinematic ambitions as him chipping away at a blemished façade in search of his real purpose.

Yet he would never lose his theatrical flair; it would become his most striking teacherly quality.

With the photocopied text of "The Poet" in front of each student, Gabriel took a steady breath.

And then he read aloud: "'The story is told of the Chinese poet Han Fook that from early youth he was animated by the intense desire to learn all about the poet's art …'"

Han Fook is to be married but he meets a sage poet who invites him to study with him in the far-off mountains. Han Fook asks his father if he will allow him to postpone the wedding, and his father gives him a year.

As Gabriel read he floated around the classroom and the students were silent, listening, some turning to watch as he moved behind them. The story had no gunshots, no murders, little intrigue, but because of the way Gabriel delivered Hesse's dazzling words, growing quiet with enunciation, the students leaned in to hear every sound.

Han Fook never returns to his life. One morning he awakes and his master has vanished. The seasons seemed to have changed overnight. He descends the mountain to his old village and discovers that his father and his bride, in fact all his relations, have died, and strangers now live in their houses.

Gabriel hovered in back, letting the silence settle.

"How many years do you think passed from the beginning of the story to the end?"

No one answered. Gabriel moved to the center of the room. He addressed a specific student.

"I don't know," she said. "Twenty?"

"Twenty—okay. Anybody else?"

"Can I go to the bathroom?"

"Fine. Anybody else?"

"I have to go too."

"No, I mean how many years passed?"

"Thirty."

"Ten."

"Fifty," a boy shouted from the back.

"How about a hundred and fifty," Gabriel said. "How about two hundred and fifty."

"Everyone did greet him as an old man."

"Han Fook became the Poet!" a student said, bristling with excitement.

Sentence after sentence, comment after comment, an exchange of an idea from teacher to student to student to teacher to student, the bell ringing, class after class, swept up in the gathered momentum, Gabriel taught without the interference of his brain. He moved forward, reading the story, leading the discussion, encouraging students without his thoughts disturbing him. He was on autopilot. No, not autopilot, for auto-pilot suggests a state of absence. Gabriel's mind-set was just the opposite. He was ultra-aware. He interacted without considering how he was doing. He thought of nothing—only the present instant: a student's expression, a student's response, a Hermann Hesse sentence. Not even a sentence—a single word—'lute'. Gabriel spun around and drew a pair-shaped guitar-like instrument on the board and then was back in the story. The classroom was electrified with implication. It felt like grace. Every word he said, every question he asked, every inflection in his voice seemed to be the perfect pitch. The brain has a tendency to censor itself, second-guess itself; wanting to be just right, the brain pauses for a split-second missing its cue. Gabriel skipped that neurosis, ran on instinct, and taught like a master.

"What was Hon Fook's motto? What did he give up to live it? What are you willing to give up to live your motto?"

Gabriel may have been getting the wrong impression. For him the first week was a challenge—but not a catastrophe. His awkward freshmen students, net yet comfortable, had almost been polite as they stumbled around the strange new environment of this vast high school.

At the beginning of the second week, as if cushioned from all unpleasantries, Gabriel strolled out the door for lunch outside somewhere in the sun. In the hall he spotted a short, round student who hadn't rushed from the building to the cafeteria with all the other students. He looked tormented. Gabriel thought to relay a joke or a smile to elevate him, but as he approached he noticed two other boys around the corner moving away.

"... over fatty fuck!"

"Yeah ya fat fuck—"

Gabriel's appearance hastened the bullies' departure.

When the taunted student turned towards Gabriel—and saw him—he pulled back a full-sized sob like a hiccup. The kid's face was heavy and sodden. He looked up at Gabriel, but before Gabriel could speak, the kid hurried away, down the hall, out the door.

On the ground where the kid last stood, Gabriel noticed a cushioned pair of headphones. He bent down to pick them up.

The next day this same, round kid shuffled into Gabriel's third period.

"I'm supposed to be in this class," he said, handing Gabriel a pink admission slip.

"Great. Take a seat."

Later, as he swept past, Gabriel set the headphones on the kid's desk.

"These aren't mine!" The kid pushed the headphones to the floor.

Gabriel paused, perplexed.

The student next to him laughed, and the round kid took notice and sat back satisfied as the rest of the class peeked up to see.

Gabriel had not anticipated such a reaction. He was sure the headphones were his. He had expected the kid to break out in a huge grin realizing that someone was looking out for him.

Gabriel bent down and scooped up the headphones.

"Yeaah," the round kid challenged under his breath and his neighbor laughed again.

Puzzled, Gabriel stood up in front of him, looking down upon him, not trying to intimidate at all, but ... amazed.

And shocked.

And the kid started laughing, his big body rolling, sitting back in his chair, laughing and pointing his finger at Gabriel.

A primal sense of embarrassment welled up in Gabriel's throat. There is no class in Teacher College that prepares a future teacher for this moment. As the kid laughed and pointed, other students started laughing, and a chill shuddered up Gabriel's spine. I've had this dream where I go to school having forgotten my pants. It's a common dream. There's this moment in the dream when you realize you have no pants and everybody in the auditorium is looking at you. This was Gabriel, and the moment even felt dreamlike: all his tiny body hairs tingling, these bright bouncy faces bobbing in front of him, and the sound of mocking laughter growing slower and slower as if morphed by a hidden technician. Even his own voice came out as if through a foreign sound system:

"Take out a piece of paper. Everyone take out a piece of paper."

"A piece of paper?" Laughter boomed out of the round kid like bursts of gas. "A piece of paper!"

"Take out your notebook, a pen, a pencil—whatever you got."

"I got crabs—" A spasm of laughter from the class. "What do you got?"

"Do the Do Now now," Gabriel said.

"Do the Do Now now now now."

"Do do do now now now," another student joined in.

"Let's go, take out your notebooks and do the Do Now."

"Love is for losers," Jorge sneered.

The Do Now on the board asked the students to define love.

"Losers," Jorge repeated, his ears twitching.

"Yeah, losers," the round kid with his big mouth said.

Gabriel moved towards Jorge.

"You don't love your family?"

"No."

"No girlfriend?"

"Plenty, but I don't love 'em," Jorge said, turning to his friends for a braggart's laugh, and the round kid laughed loudest.

Gabriel turned back to the class. "Come on guys, do the Do Now."

"Do de de."

"Please."

"De de do."

"Stop!"

"Do do do."

"Stop! Now!"

"La la la."

In the classroom a car crash—Gabriel had been cruising along admiring the mountains when from nowhere a truck slammed into him.

Creatures test boundaries. It's instinct. If thrown into an unfamiliar yard, students, especially freshmen, will sit in shock at first, but eventually they'll start sniffing around, nudging the far reaches of the boundary. And it starts with great subtlety. A student whispers while the teacher addresses the class, yet, because it's not quite interrupting, the new teacher continues without reprimanding the student. The next time the student won't be whispering: she'll be talking. And if her activities continue unchecked, soon she'll be chomping on her gum, curling up her hair, arguing on her cellphone all while the teacher's teaching.

A week before on the second day in his second period class, two girls quietly whispered to each other. Amanda and Lissa, Siamese-twin-like friends, seemed to need to converse as if that were how they procured their oxygen. When Gabriel finally asked them to please be quiet, they were so polite.

"We're sorry, we're so sorry," they said.

And Gabriel could tell they were.

But within three minutes they were talking again.

Gabriel asked them to stop, and once more—perfectly portrayed attrition: "We're sorry, we're sorry, we're so sorry."

Gabriel couldn't help but to believe them a second time.

Yet within a minute they were talking again, but the end of class was near and Gabriel wanted to finish the mottos, so, letting them continue to talk, he ignored them, pushed through, and the bell rang.

Amanda and Lissa would never unlearn that moment. And neither would the other students. Mr. Abrams had 'allowed' them to talk.

And now under the onslaught of a tidal wave of rudeness, Gabriel tried to get his students to read their Do Nows, but every time he was close—

"Love is for losers," Jorge would say, and from across the room the round kid, who was fast becoming known to Gabriel as the Mouth, would laugh.

Gabriel's third period was the first to burst.

"Please! Let her finish," Gabriel said. "Go ahead."

"I think," the girl said, "in everything there is love."

"Loser," Jorge said.

"Loser," the Mouth echoed.

"What a loser," another student said.

"Stop! Now! Have some respect. Please," Gabriel said.

"Loser," Jorge coughed beneath his breath.

"Excuse me?"

"I didn't say anything."

The fate of a rock tumbling downhill is easily predicted: It will gain momentum and crash to bits at the mountain's bottom. On the first day of the new school year, a teacher must set down the tone in the classroom, for it's easier to let an obedient dog out of a pen than to get a wild one in. Gabriel had no clue, and, when he gained a glimpse, it was too late. His students were wild beasts.

Gabriel woke with a start—or maybe he was still awake and the image shocked him as she danced through his head wrapped in red silk. Thoughts of her had both comforted and tormented simultaneously. He couldn't escape it, he couldn't get it out of his head or the feeling away from his body. Sasha and Gabriel—from that first night in the Green Tea Guesthouse in Dharmsala—slept in a tangle of each other. To Gabriel, this was Exhibit A of their union's perfection. In his life Gabriel had had many girlfriends, and it seemed as if they all fell in love with him only to be dumped in a week. As it's often meant to be, the girl who Gabriel fell for was destined to break his heart.

Squished alone in the dark at the bottom of his bed he tried to sense the warmth of her breath on his own skin. His cheeks soaked in so many tears—they wrinkled and hurt.

They had met in India, traveled through Indonesia, and settled in Santa Fe, New Mexico—of all places. A little older than Gabriel, beautiful Sasha Samson from Australia wanted to attend Tuwa Institute, a Santa Fe environmental school her aunt had helped establish some years before.

Often during a thorny breakup there is a buffer zone of *maybe*. Maybe we'll get back together. Maybe not today, maybe not tomorrow. But maybe. Gabriel never had that shock absorber. When Sasha left, she was gone—to the other side of the world, to the arms of another man. Gabriel was devastated, and I had never experienced my brother in such a state. I was afraid. That last month of summer, after Sasha left but before Gabriel started his new career at Los Pinos High School, I talked to him every day, though I had to call four or five times in a row to get him to pick up the phone.

"What about the way we slept?" would be the first thing he'd say. "We were perfect."

And then one day he just stopped answering his phone. I talked with him on his birthday and then that was it. I couldn't help but to imagine the worst. I can get pretty down and, in that hole, I sometimes feel capable of the nastiest of acts aimed at myself, but I didn't think Gabriel was capable, yet his heart had never been ripped from his chest and left in a puddle on his kitchen floor for him to contemplate alone for a month. I know he was excited about teaching, but still I worried. Reading and rereading, he was preparing *Romeo & Juliet* in which the two young lovers kill themselves in the end. I put myself in his place. I don't know, I was anxious, and I called and called yet he never answered. I guess I also worried that he would take off again in an attempt to bury his wounded heart in another frivolous international adventure. It felt like a poke at me.

Many months later, on the night I received the missing persons call from the New Mexican state trooper, I found Sasha's phone number on the internet and, in the middle of my disturbed night, I called her, thinking maybe she had taken Gabriel back and he had abandoned his students and split to Australia. But that was quickly dispelled. She was very sweet on the phone, but curt. She planned to marry her university boyfriend the following week.

The unforgiving onslaught, the crush on his every breath, the hastiness of Sasha's devastating departure helped him to process his heartbreak in an abrupt explosion that bled profusely. Because there was no *maybe*, Gabriel had no choice but to move forward. During that month before school started Gabriel was forced to exorcize Sasha's spirit from his life and from his body like a man pressing venom out from a hole in his chest.

When he finally returned my thirty-seven calls, an elevated tone surrounded his voice, a quality that lacked the strain and torment that I had heard in all our previous calls that August, but I attributed it to the fact that he started teaching the next day—and not a new woman. On the phone he didn't even mention her. I only know because of much later, when Holly called to beg me to come to New Mexico to join the search party.

*If you had to give up one of your senses
which one would you relinquish?
And why?*

A stack of printer paper sat neglected on a table. As students from Gabriel's third period shuffled in, the whole stack, a few sheets at a time, dripped over the edge and spilt to the floor. Nathan stooped over and straightened them up even though he hadn't knocked them over.

Right away Gabriel liked Nathan.

Most students reasoned that they would give up their sense of smell or their hearing or their sense of touch, but not Nathan; a self-described music lover, a food lover, a fine-body observer, he insisted he would surrender his common sense. Gabriel wanted his students to enter his classroom and immediately focus—and the daily Do Now gave them the opportunity to fix their attention on something creative, on something that related to them, on something to which there were no wrong answers.

A few days later, while roughhousing with another student, Nathan knocked the same stack of paper to the floor.

Gabriel rushed over. "Hey hey hey!"

The boys released each other's arms.

"Pick the paper up please."

"No," Nathan said, took two steps, and sunk down into his desk chair.

"Nathan."

"No."

"Nathan …"

"He said, 'no,'" the Mouth said, grinning.

"Nathan, you knocked them over now please pick them up. Nathan … Nathan … I'll give you three seconds—"

"One two three," shot from Nathan's mouth—he threw back his chair and stormed out of the room.

"Good one," the Mouth said, stretching up tall in his chair and then with a dollop of drama he peeked back over his shoulder at the white sheets splayed out over the floor.

By this time, Carl, the redheaded student who had been wrestling with Nathan, was at his desk on the other side of the room.

"Carl, will you please pick up the paper?"

"Carl?" the Mouth said, "Carl didn't do it."

"Carl, please."

"You do it," Carl said to the teacher.

The class laughed.

"Yeah, you pick them up," the Mouth said.

Gabriel was shocked into silence.

About two-thirds guys, Gabriel's third period had a discordant amount of vocal boys who seemed to need to prove themselves by being rude, while the handful of girls crowded in the desks closest to the teacher's.

Off the podium, Gabriel seized *Romeo & Juliet*, and the rumpled ridges of the overused paperback felt like redemption in his hands. Let the Montagues and the Capulets fight it out.

"Take out your books and turn to page—"

"What? We're gonna read!" The Mouth would not be satisfied.

"Act I, Scene III: 'Nurse, where's my daughter?'"

"What about the paper on the floor?" The Mouth. "Who's gonna pick them up?"

Gabriel tried to ignore him. "'Call her forth to me,'" he read.

"I'll pick them up," the Mouth said. "Should I pick them up, do you want me to pick them up?"

"Just leave them."

"Why, you think Nathan's gonna come back and pick them up?" With this the Mouth let out a joyous roar, leaning back in his chair, his head rolling around on his shoulders, looking at everyone to get them to laugh, to see if they were laughing. And they were.

When the bell rang, the students rose up out of their seats, collected their belongings, and headed to the back of the room and out the door to their hallway encounters, their cheese pizza lunches, their teenage lives. Gabriel on the other hand sunk into his funk. He felt demoralized. As he watched the students clear out of the room, he judged each one's character as he or she either stepped over, skirted by, or plopped a sneaker right down into the center of the scatter of paper on the floor near the door.

Gabriel's empty classroom felt like a temple. The dust and whirl settled as silence overtook activity. The hallways were now quiet, for the students were all at lunch and the cafeteria was clear across campus. Gabriel hadn't sat down yet; instead, he stood in the middle of his classroom. Something inside of him had collapsed. He lost his confidence, and the students, seeing that crack, charged in with their spears.

He glanced at the scattered pile of paper; maybe he should leave it till tomorrow so Nathan or Carl or the Mouth could pick it up.

Without his consent, nicknames for his students had gathered in his head. They helped Gabriel identify faces and, as he learned their names as the passing days turned to weeks, he forgot the nicknames. Except 'the Mouth' stuck. As inappropriate as it was for a teacher to refer to one of his students with such a derogatory name, Gabriel's mind just could not let it go. It was involuntary, and, although he never once called him it, whenever he looked at him he saw him as thus. The Mouth. From the day he had rejected ownership of his own headphones all the way to the moment he was withdrawn from Gabriel's class, the Mouth proved himself to be the Mouth by sabotaging Gabriel's intentions at every opportunity.

Gabriel felt unprepared to handle the Mouth. In Teacher College they spent so much time on lesson preparation when all they really needed, all they should have studied every minute in every class for the entire year, was classroom management. Lesson plans become irrelevant in a classroom for a teacher who presides over an out-of-control mob. If the students refuse to sit down, the teacher will never get to that brilliant lesson.

Gabriel's classroom was a box filled with desks. Made of plastic, metal, and fake wood, the thirty-two student desks, in two concentric semi-circles, opened up to the blackboard at the front of the room. Opposite the two windows was a long closet that took up the whole wall. On a table in the back sat three ancient computers that surely needed to be replaced, and covering the entire wall above hung a blank bulletin board that Gabriel would slowly fill with student artwork. The teacher's desk squished into the front corner, while the floor was made up of hundreds of hideous beige tiles.

Gabriel gazed at the white paper splayed across the floor. He didn't want his beautiful fifth period creative writing class to have to step over someone else's mess. He moved across the room, sunk down to his knees, and began to scoop up the paper. Big dark footprints marred the pages.

Because Nathan had stormed out of the classroom and never returned, Gabriel filled out a discipline referral form for him. And then he ripped it up. He sat there for ten more minutes before he wrote another. Then he ripped that up too. He didn't want to drop his troubles onto a principal who might judge Gabriel's teaching ability, or lack thereof.

The next morning in the hallway Gabriel spotted Nathan alone, so he intercepted his path and asked if he could have a word with him. Nathan shrugged and followed Gabriel out the door. Though class was about to begin, they paused in the parking lot between two Toyotas. There was no animosity between them.

"You're a leader you know Nathan."

Nathan gazed through the haze, out at the mountains in the distance.

"The other students listen to you. They look up to you. Do you know that?"

"Yeah."

"When you act in an inappropriate manner, it encourages the others to do the same. And when you're listening and you're in to what we're doing, the other students are too. You're really smart, Nathan, and I expect exceptional work from you."

Nathan pulled up his sagging pants.

"Will you help me with this class?"

The bell rang, but they remained unaffected.

"Can I expect exceptional work from you?"

Nathan glanced up at Gabriel and then looked back down. "Yeah," he said.

"Yeah?"

"Yeah."

Then for a moment they were looking at each other.

Gabriel hadn't planned this meeting. He did what felt natural—he found a moment to talk to Nathan alone. Gabriel never anticipated that in front of a class he'd be so out of his element. But here, one on one, he worked his magic.

The last time Gabriel was in Chicago (for our grandmother's funeral), I witnessed him break up a fight without touching anyone. We had gone out to see a reggae band at the *Wild Hare* and outside the bar after the show we encountered a crowd watching these two menacing drunks circling each other about ready to brawl, and this idiot gets between them—and it's Gabriel. I had to look to my left to see that he was no longer standing next to me. He had walked right into the scrum.

"Yo tough guys!" Gabriel had shouted to distract them. "Yeah you, tough guys, this is crazy, this is nuts." And then motioning to a crying woman at the curb—"She doesn't wanna spend the rest of the night bailing your ass out of jail. You're both probably gonna go to jail."

And that was it. Gabriel's short diversion dissolved the urgent tension and the girlfriend stepped up, grabbed onto her boyfriend's elbow, and the other combatant watched as they walked away and the crowd dissolved.

Gabriel loved when situations like that presented themselves, for he was equipped to deal. His own sense of self didn't get caught up in the moment; he didn't need to weigh his ego against theirs. I'm not saying Gabriel didn't have an ego—he did, trust me—he just didn't need to prove he was cool. He already was. There was no competition. Being the peacemaker invigorated him.

He had this mystical touch with people. He sensed what they needed—praise or a sharp new perspective. He knew Nathan needed coddling, a compliment—first—before anything else. Just to get him to listen, he had to be positive and not with false praise, but with some bit of truth. "Nathan, you're a leader." And then Gabriel said what he needed to say. I've realized from Gabriel's example that if you want to be heard, if you really want people to listen to you, you have to feel each situation and act accordingly. If outside the *Wild Hair* that night Gabriel would have started by pushing the drunks apart, it would have been a different scene for sure, and if he had started by scolding Nathan, nothing could have been accomplished.

Back in class, Nathan sat poised in his seat, did his work, and contributed to the class discussion. Nathan could affect the others with his emotions; he could set the mood without saying a word, and when he stepped forward and spoke he was a commanding presence. Nathan's enthusiasm was contagious.

"Juliet's way too young to get married," he said, leaning forward in his desk. "Her mother's a dog. What's her problem? She doesn't care about her." Nathan slammed back in his chair all bothered by Juliet's callous, self-serving mother.

"Anyways she's supposed to be with Romeo—right?" Clarissa said, genuine teenage heat burning up off a Shakespearian play.

The next two days, Nathan was absent.

When he returned, he sat tight-lipped and silent. He sneered. Participating in neither classroom projects nor social interactions, he sunk low in his seat with his arms wound round his chest. Something had happened to Nathan during those two days he was absent, yet Gabriel would never know what. When Nathan wasn't staring out the window, he was glaring at Gabriel. Nathan couldn't sink into the shadows to suck on his sorrows. When mad, no one could get away from him—even if he said nothing. Nathan led the class in a positive direction only for that one day. Now he sat back in his secret silent dissent, watching as the Mouth made a mess.

At first the Mouth's demands were a low-grade annoyance, but with Nathan ceding center stage, the Mouth coasted into the spotlight. Every syllable originating from any lip became fair game for the Mouth's commentary:

"That's whack. ... That sucks. ... You can't do that. ... That's the gayest music ever. ... I don't have to do that. ... What are you a fag? ... That's stupid. ... I've done that. ... You have to relax. ... That's stupid. ... Are you retarded?"

A big round kid decked out day after day in a different sports team's jersey, hat, and jacket, the Mouth trounced into the classroom laughing with his new headphones on, his mouth jabbering away at an extreme volume so he could hear himself over his music, which everyone else experienced as a high-pitched, screeching squall. When class started and Gabriel asked him to take off his headphones, the Mouth would bellow, "What?" as if he couldn't hear. When Gabriel motioned to take off the headphones, the Mouth would bellow louder, "What?" And then he'd laugh with his shoulders bouncing.

Gabriel was not a hateful person, but dealing with the Mouth was like nails being driven into his face. The Mouth seemed so satisfied with his antics. Gabriel could have smacked those headphones right off his head.

Gabriel judged himself.

After class, distraught and looking for the bathroom, he made his way into the teachers' lounge bumping face to face with an elder teacher.

"Sheeet," Ms. Bimble said, full of compassion. "Looks like you could use a latte."

A modest silver espresso maker sat brewing on the stove.

Gabriel made his way back to his classroom without having gone to the bathroom. For the first time, he shuffled through his class information sheets, found a phone number, and called a parent.

"This is Gabriel Abrams, I'm your son's English teacher."

"Hello Mr. Abrams, I'm glad you called."

The Mouth's mother, Mrs. Rudolph, wasn't surprised at any of her son's behaviors. She listened and, after Gabriel had exhausted his litany of complaints, she exhaled a long sigh.

"Mr. Abrams," she said, "I am so sorry, but you must place this in context."

She began by listing off a slew of letters—ADD, ADHD, BPD—which had little immediate effect on Gabriel, but the story of her son's life did.

Mr. and Mrs. Rudolph were not his real parents. They had adopted him five years before from his mother, Mr. Rudolph's sister, who was a methamphetamine addict. Mrs. Rudolph clarified that her husband's sister came from a good family but had collapsed into drug addiction. Alex, the Mouth's real name, never met his father, yet endured a succession of johns and boyfriends throughout his first nine years.

"You can imagine how this column of men treated Alex."

Mrs. Rudolph paused for a good twenty seconds, leaving space for Gabriel's imagination.

"Alex has issues with male authority," she said.

Through the phone she let loose another long pause.

Gabriel was dumbfounded. He didn't know what to say, wasn't sure if she was finished, but he prayed she was.

"I'm sorry," Gabriel said, "I'm so sorry."

"I know you are, of course you are."

Gabriel rubbed his ear—it hurt. He glanced up at the clock. He'd been on the phone for thirty-five minutes. From afar the Mouth appeared to be a normal kid. Up close, he was impossible. And now this third perspective. Gabriel could never have imagined his history. He felt nauseous. He hadn't eaten his lunch. Or gone to the bathroom.

The Mouth and Alex seemed like two separate entities. Gabriel's anger still crawled out over his skin, and he just couldn't attach this heartbreaking story to the Mouth. He unraveled his lunch and poked at it. Gabriel struggled for this one student's two divergent elements to meld. He told himself that those of us who need the most, often push away the hardest. Gabriel would try to treat him with more patience, but that didn't mean that the Mouth—or Alex—would behave in class. The problem remained; it just got a lot deeper—and more tragic—and beyond Gabriel's ability. He felt as if a wall was being erected brick by brick to keep him from teaching and it wasn't just Alex and Nathan and Jorge but all his freshmen who seemed lethargic and whiny and determined to hassle the teacher or do nothing at all. Day after day it wore him down.

Teaching can be an endurance test. Gabriel taught four classes, each an hour and ten minutes long—three freshmen English classes in the morning and a creative writing class in the afternoon that ended the day. In the middle, between his freshmen and his fifth period creative writing, he had forty minutes for lunch as well as his fourth period prep during which he was supposed to prepare his lessons. Eight to three. Every day. And then he went home to create more lessons, grade papers, and do required clerical work that often lasted for hours. His classes averaged twenty-nine students, so daily almost a hundred and twenty kids needed his attention, demanded his attention, vied for his attention. Personalities danced into view, begged for his energy, and then sashayed away only to be supplanted by another pressing personality, or two, or three, or twenty-nine.

But once fifth period rolled around Gabriel got his daily dose of redemption. Though he knew nothing of creative writing, his fifth period students attacked their assignments with an unrivalled passion, which, at the end of every day, lent Gabriel a bit of grace.

Two minutes after the final bell, the classroom phone rang.

"Mr. Abrams, this is Chuck Rudolph, I'm Alex's father. You spoke with my wife earlier today."

"Oh yes of course hello."

Teaching is one thing after another and no pause to take it all in. Just forward forward forward. Gabriel cherished his time after school when the entire building grew quiet. It would seem a teacher needs these moments of reflection. But not today. Not this week. Or this month. Maybe this summer.

"I am so sorry about my son." A ring of remorse hemmed in his voice, but as the conversation went on Gabriel realized it wasn't remorse—it was a profound understanding of what Gabriel was going through with his son.

"I too am a target," Mr. Rudolph said. "Alex struggles with men. And understandably so. He's two completely different people with me or with Judith."

Judith was his wife—Alex's adopted mother.

"She often doesn't understand. Not that I don't love Alex—I most certainly do, he's been through so much, but I get frustrated. I know how it must be for you."

Mr. Rudolph suggested that if things don't improve, he'll come and sit in Gabriel's class and monitor Alex's behavior.

"Maybe something good can come of it," Mr. Rudolph said.

The next day Nathan came into the classroom and plopped down in front of a computer. When the bell rang, Gabriel asked him to take his seat, but Nathan made no move, his focus pressed to the computer screen.

"Nathan."

"Okay."

When Gabriel turned to the class, an unsettling calm gripped the room; someone had done something and now everyone sat frozen guilty saying nothing. Gabriel moved around the room, coaxing students to take out their notebooks and do the Do Now. When he glanced down at a student's work, a burst of activity exploded through his peripheral vision. Gabriel jerked around to see the Mouth—or Alex—fall down into his seat.

"Alex please take out your notebook."

"I am," he said, stifling a giggle.

Nathan was still riveted to the computer.

"Nathan, class has started."

"I'm almost done."

"Yeah, he's almost done," Alex said.

"Now! Nathan."

"What's your problem?"

"Yeah, what's your problem?"

Alex wound up and threw a wadded-up ball of paper across the room.

"Alex!"

"I didn't do anything."

"I saw you."

"No you didn't."

"Would you please pick up what you threw?"

"I didn't throw anything."

"I saw you throw it and I can see it right over there now."

Girls were talking, boys roughhousing, people texting. And Nathan was still on the computer.

"Nathan, will you please take your seat?"

"He's just on the computer," Alex said.

"Please pick up the paper you threw."

"Why you have to be so mad all the time?" Jorge said, and he said it with such a sneer Gabriel had to look, and what was so weird was that Gabriel was remaining calm. Sort of.

"Nathan," Gabriel said. "Now."

Noticing that Nathan was watching a real-life filmed streetfight on the computer, Gabriel bent down and pulled the plug.

"What's your problem! I'm just checking one thing out."

"He's just checking one thing out."

Nathan pushed his chair back, slamming it into Gabriel's leg. Gabriel sucked in his lips, stifling any sign of pain as Nathan thumped past, threw back his own desk chair, dumped himself into it, and hammered his book bag onto the desktop.

Someone had entered the room. Just inside the door, a small man in his early fifties stood there holding his baseball cap in his fingers, a visitor's name tag affixed to his shirt. Embarrassed Gabriel wondered how long he had been there. The students turned to see what their teacher was looking at. When Alex turned he snapped back in his seat, sinking down into his chair. Gabriel knew who this man must be.

"Mr. Rudolph? Hello."

"Mr. Abrams, nice to meet you."

They shook hands. It was Alex's dad.

"I didn't expect you."

"I was in the neighborhood."

"Okay, great," Gabriel said, not feeling okay or great. On the phone the two men had made no specific plan for him to visit his classroom.

"Please, have a seat."

"Oh no no."

"Yeah you stay there," Alex, slunk down in his seat, said without turning around.

Mr. Rudolph forced a rickety smile for Gabriel, and Gabriel thought maybe Mr. Rudolph would say something to his son, he thought maybe he should say something to his son. But it became apparent that he would not.

Gabriel was shaken. He felt judged by Mr. Rudolph as he hovered there saying nothing. Gabriel couldn't move forward with a class discussion or any sort of real teaching. So:

"Open your books to act I, scene VI and read to yourselves and answer the questions I will write on the board."

Instead of discussing them, Gabriel wrote the discussion questions from his first two periods on the board.

Nathan didn't take his book out of his bag. Alex didn't even have a bag.

Finally the bell rang and the students headed for the exit.

"Alex, will you please wait a moment?" Gabriel said.

Alex paused, but when the classroom emptied and his father and Gabriel turned to him he suddenly rushed past, out the door, down the hall.

Mr. Rudolph gave Gabriel a panicked expression, then he too hurried out the door. Gabriel thought maybe they both would return—Alex under his father's clutches, but neither did.

Not for a week.

*Some say we choose our parents
before we're born. Did you? Why or why not?*

I couldn't help but to suspect something as Gabriel kept mentioning his landlord in tones of secrecy. When someone is having an effect on your life it's hard not to reference her in intimate conversation with your brother. Even as he had tried to keep from me his feelings, Gabriel had cited the facts. After his girlfriend Sasha left, Gabriel couldn't continue to pay the rent alone. He had meant to break his lease, move somewhere cheaper, yet his landlord, Holly, presented an alternative. She wanted to move back into her house where Gabriel was living and offered to be roommates—Holly and her young daughter would move into the master bedroom and Gabriel could switch to the small back bedroom at a much-reduced rent. Crippled by his broken heart and about to start teaching, the arrangement seemed affordable and easy, and Holly seemed nice and her daughter, Chloe, well-behaved. Those were the facts, sort of.

The truth was Gabriel and Holly liked each other.

But struggled not to.

Before he was to start his new job at Los Pinos High on Monday, on that Saturday while I imagined Gabriel suffering in the shadows with his wrecked heart over Sasha, he drove Holly and Chloe up into the mountains for a hike to get to know each other, to see if they could live as roommates. With Holly and Chloe's dog weaving through their legs, they wandered the woods tapping trees until they ended at a simple and clandestine campsite. Up towards the ski basin, tucked into the woods, a mini *North Face* tent was pitched beside a creak. A circle of rocks formed a fire pit over which three steel rods had been fashioned into a tripod that held a swaying Dutch oven. Two stumps as chairs sat in perfect position. In a nearby clearing a laundry line stretched between two trees on which hung in the sun one little girl's green T-shirt.

"You live here?" Gabriel asked.

"Yeah," Chloe said scrambling to the tent, unzipping it, and disappearing inside.

"How long have you lived here?"

"Some time," Holly said.

Chloe emerged from the tent with a plastic dinosaur, a gaping hole in its belly. "Here's my Tyrannosaurus Rex."

"Cool."

"Tea?"

"Sure."

Gabriel was captivated. The site was in flawless order, almost camouflaged. Covered in ivy, a long narrow plywood board leaned lengthwise against a downed tree. Holly lifted it as if opening a cupboard. Beneath was stored their supplies. She drew out two mugs.

"We only have two."

"We'll share," Chloe said, looping a tiny arm through Gabriel's.

From a nearby tree Holly untied a rope and lowered a canvas bag, from which she plucked her tea bags. The dog laid in her mound of pine needles.

"Can I light the fire, can I mamma?"

"Let's do it together."

As they set a few twigs ablaze Gabriel sat on a stump and watched. Side by side Holly and her daughter squatted, balancing on their feet, placing the kindling with such care. Holly peeked up at Gabriel and then back into the emerging flames, but Gabriel kept looking—what was it about her that so enchanted him? She was so certain, so easy in the woods, a mother. And his landlord! The fire flicked up through the twigs and she sat back on a stump facing him and at each other they gazed without a word. They weren't staring, they were noticing, looking as if curious, intrigued. Chloe handed Holly the blackened kettle. The plastic T-Rex in mid-roar balanced on a rock.

They never considered that if they felt that tweak between breaths in their hearts that maybe they shouldn't become roommates.

The next day, Sunday, they went on a mini roadtrip out to western New Mexico to crawl through the lava tubes. No wonder Gabriel didn't return my calls—and there I was scowling all weekend in my apartment worrying if my brother would off himself in some stunning attempt to alleviate his broken heart.

Without a word Gabriel stepped into the spot in the middle of the classroom, clasped his hands behind his back, and stared straight ahead. His creative writing students settled down, drawn to his presence, yet Gabriel remained a stiff arrow stuck in the floor.

And then he began:

"There once was a young man who was driven by passion, and this passion promised him perfection, and because of this promise nothing ever satisfied him. He thought the truth was around the corner. He was always looking past what was right in front of him, thinking it must only be a shadow of the truth. He kept searching, never settling, never losing faith.

"Until one day he woke up and he was no longer young. It seemed as if so much had passed him by. So he married someone he did not love, had children, and took a job where he made the right amount of money, but paid for it with his passion. Ten years passed in the span of a meme. And then five more."

Gabriel broke from his stance and began to stroll, engaging the students as he passed, looking into their eyes, speaking deliberately to them.

"He had these piercing gray eyes that could look deep into you and if you looked back, deep enough, you could see a hint of his lost passion. It hurt, but it was there. One day—in the middle of the day—he left work. He took the elevator down to the ground and walked across the street to a courtyard where a gypsy woman was dancing for coins. He watched her, and she shifted her body towards him. Right away they both knew—as it is with things like this. For her he left his life; for him she righted the universe."

Gabriel marched to the center of the classroom.

"The lovers traveled everywhere on nothing, yet had everything. They loved harder and deeper than broken bits of planets plunged into the depths of space. They loved like children, they loved like gods. They loved with their bodies and their breath, with their histories and their future. They loved up every morsel of their sustenance. Their cup filled and then emptied and filled again. All that the man had been promised had been granted.

"And then one day she died. But the man wouldn't believe it to be so. He couldn't. For a week he shed not one tear. He was in shock. He waited for her, but she never returned. Not that he refused to sleep, he just didn't, and sleep never forced itself upon him. Instead of sleep, reality sunk into his bones like a handful of sand sinking deeper into the sea; at some point it must reach the bottom, and when it does, it doesn't crash to the floor—rather, it settles. When the harsh reality reached its sandy mark in the depths of his heart, the man knew it inside and out. Tears didn't explode from his eyes—they simply began to fall, never to cease, not for the rest of his life.

"His passion whirled inside him like a forest of fire consuming itself. He left his chamber. He stepped out into the night. He walked a couple blocks and then in a different direction he walked a few more. He didn't know where he was; he didn't think to know where he was. In a city he once lived, he no longer saw. Every one of his tears rolled out of his eyes like liquid silver, and these burning silver tears filled his mouth. And he began to sing.

"The sound that emerged was pure sorrow."

Gabriel had now been speaking to himself and the class strained to hear. He looked up, he looked around at all his students.

"This sad gray-eyed man roamed the streets singing his sorrow. He became a homeless fixture in the city. You'd see him all over. When I was your guys' age, I'd pass him on my way to school. And I would stop and listen. At first it sounded like the sweetest song in the world, but if you kept listening its grief could sneak in and collapse your heart."

As affected as they were, the students were no longer looking at Gabriel, or at anyone for that matter.

After a few moments, "Is that a true story?" a boy in the back asked.

A student remained after all the others had left. Isabel—a tall and striking presence—her eyes fixed on Gabriel's.

"That was an amazing class, Mr. Abrams."

Gabriel smiled, maybe a bit bashful in the light of a compliment.

In class after Gabriel had told his story, he prompted his creative writing students to think of someone they knew, or someone they saw around but didn't know, someone they wished they knew—or were glad they didn't—anyone who captured their curiosity.

"Think of that person," Gabriel had said. "What they look like, how they dress, something weird you might've heard them say—and make up a story, not necessarily about them exactly, but inspired by what you imagine them to be."

Many started writing right away, and after forty minutes, his students had presented the most creative inspiring tragic funny and insightful narratives.

"There used to be a poetry club," Isabel said after school alone with her teacher, "but there hasn't been for a while and I want to organize one. I know you said you're not a poet, but I need a sponsor and I'd really like it if you'd be the sponsor."

Enunciating, Isabel introduced this as if it were some honor and Gabriel felt as if it were. But he was cautious.

"What do I do as the sponsor?"

"Well, we hold meetings in your classroom during lunch one day a week and you have to be there—but you don't have to do anything—you can, if you want, but I'll run it."

If a hummingbird had peeked in through the window at that first poetry club meeting, she might have flown on after only a few flutters. There were just three people there, and that included Gabriel, yet Isabel was all business.

"Welcome to the first installment of poetry club. We're glad to be here and thank you to Mr. Abrams for sponsoring us."

The meeting didn't last long both because there wasn't a lot to be done and the lunch period was barely forty minutes.

Isabel asked if anyone wanted to read a poem. She looked at Gabriel, and for a split-second he was embarrassed—he didn't have a poem, he didn't know he was expected to have a poem. He shrugged his shoulders and declined. Isabel looked at Lori, the third attendee, and she was even more embarrassed. Her lips quivered.

"Lori, I know you do," Isabel said.

"I don't know."

"C'mon, it's just me."

Lori's eyes slid over to Gabriel as if pointing.

"He's not so scary," Isabel said and Gabriel growled and Lori smiled.

Lori dug into her knapsack. A chubby girl with perfect tresses of blond hair, Lori pulled out her pink spiral notebook from which a mess of papers spilt. It took her most of the rest of the time to weed through her spiral and find her poem. When she found it and read it, it was all of three lines. She could have said it from memory without having to dig through her confused pile. The poem was about how red a bowl of cherries were.

"Thank you Lori, that was great," Isabel said. "Really, thank you. Wonderful." She glanced at Gabriel—"Anyone else?"

Gabriel again declined.

Isabel waited an appropriate moment.

And then she said: "I have a poem."

Isabel rose up out of her chair. She moved to the front of the room and closed her eyes, which then flashed open—all fire—she enunciated a poem as if she were center stage. She lit up and bloomed out, her hands reaching, fingers gesturing flairs against a black night. Disregarding the humdrum of the classroom—the near emptiness of it, she weighted her poem and her presentation with significance. She transformed the room into the colors she painted, and when she finished and stood there motionless, applause broke out (Lori and Gabriel). A wide smile blossomed onto Lori's face and Gabriel's insides thumped. They were elevated.

*C*ome, we burn daylight, ho!'"

"'Nay, that's not so,'" a student as Romeo answered as they read the play aloud.

"'I mean, sir, in delay—'"

"*Que pasa que pasa?*"—Alejandro burst through the door, calling out to his friends, "*Que pasa que pasa?*" And then, "*Que?*" in response to Gabriel's glare.

"You're late," Gabriel said.

"We ran out of gas," Alejandro said.

"You ran out of gas last week."

"We live way outa town, *pendejo*, should I not come at all?"

"You should try …" Gabriel stopped himself, too tired to engage.

"'Cause I could leave," Alejandro pushed. "Should I leave?"

No matter how many times Gabriel wiped his eyes, sleep stuck in the corners, for the night before he'd been up till two creating lesson plans.

In second period as *Romeo & Juliet* stumbled through his students' lips, Gabriel noticed that Steven hadn't opened his book. Redirecting his slow stroll, Gabriel came upon Steven's desk, off of which he took the book, opened it to the right page, and slid it in front of him—then resumed his stroll. A slap to the floor! Gabriel turned to see that Steven had pushed the book off his desk.

"Pick it up."

"No."

"Pick it up."

"No."

"Pick it up."
"No."
Gabriel felt the bridge of his sanity begin to buckle.
"Pick it up."
"No."
"Pick it up."
"No."
"Pick it up."
"No."

Gabriel could not, in all his wisdom, say it again even as the words raced up his throat.

When third period appeared he could hardly stand, so he ordered his students to read *Romeo & Juliet* to themselves.

Nathan sat with his book closed on his desk.
"You're not reading?"
"I can't."
"Of course you can."
"I can't."
"Come on Nathan, pick up your book and start reading."
"I can't."
"Why not?"
"Because."
"Because why?"
"'Cause."
"Why?"
"I read at a third-grade level! ... There! Are you happy?"

He shouted this for the entire class and then covered his head in his arms on his desk. Gabriel glanced up and noticed the Mouth (I mean Alex) and his father standing in the doorway.

"Can we talk outside?" Mr. Rudolph said.

"Keep reading," Gabriel said to his class, not wanting to leave them alone.

Outside Alex said nothing. He kept his eyes heavy on the floor. His father prodded him.

"Uhm," Alex said, "uhm, I'm sorry."

"And?" his father said.

"And, uhm, I'll do better."

They slunk back into the classroom. Mr. Rudolph stayed at the door, and, just before shutting it and leaving, he gave Gabriel a thumbs up.

Re-invigorated (sort of) Gabriel took a chance. He arranged his students into small groups with the task of listing as many examples, from their lives and from the play, that support the themes in *Romeo & Juliet*. Nathan refused, sitting off by himself, but Alex participated, his headphones nowhere in sight.

Gabriel drifted around the room checking the progress of the various groups. Off a desk a pencil rolled and bounced to the floor. Both Gabriel and Robertson leaned over to pick it up and their heads bumped—not a hard bump, but startling nonetheless.

"Are you okay?" Gabriel asked, holding his head.

With watery eyes Robertson rose up from under the desk but didn't answer. Gabriel looked at him. Every day, no matter what, Robertson wore these thin gray gloves.

"You alright? ... Robertson? ... It hurt—didn't it? ... Quite a shock."

"Fuck," Robertson finally said.

Someone giggled.

"Fuck," he said louder.

"Please don't swear in this class."

"He didn't," Jorge said.

"Fuck," Robertson repeated.

Leaning forward to speak just to him—"Robertson, please don't swear in my class."

Pushing himself back—"What're ya trying to kiss me!"

The class laughed. Alex laughed, leaning back—a good belly laugh.

"Robertson," Gabriel warned.

"What? You banged my head and now you're telling me what to do?"

"You banged his head?" Jorge said.

"Why'd you bang his head?" Alex said.

"It's not your business."

"Of course it's my business," Alex said, the Mouth re-emerging. "It's his business and his business and her business—it's everyone's business: You hit a student."

"Who hit a student?"

"He did."

The thick tick of the wall clock clicked forward. At the second meeting of the poetry club, Isabel, Lori, and Gabriel lingered. Generally, they were waiting for new members to arrive, specifically, for Isabel's friend Justin, who had promised to come.

After half of their allotted time Gabriel felt compelled—

"Isabel, why don't you give us a poem."

"This isn't much of a club," Lori said. "No one's here."

"I'm here."

"I'm here too."

"You're the sponsor, you have to be here. And you're like the head of it, you have to be here too. Justin's not even here."

"He said he was coming."

"But he's not."

"But he said he was."

"We have to get people who aren't just friends," Gabriel said.

"I don't have any friends."

"I'm your friend," Isabel said.

"Yeah but we're geeks."

"Lori."

"What?"

"You don't have to put yourself down."

"I'm not putting myself down—I'm putting us all down. Nobody wants to be in a geek club. Not even Justin. Especially Justin. That's probably why he's not here."

"That's not true."

"Then where is he?"

"I don't know."

"See."

"At least try," Isabel said.

"Fine," Lori said. "But, it's like—nothing ever works. I don't know why I care, or come, or breathe at all by the way."

"Lori."

"What?"

"Please."

"Fine."

"So how do we attract more members?" Gabriel asked.

"Posters," Lori said, "duh."

Early the next morning Gabriel entered the main school building. Light from a few scattered classrooms twinkled, and the far-off noise of a chair scrapping over the floor echoed through the hallway. The rubber from Gabriel's shoes squeaked each time they met and left the floor. Looking up, he saw a colorful poster hanging at the end of the corridor:

'Be a Geek, Join the Poetry Club, Tuesdays at lunch, room 103'.

Gabriel didn't laugh—it was too early for that—but a smile slipped through his fatigue.

Not even for one full period could Alex (the Mouth) act in an acceptable manner. One good belly laugh shattered the eggshell veneer that kept him quiet and studious. Never in Gabriel's classroom would Alex be the docile student doing his work. Alex regained his momentum, tumbling further and bringing with him anyone stupid enough to engage him, e.g. Mr. Abrams.

Alex: "That sucks. ... You can't do that. ... That's whack. ... I don't have to do that. ... What are you a fag? ... That's stupid. ... Relaaax."

Gabriel: "Take off your headphones. ... Open your book. ... Stop talking. ... Don't say that. ... You can't say that. ... That's rude."

Gabriel found himself an intricate part of Alex's soundtrack—all mixed with the class' laughter and Alex's furious screeching rap music. Alex never took off his headphones, he never did any work, and he never stopped talking. Universal wisdom claims the best way to quiet a student like this is to ignore him, but this proved impossible because Alex's running commentary was louder than Gabriel could be. Gabriel kept in contact with Alex's parents, but his mother became less and less sympathetic, and Alex's father grew more and more frustrated.

Gabriel yearned to keep his problems in his classroom. He had heard that if a teacher wrote too many discipline referral forms he could get fired. He understood that the principals were busy and might develop a bit of contempt for him if he asked too much of them. Every time he wrote a discipline referral form, instead of turning it in to a principal, he ended up ripping it up or stuffing it in a book. He had a pile of them at home.

But one day the class grew so rowdy Gabriel didn't know what he was teaching. When he turned towards Alex, Alex flung a blue plastic toy football that spiraled right towards Gabriel's face. Gabriel's always been athletic—not as the high school football star, but more like the agile kid prowling the halls; he's very graceful in his movements. So with this football zooming towards his face, Gabriel, without thinking, dipped a shoulder—ever so slightly—and his head moved an inch and the football zipped past and banged into a filing cabinet. If not for this move the fist-sized football would have smacked him square in the face.

For a moment, Gabriel and Alex stared at each other.

The class too was silent.

There was no confusion as to what had just happened. Alex threw it, Gabriel saw him throw it, and Alex saw Gabriel see him throw it. And most of the students saw as well.

But still: "I didn't throw it," Alex said.

The comment clung to the dust floating in a ray of sunlight.

Gabriel was not mad. His emotions remained intact. Alex had stretched his situation into a different realm, and this pacified Gabriel, distanced Alex from him.

Gabriel simply said, "Alex, come with me," turned, and left the room.

Gabriel walked to the end of the hall and looked back down the empty corridor. Alex was not there and Gabriel didn't mind that he disobeyed. Searching for a security guard who could remove Alex from his classroom, Gabriel stepped out of the building, and, as he headed towards the security offices, he spotted Dr. Fitzpatrick, the head principal, across the courtyard. Gabriel had never personally met Dr. Fitzpatrick, but during teacher orientation, she had given an impassioned speech that electrified Gabriel. In her speech she had acknowledged that many teachers didn't like her, but her objective was to turn this school around for the students. Her speech appealed to Gabriel's idealistic charge into his teaching career. He felt Dr. Fitzpatrick could be an ally. Without fear he marched up to her and told her he needed a student removed from his classroom.

From down the hall they could hear the chaos coming from Gabriel's room. When they opened the door it was like a tornado bursting out, but the class quickly calmed as they realized who was with Mr. Abrams. As they climbed back into their seats, Gabriel pointed out Alex.

"Let's go," Dr. Fitzpatrick said. "Bring your things."

And Alex obeyed.

"Mr. Abrams," Isabel said, "do you have a poem?"

Now there were five. Isabel, Lori, and Gabriel, and two new members—Sammy from Gabriel's first period freshmen class and Perry, a giant of a boy, from Gabriel's creative writing class. (Gabriel had announced the poetry club to all his classes.)

After welcoming the new members, Isabel asked if anyone had a poem to share. Perry and Sammy declined and Lori shook her head like a twitch.

Gabriel felt it, he hated it, and he tried to look away—

"Mr. Abrams? Do you have a poem?"

Wanting to deny Isabel's request, Gabriel felt obliged to comply, for he was the teacher, the sponsor, and he sensed a certain responsibility to do what he could to encourage the club's success. And this was what frustrated him, because he was not a poet; in fact, he had never written a poem, yet, after feeling embarrassed when asked to read one during that first poetry meeting, he felt compelled. Last Tuesday after school Gabriel had sat at a student desk in his empty classroom struggling to compose a few lines he could share. After an hour he had nothing but a jumble of words. Heaping more and more awful phrases on top of each other all week long he endeavored to come up with something that would not embarrass him. He felt the days clicking away as Tuesday's poetry meeting approached. In the end, in a moment of panic, he scratched out all but nine words. And these were the words he read:

The steam
Rose up
Off his back
Signifying
Grace

"Mr. Abrams!" Isabel beamed. "That was wonderful."

Even though he was the teacher, Gabriel basked in Isabel's praise.

Sammy showed his palm—he was raising his hand. He too wanted to read a poem. When Isabel motioned, her shirtsleeve rose and Gabriel saw a textured, purple and black bruise on her bicep. Even though he didn't think she saw him notice, she pulled down her shirtsleeve and never again in Gabriel's classroom wore a short sleeve shirt.

Sammy pulled a scribbled piece of paper from his backpack. He tried to smooth it out over the desk. He stretched and scrunched his lips over his mouthful of metal braces. And then: a sudden onslaught, exploding words, Sammy shouted his poem from his chair never looking up but the words bounced off the desktop and shot to the corners, ricocheting off the ceiling and filling the room. What a shock! Gabriel thought to cover his ears, and the poem went on and on. When he finally finished the room went silent. No one said a thing, and Gabriel needed to say something, but all he could think to say was, 'Whew'.

"Sammy, thank you so much," Isabel said. "Your energy is impressive. And wanted. Thank you."

Sammy smiled, showing all the metal in his mouth. He was in the right place.

"Gabriel Abrams to Dr. Fitzpatrick's office. Gabriel Abrams to Dr. Fitzpatrick's office."

The public address system boomed through the school five minutes into fourth period, Gabriel's prep period.

When Gabriel arrived, her door was closed and Gabriel was unsure if he should enter. He knocked and was invited in.

A picture window looked out over the quad, several framed prints of famous paintings hung on the walls, a bunch of potted plants were scattered around the room. Dr. Fitzpatrick sat behind her wide wooden desk, and Alex lounged on a plush couch, a half-eaten Butterfinger in his hand. He straightened up upon seeing Gabriel.

"Please sit down." Dr. Fitzpatrick motioned to one of the ivy patterned chairs in front of her desk. Gabriel sat and now Alex was behind him, just out of his peripheral vision.

"Mr. Abrams," Dr. Fitzpatrick said, "Alex tells me you have a problem with his race."

"Excuse me?"

"Mr. Abrams, I know there are not a lot of African-American students here at Los Pinos High, and we don't offer specific training in reference to our small African-American community, yet we strive for understanding."

Confused, Gabriel turned around and looked at Alex who refused to look at him. The couch too was patterned in textured ivy.

"I'm sorry, I'm not sure what you're referring to."

"I'm referring to the incident in your classroom today."

"Alex threw a football at me. I'm not sure what that has to do with race."

"Alex threw the football, as he says, to see how you would react."

According to Alex, Gabriel had treated him unfairly because of his skin color (Alex was half-black). The other day a student threw a baseball in class and Gabriel did nothing, so today, apparently,

Alex decided to do an experiment. He threw the football to see if Mr. Abrams would react in a dissimilar way. Turned out he did.

"Dr. Fitzpatrick …" Gabriel twisted around to look at Alex. "Alex, in no way does the way you look have anything to do with how I treat you in my class. You threw a football at me, which is different than tossing a baseball to another student—which, by the way, is also inappropriate."

Gabriel paused, giving Alex space to say something, but he was silent. He was a different person in the principal's office, streaked tears painted down his face.

"Mr. Abrams, we can't tolerate racism at this school," Dr. Fitzpatrick said. "There needs to be zero-tolerance for racism. Don't you agree?"

"Dr. Fitzpatrick, I resent the accusation. The way I treat Alex in my classroom and the problems we have stem from Alex's behavior—not his skin color."

Dr. Fitzpatrick had stopped looking at Gabriel and was now looking at Alex. Gabriel turned to see Alex's face scrunched up like a gnarled fist struggling to hold back a new burst of tears. A sound squeaked out of his face. Gabriel could have laughed if it all weren't so pathetic … and potentially damaging to his career. The accusation floated above Gabriel's head and he shifted away from it. He tried to remember all of Alex's struggles.

"Dr. Fitzpatrick, Alex is a constant disruption in my class and it affects the other students who deserve a chance to learn and not be bombarded with Alex's endless commentary. There are many issues regarding Alex that we need to—"

"I am aware Mr. Abrams and I do agree that a classroom needs a certain sense of order, and I'm here to make sure the entire school runs smoothly, but also to make sure the individual student feels a certain connection. The grand as well as the—"

A knock on the door, a secretary poked her head in, but before she could say anything, Dr. Fitzpatrick said—

"Yes yes yes I'm aware." The secretary popped back out. "I'm sorry but that's going to have to be all for now."

She looked at Gabriel and he realized that he was being asked to leave.

"Mr. Abrams," she said standing up, dumping the remains of her coffee into a spider plant, "I promise further action."

As Gabriel walked back to his classroom he was unclear whether she meant further action on Alex's behavior or further inquiry into Gabriel's alleged racism. What had he done to cause Alex to accuse him? Gabriel thought back to all their horrible encounters. As he struggled to navigate their conflicts, he had never thought of Alex's race—not until just then in Dr. Fitzpatrick's office. What had Gabriel done? He didn't want to treat anyone unfairly—not even Alex.

On Friday Gabriel found a note in his box informing him of a meeting on Monday he was required to attend. Written at the bottom was a simple: 're: Alex Rudolph'.

Right there in the teacher's lounge Gabriel began to sweat. He didn't think he was a racist, yet being accused was in affect being labeled. If whispered from person to person the community may start believing it—and then teaching would get even harder. There's a certain negative real-world power in hearsay. If the establishment determines a person a threat to their agenda, they may paint him in a perverse light, so the average person no longer sees an insightful eccentric, but now they see only the rumored transgressions and they disregard the truths he may profess. Character assassination works. Gabriel felt the guilt being thrust upon him. He didn't want to be a racist.

*G*abriel drove out alone to the lava tubes where he sought refuge. He could accept being confronted by befuddled students, but an antagonistic principal? The administrators should support teachers no matter what—at least not make their jobs harder. Right?

As Gabriel snuck through the caves following his flashlight's beam of light, he was enveloped in an alternate reality. Dense sharpness squeezed him in in every direction, including above and below—especially above and below—he banged his head. He wasn't escaping, but being underground in the dark and muffled silence, Gabriel felt far away from his classroom. He pressed his tongue to the roof of his mouth and stopped breathing as if he didn't have to anymore. He was comfortable—comfortable with the cold, comfortable with the solid rock on which he sat, comfortable not breathing.

When his breath burst back without his consent, he opened his eyes and the streak from his flashlight blinded him—he knocked it against a rock and it blinked off. Under the earth Gabriel sat in the dark, his wounded flashlight in his lap. Yes, the sharp-edged walls and the serrated ceiling crowded in close, but it was the darkness that pressed together his knees, his shoulders, his cheeks. The wider he opened his eyes the darker it got. The blackness, as fierce as the bright sun yet its opposite, streaked into his eyes. It slithered inside his head and crept under his skull—warm hands cradling his brain. In the dark he floated. He found himself breathing slow, deep, satisfying breaths.

With his fingers, he toyed with the flashlight and it blinked back on.

As a teacher trying to help, all he found was persecution. He had craved to support and contribute and the frustration and realization that in every moment someone or something hobbled that effort crushed him all the way to the core. Every breath he took exposed the hole inside of him. He could have cried all night, he could have cried for the rest of his life. It made him sad for his students, for all students, for all the teachers who were fighting for the goodwill of our world. I could see Gabriel just picking up and going. Leaving. Splitting town. Things get tough, his brain shuts off, and his run instinct kicks in, and off he goes without consideration for anyone else—including those who love him most. That's what he did in Hollywood. He was there for a month. One month. He gave his whole life to acting and then he goes to make it happen and lasts not thirty days. It made me question what was really in his heart. He didn't go right to teaching from there—he disappeared to India and we barely heard from him for almost two years.

Our every action affects those around us. It's not bad to hear and obey our inner longings, but to act without regard can be detrimental. I struggled for years to make sense of the choices our father made, the choices that took him away from us, while Gabriel transformed our father's selfish acts into some sort of heroic proverb—the singing bum, or whatever.

When Gabriel graduated from college, I got him a job at Oberville—the company where I worked. Gabriel was lucky to get it, but, of course, he didn't see it that way. Many people can do nothing other than what is expected of them and that's not a problem because we often have that same expectation for ourselves. House, family, security. That was what I wanted. I liked my job, I saw my future, and I could appreciate that. But Gabriel split. Yup, he split there too. He wanted none of it. After less than two months at Oberville, without even a two-week notice, Gabriel quit and left town, leaving me to vouch for him.

"Mark, I'm sorry," Gabriel had said, "I'm outa here."

'Screw you' was all I could think at the time. He left me having to face everyone at Oberville. I was so mad and disappointed and embarrassed. And to make matters worse Gabriel was gone, and month after month after month we heard nothing from him. Not one word. I was left to chew on my curses, and into my mind crept tragic imaginings of his death. It was awful. My anger and resentment was overrun with the fear of his demise and the regret at the way I had treated him the last time I saw him. And then we got the postcard that proved he was alive and the anger and resentment returned, renewed.

Brothers can be brothers and not friends, but when brothers are also friends their relationship transcends both labels because it's unusual to have a friend with whom you share so much from such a young age and with such consistency—and sometimes siblings for those same reasons can't stand each other. Gabriel and I had always been very close. We shared a room for most of our lives and confided more than we fought. So when I hadn't heard from him in months, I suffered. It's hard to be so close to someone and then not. After he left Chicago and after he left Hollywood and after his years in Asia, finally when he settled in Santa Fe our brotherhood and friendship revitalized. You can see why I'm so upset at his latest disappearance. We were just beginning to be close again. How long will his newest mysterious absence last? For how long do I have to wait for that lone postcard with five fucking words on it to arrive with a clue of his latest escapade?

After he left Oberville, five months passed without a word from him. And then the postcard arrived.

You can't fit much information on a postcard, and Gabriel wasn't going for any world record. I received the postcard postmarked January 7 from Shawnee, Illinois. In all that time could he have never left the state? Besides my address, the five words were: "Been livin' in the woods." That was it. And the picture on the front was of a rock formation in Shawnee National Forest. The postcard confused me and made me more angry. "Been livin' in the woods." I had no idea what that meant, and if I had understood at the time I probably wouldn't have believed him. So, in retrospect, what he had written was about the extent of what I needed to know: he was alive and still an asshole.

A large conference room with a dry erase board and no windows served as the meeting's location. Although Gabriel arrived early everyone was already there. Dr. Fitzpatrick sat in the middle of the oblong table with Alex at one end, his parents next to him, and a school counselor at the other end. Alex's face looked sopped, stretched, and tired.

When Gabriel entered, no one looked at him. He slid into a seat next to the counselor. He nodded greetings to Mr. Rudolph who introduced him to his wife. Gabriel nodded to Alex, who didn't respond, and then to the councilor, but when he turned to Dr. Fitzpatrick she preceded to say—

"We're here to see how we can help Alex succeed in school."

Mrs. Rudolph shifted around in her chair.

"Alex is our main concern," Dr. Fitzpatrick continued, but Mrs. Rudolph interrupted—

"I have been trying since the summer to get my son the attention he needs. You promised me everything and then I never heard from you again."

"Mrs. Rudolph, we try to give our students what—"

"Well you've given my student nothing."

"Let's see what our counselor has to say. Ms. Hedge—"

"Ms. Hedge?" Mrs. Rudolph said. "His counselor? I don't even know this lady. Dr. Fitzpatrick, you promised me special classes, including a cooking class, and even to provide counseling for our son. And now so much time has passed and nothing. You stuck him in any class that accommodated your schedule, and I've been shuttled from one councilor to the next—first Ms. Baker and then Mr. Sheldon and now … Ms. Hedge? I don't mean to be rude, but I have never heard of you and my son's life is deteriorating. The only idiot at this school who cared was Mr. Abrams and he's a disaster."

Mr. Rudolph grabbed his wife's arm in mid-gesture. Mrs. Rudolph sat back in her seat and looked at her husband with a drained, vacuous expression.

"I've had it, Chuck," she said. "I've had it."

To Gabriel, Dr. Fitzpatrick said, "You can go."

And that was it. The end of the meeting and the end of Gabriel's association with Alex. He was pulled from Gabriel's class and put in a special education program, a cooking class, and forced into regular appointments with a (new) school counselor. Alex's problems didn't end of course, but his wrath was redirected towards a different teacher.

Write the best excuse you got.
For what would you use it?
Is it valid?

Holly and Chloe's belongings had been stored in the locked shed in back of the house. Amongst all the boxes was a bed, a TV, and a supply of pots and pans and spatulas and ladles. After they moved in and all through the fall Holly cooked monstrous vessels of stew and couldn't help but to share and Gabriel, so overwhelmed at school, couldn't help but to accept, and sitting at the table with Holly and Chloe laughing was a lightening contrast to his grim reality in the classroom.

At first he had tried to keep to himself.

Holly and Chloe would invite him to watch a movie and Chloe would fall asleep in her mamma's arms and Gabriel and Holly would end up talking instead of watching. They'd mute the volume and whisper into the night. Holly would ask a question and then listen as if, not just hearing, but sensing Gabriel. The attention encouraged him. They'd ask each other intimate questions. Gabriel wondered how she had a daughter at such a young age.

"Idealism," she said.

Her parents and her professors had hoped she'd become a lawyer, yet she wanted to prove that motherhood was as important if not more so than all the professional possibilities.

"It was a revolutionary act," Holly said.

"How so?"

"I was an 'A' student and some of the top law schools were … I didn't appreciate—and I don't appreciate—how our society subjugates mothers. It was—and is—the most profound experience of my life, yet people would see my growing belly and shake their heads as if I were on drugs or something."

"That's awful."

"I know."

In her lap she brushed her sleeping daughter's hair from her face.

"How'd you become a teacher?"

"Idealism."

They laughed.

"It's ingrained," Holly said. "Teachers and mothers—it's a radical, even innovative act if someone with any sort of merit becomes one. Like you, you just don't look like a teacher."

"Thanks a lot."

"I mean that in the right way. Those who could be the best teachers often veer off into something else. People still ask me what I'm going to do with my life."

"Like who?"

"My dad. Some friends. People think I spend my day in pajamas eating ice cream."

"You have a job."

"But it doesn't fulfill the career expectation that's been thrust upon me."

Holly's eyes found Gabriel's, and for a moment they grimaced at each other in agreement.

"Where's Chloe's father?"

Holly closed her eyes, slowly shook her heavy head. "He's in L.A. What do you tell a child? At first to Chloe I said nothing, but kids are pretty perceptive."

"So what did you tell her?"

"I told her Santa Claus loves her."

Gabriel laughed.

"I needed some higher power to help discipline. It's like—" She takes on a nasal inflection, "'Wait till your father gets home ...'" She laughed. "For years I would say, '*Santa's watching*'. And it worked. Chloe always behaved at the mention of Santa."

"How did you tell her the truth?"

"About Santa? She still believes."

"Really?"

"I guess, I mean I'm not going to shatter it for her."

"Perpetuate the lie?"

"Gabriel, you are such a strict idealist. The moment I became a mom—ethics, morality—all that vanished. I lost my purity. Sometimes you just want your child to be safe, or to behave, or to understand."

"I just ... I think honesty is important."

"So do I," Holly said, "though some things are more important."

"Like what?"

"Would you lie to help a student?"

"No."

"What if he's in danger?"

"I just think our life is an example and a lie can—proliferate."

"Sometimes it's—not necessarily easier—but more effective," Holly said, "especially when dealing with someone who could care less about honesty or fairness and may very well mean you serious harm. Then what?"

"Like who?"

"Like if some figure of authority threatened to take Chloe from me because he believed I was an unfit mother because we lived in some weird way. You're damn right I would lie, and more."

"Like living in the woods?"

"Yes."

"Can that happen?"

"Yes."

An energy seethed beneath her words and at first she returned Gabriel's gaze but then looked away. The light of the TV flickered off Holly's face. Gabriel glanced up at the vega beams—the long, cracked logs that spanned the length of the house, which was basically one big room—the living room and the kitchen—with two adjoining bedrooms.

"I became a teacher accidentally, I guess." Gabriel stepped into the spotlight so Holly could retreat. "I'd been all through the States but never out. I figured the quickest way to get worldly was to go to the most different place I could think of."

"India."

"Yup. Even the smells were different. I ended up in upper Dharmsala where a huge community of exiled Tibetans live, and some English guy asked if I was a Yank. He needed someone to take over his class and they wanted to learn American English. I figured it was another experience to absorb."

"What do you mean?"

"I mean I never imagined being a teacher—I hated school. I didn't know what a lesson plan was, I didn't have any guidelines or benchmarks or requirements. It was a pure experience. Like something amazing you do before you know how amazing it is—you experience it without any sort of expectation—I just stepped in front of the class, smiled, and waited for liftoff."

The class had consisted of one woman and eighteen guys, half wore the Tibetan monk's saffron robes and all were in their early twenties. Six were named Tenzin, three Lobsong, and all were eager for anything Gabriel had to say, and Gabriel had no idea teaching could be any different.

"But it *was* different," Holly said.

"Yes," Gabriel said. "It was India and they were Tibetans and I knew nothing about teaching. In class we'd make fake phone calls or do acting exercises that I've done for years. Once the word 'life' came up and trying to translate it I acted out an entire scenario as a definition: I started as a crying baby and did each stage of life— from little boy to nasty teen to working stiff, all the way to hobbled old man—until I died a painful death in the corner of the classroom. They loved it, I loved it. Once during a game of hangman my answer was 'angel' and they got it even though their culture's steeped in reincarnation. They don't really have angels, at least not the way we do."

After class Gabriel's students would invite him into their cramped rooms for butter tea, which Gabriel could hardly stomach. Unable to exchange many words, Gabriel and Lobsong sat together in Lobsong's room. This was the Lobsong who spoke no English, yet he arrived every day for class with a huge smile and in his prized blue jeans. As they sat grinning at each other holding their cups of butter tea, there was a knock on the door and a heavyset monk wrapped in his maroon robes entered. Lobsong leapt over to greet him. The monk was a bit older and had eyes that were glowing, smiling slivers of silver moons. Lobsong turned to introduce him to Gabriel.

"This," Lobsong had said, "Angel."

To Holly Gabriel said: "Lobsong was understanding! He was learning. I was so excited—they must have heard my heart beating."

Maybe Holly could hear Gabriel's heart beating now—thumping, thumping. Gabriel felt her feeling him—felt her concern, her curiosity, felt her empathy. When they looked at each other a pause filled with relevance bulged between them. Gabriel observed the smooth lean of her jaw and he wanted to brush her cheek with his fingertips, he wanted to bow forward and close his eyes and press his lips to hers. His body shuddered with excitement or anxiety or both and she must have noticed.

"I know Gabriel," was what she said in response. "I know, everything's been so nice, and natural. Can we just, you know, can we just see?"

"Oh, sure yeah of course," Gabriel said bumping himself to his feet.

"Gabriel, I feel—a lot of things. We live together already. I don't want this all to go wrong. Chloe likes you so much."

Gabriel ended in his room pacing. Did he blow it? What was he thinking? So stupid. Of course they were living in the same house, of course Chloe was young and fragile and for her any movement required prudence, and of course thoughts and feelings of Sasha, his old girlfriend, still lingered, but it was different—Holly was different. She was magnificent, opinionated and directed and sane. So kind and such a great mom. And she was right about so much even as she pushed upstream as a single mother. Gabriel didn't just like her—he liked himself with her. Her attention lent Gabriel's words weight. He loved how she had lived and the choices she made seemed so radical and pure. Gabriel wanted to live a unique life, yet growing up and living as an anomaly in this society had always seemed to Gabriel to be mutually exclusive—they could not exist as one, yet Holly embodied both, grown up and still idealistic. Shit. Did he blow it? He didn't want things in their home to now be awkward. He paced. He couldn't lie down and sleep with these crinkled issues lingering.

He tapped on their bedroom door, but no one answered, so he pushed and it creaked an inch open.

"Holly," he whispered, "Holly. I'm so sorry. I wasn't thinking. I uhm, I don't want things to be weird, things won't be weird. Okay?"

"Okay," she said, and it shocked Gabriel, for he thought maybe he had been talking to the air in the dark as they slept.

He started to his own room but turned back for a moment—

"Goodnight."

"Goodnight."

Gabriel counted seven—and he hadn't included himself. Not a roomful, but enough to call it a club.

Signs in school hung up in the hallways often get defaced or torn down. Their 'Be a Geek, Join the Poetry Club' sign did not escape that fate. Someone had ripped it, leaving one half and taking the other. Either by design or fate, the sign now read 'Geek Poetry'. And the sign, in its new altered state, hung for longer than the original.

To Gabriel, it wasn't a geek club. At least not in the way 'geek' was meant as a putdown. Some kids were too busy dressing right, too concerned with what not to say, too cool to put any effort into their work—any emotion into anything, busy on their phones, whereas the members of the poetry club fired their emotion and energy into their poems. They might have been timid outside Gabriel's classroom, but here they showed themselves.

From his seat Sammy shouted a poem. His eyes closed, his head cast back on his shoulders, he was unconstrained and vulnerable when the door banged open and two boys stood in the back sizing up the room. All the members of the club turned to see, and the two in the back said nothing and made no movement. They waited. They posed. Gabriel felt the candid energy in the room cap to a halt.

"Geek Poetry?" the curly blond-headed boy asked.

"It is," Gabriel answered.

"We have arrived," the blond boy said and leapt up to sit on a desk.

His friend moved like a cat, cautious yet confident. He pulled a chair back and slid down into it.

Everyone remained still, watching, unsure.

"Proceed," the blond boy said.

Isabel stood to her full stature as if to meet this kid's confidence with her own composure.

"Can you please shut the door," she said.

The blond kid turned to see that they had left the door wide open. He inched back around to look at Isabel.

"Of course," he said, and he eased up onto his feet.

At the door he turned to Isabel and with exaggerated theatrics he set the door closed without a sound. He tiptoed back to his seat and motioned for Isabel to continue.

"Okay," Isabel said. "Sammy was in the middle of his poem."

"I was finished."

"Okay, uhm, ah, how about either of you? I'm sorry, what were your names?"

"I'm Drew and this is Ned," the curly blond boy said.

"Greetings. Welcome. I'm Isabel and this is Mr. Abrams, our sponsor, and—"

They went around the room and everyone forced out their names.

"How y'all doin'?" Drew said.

"Do either of you want to share a poem?"

"I sure do," Drew said and from his pocket he pulled out his phone. He cleared his throat and started laughing. Then he cleared his throat again. "The tundra glances at the sky." He laughed his cool laugh. "The tundra glances at the sky as if to say I want to embrace you." From his phone he read his whole poem, and it was good, but his flippancy took away from his flow.

"Thank you, Drew," Isabel said. "That was wonderful. Very unique."

"Yup," Drew said.

But after that no one else wanted to read.

And the lunch period ended.

And after everyone left, Lori and Isabel lingered.

"Why are they here? Why do they have to be here?" Lori said. "They just wanna mess with us."

"No they don't," Isabel said. "Did you hear Drew's poem?"

"If only Justin had come. He would have had *something* to say."

Lori laced that word—'something'—with so much indignation it stunk as soon as it left her mouth in a flash of anger.

"We should at least give them a chance," Gabriel said.

"Are you kidding?" Lori said. "Do you know who that kid is—Ned—that kid that said nothing? That's the kid who poisoned the milk freshmen year."

"No one poisoned the milk," Isabel said.

"You don't know that," Lori said. "There's a reason he sat in back not saying anything."

"What reason?"

"Just that."

"Just what?"

"Just that."

Always and endlessly styled or brushed or curled, Lori's bumblebee hair could have been a poem unto itself, for so much energy went into it. She wasn't unattractive, but when she slumped into the classroom hiding behind a stack of books or a wisp of her fallen hair you'd think she'd cower from a leaf in a breeze. She walked in a protective position. That was why it was such a shock when she had her acute outbreaks of anger. Underneath her eggshell, *something* was ticking.

Lori had been obsessed with the ghostly presence of Justin, her friend and supposed savior of the poetry club who never came after promising Lori and Isabel that he would. At the beginning of those first meetings they anticipated his arrival. When it became clear that he was never going to show, Lori wrote a poem in which she likened him to a smooshed mosquito, and when the group discussed a name for their poetry group, the first offering came from a sarcastic Lori—"Justin's Poetry Club."

No one laughed. Gabriel thought it kind of creepy, and the group skirted around the offering. Besides, the discussion seemed but a formality, for Isabel presented the group with its name: the Poets' Circle.

When Perry rose to recite a poem, Lori shrunk away from his girth, and Perry noticed. Perry was huge, six-eight, maybe three hundred pounds, a face a mess of acne, and as if to accent it all he wore only black vintage concert T-shirts. Today was *Black Death*.

With his poem on a piece of paper in his hands, Perry's shoulders curled in over his chest as if to reduce his size. Everybody saw Perry teeter—another teenage leper.

Perry glanced at his poem, his fingers loosened, and the page fell to the desktop and Perry wiped his sweaty palms on his jeans.

"Uhm—I'm sorry," he said. "I'm just ... big, I know."

Lori peeked up at him. "Are you gonna read?"

"Uhm actually," Perry said, "let me write." He dropped back to his seat, flipped his poem over, and started writing on the back.

"I'll read," Drew said, sliding open his phone.

Drew's quiet buddy Ned had not returned to the poetry group since that first day. Gabriel wouldn't admit it, but he was relieved. Ned had sat in the back dripping attitude and stinking of cigarettes.

When Drew finished Perry raised his hand, trying to get Isabel's attention.

"I think I wanna read now."

Perry stood all the way up.

"This poem is called *Tiny*. It's autobiographical."

Perry took a deep breath, and then began the poem he had just written:

As big as a bee sting
As big as a thorn
As big as a grain of sand—

Just then the bell rang.

The Poets' Circle had gained a bit of momentum. The classroom was never crowded, yet consistently there were seven or eight students, and there was never enough time for everyone who wanted to read. Often Gabriel would write a short poem—for he too was inspired—yet two-thirds of the way through the meeting he would tuck his poem back into his notebook. He wasn't about to step in front of Sammy or Tiffany or Drew or poor Lori who ached more and more to read. One day they agreed to shift the meetings from Tuesday's forty-minute lunch to Wednesday after school where they would have an unlimited amount of time.

Isabel made a habit of asking each individual to read, encouraging everyone to share. Through her example, she influenced them to present their poems with more enthusiasm, with more energy, more performance. The others followed her lead and, instead of staying seating, began to take their place at the front of the room when they read their poems. As the weeks passed they presented their poetry with a stronger sense of purpose.

At that first after school meeting, Ned, Drew's cool-as-ice friend, walked in and took a chair in back. He said nothing. Lori couldn't help but to keep peeking back at him, and she read no poem that day. From then on week after week Ned sat in the back never offering a poem or a comment or any sort of enthusiasm. Nervously tapping his foot, he sat there menacing the others. Isabel would ask him if he wanted to read a poem and he'd lean sideways and shake his head no. Gabriel thought to corner him alone and say something to him—persuade him to share or smile or leave, but Gabriel didn't, for Isabel was the leader, and the club had its own velocity.

One day without fanfare when Isabel asked who wanted to share, an arm in the back of a forest of arms rose up without calling attention to itself. Gabriel saw it. So did Isabel.

"Ned," she said.

Ned stood up and skulked to the front of the room. No sheet of paper, no notebook, he had nothing in his hands. Forehead glistening with sweat, his eyes pointed nowhere but the floor. After a moment he started mumbling and his mumbles had the familiar cadence of the freestyle rap, yet none of his words could be understood. Gabriel listened, he focused, finally catching a few clear syllables: Ned was rapping about how nervous he was. Ned looked up and started rapping about what was hanging on the walls and the color of the classroom and the sun coming through the window. He was moving his right hand in a stereotypical rap gesture:

holding his knuckles out and moving his tense wrist in small forward circles with each accented rhyme. After counting the desks in the room, his voice grew sharper as he rapped about the power of fists, how "two was a start and four could change your heart and six fully furled could alter the world." He was moving now and Drew started knocking out a rhythm on the desk and Gabriel heard a jagged laugh and Sammy started to pound on his desk as well. Lori joined in, and Isabel's head was bobbing in rhythm, and Gabriel realized his own foot was tapping, so he joined by rapping his fingers in time on the desktop and before long everyone was pounding in unison on the desks, on the floor, on the walls. The room shook and shuddered. The room thundered. Ned, now filled with energy and assurance, snapped his rap to a close and joined the drumming which built and twisted and culminated. And stopped.

There was silence.

And then laughter.

And now applause.

Within the week all three of Gabriel's freshmen classes started *Cannery Row*, a short engrossing novel by John Steinbeck. Gabriel planned to read it aloud both for dramatic purposes and to allow Gabriel to point out poetic lines and insightful metaphors and poignant interactions—the subtle beauty of the book—to the students who might otherwise race over it.

"'Cannery Row in Monterey in California is a poem, a stink, a grating noise, a quality of light, a tone, a habit, a nostalgia, a dream.'"

What an opener. Gabriel loved how 'a poem' sat next to 'a stink' and how 'a grating noise' was juxtaposed to 'a quality of light'. It said so much of the contradictions the book would highlight.

Gabriel also loved the word 'juxtapose'. He spun around and wrote it on the board—a new vocabulary word.

Gabriel continued reading: "'Its inhabitants are, as the man once said, "whores, pimps, gamblers, and sons of bitches."'"

Gabriel read the end of that sentence hard and gritty—the language called for it. He stressed the last three words, setting up the alternate reflection: "Had the man looked through another peephole he might have said, 'saints and angels and martyrs and holy men—'" but Gabriel didn't get there.

"'Bitches? Sons of bitches?'" Jorge wasn't about to let that slide.

"You said 'bitches,'" Rodney said.

"Then we can say it?" Nathan said.

Though these students understood the rightness of sometimes using such words, and though this was about contradicting the teacher and stopping the class, and though he hated stuttering the flow of John Steinbeck, Gabriel felt compelled to address the issue.

"You guys are all certainly insightful," Gabriel said. "You know when it's appropriate to swear. And when it's not. When is it appropriate to swear?"

"Right now."

"When having sex."

"When you hit your hand with a hammer."

"If you're in your garage, maybe," Gabriel said, "but not in the library. What about in a song?"

"Totally."

"In the context of this book it's appropriate. Like in a song, it sets a tone and art has larger boundaries. If the piece needs it, then the artist, the writer, the singer must. There's an artist who paints with feces."

"What's feces?" a student asked.

"Shit," another answered.

"Now was that appropriate?"

"I'm just telling her what 'feces' is."

"Gross."

"People were deeply offended by this guy's paintings, but it's his art. Now are you going to hang it in your kitchen? Probably not. Steinbeck needs a full pallet of words to describe Cannery Row, but that doesn't give us the right to say the same things in a different context. Context is everything. A song may cuss up a storm but throw the same words around the breakfast table and your mothers'll be appalled."

Gabriel returned to the introduction. "'Its inhabitants are, as the man once said, "whores, pimps, gamblers, and sons of bitches."'"

"In context," Rodney said.

"'Had the man looked through another peephole he might have—'"

"This book is fuckin' stupid," Jorge said, "... *in context.*"

*C*ontext certainly is everything. Gabriel had witnessed the teacher who had offered him a latte, Ms. Bimble, chastise students in the hall for profanity, yet Gabriel heard her swearing up a storm in the teacher's lounge. Hypocrite? Maybe. Gabriel wanted a classroom where students didn't swear, but outside of school he felt the urge as if his cuss words were all bottled up and if he didn't release them into an appropriate space—well, he feared in a frayed emotional state he might spit one out in a bad moment. So he made a point of swearing on weekends when the house was empty—and it felt good. He'd sit in his room, gaze out the window, and let out a litany of cuss words, one right after the other like a line of razorblades.

There is a certain cathartic joy in swearing. At its best, swearing can be like poetry, or singing when the flow of the sounds exiting the mouth is as important—or more important—than the words' meanings. Check out opera. You can feel the passion without understanding the language. When we scream our swears, we aren't trying to be rational. We are expressing emotions that don't need to be articulated exactly. We hurl out a jumble of swear words so as not to explain but to communicate without the details. We are scratching the bile out of our bellies. Like walruses bellowing.

"It's pointless," she said. "A waste of fucking time. His and yours. After his sixteenth birthday, you'll never see him again. Except in the police report."

Ms. Bimble was gruff, a jagged bitter shrew. Gabriel and Ms. Bimble shared fourth period as their prep period, and Gabriel was often racing to the bathroom or to the copy machine. She'd invite him for a latte. She had a stainless-steel espresso maker from Italy that made one cup at a time and a milk steamer with a plunger for frothing.

"A waste of fucking time, a fucking waste of time. A done deal—why force him to come?"

"Maybe someone could have an effect on him," Gabriel said.

"Like who?"

"Like me. Or someone else."

"We're teachers—not wizards. We don't perform lobotomies."

The week before, a new student had appeared in Gabriel's doorway. A big guy with too much facial hair to be a freshman, Archie handed Gabriel the pink admission slip.

"I'm supposed to be in this class," he had said.

A different sort of kid, Archie never brought anything to class—not a book, not a pen, not a bag, not even a jacket when it snowed. He never flashed gang signs, he never complained about his stepfather, he never opened even a crack. He hid his shaved head with a blue bandana beneath a baseball cap. He wore oversized sports jerseys that dripped off his torso like a sickly extra layer of skin. He never showed his broken front teeth, but his knuckles—red weeping scabs—were always in fists on the desktop. He sat in the back and never said a word. He didn't have an attitude, didn't need an attitude, for his pores leaked malice, and wherever he went he carried his silent crisis. This boy was in turmoil, and cops and teachers and his mother and his parole officer would say it was too late for him. Gabriel refused to believe it, but a strong resolve alone can't redirect a plunging mass.

Archie never did a single assignment, never started one or even pretended. Most failing students make up excuses or turn in unacceptable shards of their assignments or plagiarize. Not Archie. He turned in nothing and offered no excuse.

Gabriel wondered why he even came—until he got a call from his probation officer who wanted to know if Archie Gordon was attending Gabriel's English class. Gabriel insisted on telling the man that Archie hadn't done any work, but the man didn't care.

"He's there—right?"

Gabriel was told that if Archie missed a single class he would again be incarcerated and this time not in a juvenile facility but in the state penitentiary. Until his sixteenth birthday, that is. After that, by law, he (or any student for that matter) didn't have to come to school anymore.

Archie sitting in Gabriel's class day after day doing nothing seemed such a waste. My God, he had to be there, why not do something—anything? Even doodle. Gabriel thought he could influence Archie more than another teacher could because Gabriel decided he was a different sort of teacher and maybe Archie could see that. Also, Gabriel may have had more sway with Archie than he had with other students because Archie was far removed from school—there wasn't that customary teacher/student barrier between them. Gabriel had no power over Archie and therefore Archie didn't automatically resent him for his position.

When he first arrived in Gabriel's class, Archie was two months shy of his sixteenth birthday and thus two months before he didn't have to come anymore. Gabriel counted each day that passed.

Over a latte, he asked Ms. Bimble for advice.

"They should just let go," she said.

It seemed awful.

"This is my twenty-seventh year institutionalized, hrrckhm—" She fake-cleared her throat. "—I mean teaching, not including my formative years on the other side of the barricade."

Though long past her spoil date, Ms. Bimble looked at Gabriel and probably felt his disappointment.

"I'm sorry," she said. "You come in here all idealistic. We all do. You just have to leave him alone. Let him bide his time."

"But he might as well do something as he bides his time," Gabriel said.

He wanted so much to help. He took a sip of his latte. He felt powerless.

"Getting frustrated day after day with a student who wouldn't or couldn't or shouldn't is worse than banging your head against a wall. At least the wall won't strike back."

"But still."

"Well, shit," she said, as if giving up. "I don't know, you can ask him if he wants to work. What else can you do? Every day politely, nonthreateningly, carefully ask him if he wants to do something today. Maybe one day he'll surprise us all. Unlikely."

Maybe Gabriel was naïve. From then on, every day he asked Archie if he felt like working today, and every day Archie declined, but still Gabriel persisted.

In many professions, the harder you work, the more success you enjoy. No matter how late Gabriel stayed up, no matter how long he spent on his lesson plans or how meticulously he considered his students' essays or how thoroughly he combed the internet for ideas, no matter how much energy he dedicated to helping Archie, he could do nothing. He asked him questions about his interests, he invited him to stay after class to talk, he left pamphlets in front of him for relevant courses he could take at the community college, but they were always abandoned on the desk after he left. And worst of all (Ms. Bimble would say) Gabriel grew to like Archie, a soft kid who burned with misplaced vitality. And that's what hurt the most. In Archie, Gabriel sensed intelligence buried beneath so much rage, yet he could do nothing to uncover it. Archie never hassled Gabriel. Never tried to humiliate him in front of the class. Never demanded energy or class time or attention. He sat in the back and gazed out the window. Soon the fuse would burn down.

One day feeling in a light and outgoing mood, Gabriel slid a pencil and a piece of paper onto Archie's desk. Archie kept staring out the window.

"Today's the day, Archie. Today's the day."

"No, not today," Archie replied, still looking out the window.

"Are you sure? I can feel it—can't you feel it?"

And then Archie did something amazing. He turned and looked up at Gabriel and gave him a small smile.

Less than a week shy of his sixteenth birthday, Archie stopped coming to class. Gabriel waited for him every day. He marked him present until his name no longer appeared on his attendance sheet.

Shifting the Poets' Circle from Tuesday lunches to Wednesday after school removed time as a pressing factor, but it was more. During their lunchtime meetings, they stepped out of their day, out of the chaos of Los Pinos High, but when the bell rang they were thrust out of their sanctuary back into the current of students and classes and hassles. Meeting after school, they no longer had to exit into a condemning high school hallway. Wednesday afternoons, when they left, the school was empty. The halls were theirs. Their haven didn't have to remain cooped up and left behind in Mr. Abram's classroom. It flowed out of the room and powered seamlessly into their lives.

Wednesday afternoon long after the poetry meeting had begun, Ned arrived. He didn't join the circle, he didn't take a seat, not even in the back. He stood by the door with his arms thrust in his pockets. His hair messier than usual, his shirt torn at the neck.

After Sammy recited his poem Isabel motioned to Ned even though he hadn't raised his hand or gestured for attention at all. Ned made his way to the front of the room and then, looking down, he stood there for a moment, for two moments. His hand began his circular motions as if winding up his words.

Dr. Fitzpatrick is a cunt
Dr. Fitzpatrick is a cunt
Dr. Fitzpatrick is a cunt ...

Gabriel should've stopped him. If it were during their lunchtime meetings he would have stopped him, yet after school with a mostly empty building ... he still should have stopped him.

Dr. Fitzpatrick is a cunt
Dr. Fitzpatrick is a cunt
A frickin' affront
To my sensibili-tee
Dr. Fitzpatrick the cunt
On her witchhunt
Like a dog and his
Big ass motherfuckin' blunt

Higher on power
A top her witchtower
And me in my cower ...

And off he went describing getting blamed for something he didn't do. His repeated rhythm grew tedious, but he showed his emotions with unwavering courage—how could Gabriel not admire that?

The rhythm stopped and Ned, his hands now at his side, looked out at everyone.

Nobody clapped. Ned sat on a desktop next to Drew, who nodded to him like a soldier.

"How'd they get to have so much power over us?" Perry asked.

"They've lived longer."

"That's so random."

"All teachers are like that."

"Except Mr. Abrams."

"Yeah, except for you Mr. A."

"Thanks."

"This prick, this effing prick." Lori was grumbling. "It's like everybody at this school is so out for themselves—and, and so into themselves—not even an apology can be mustered for something that they did." Lori had sat quietly simmering until Ned's piece cracked her open. "I wanna explode—or scratch or cry or do something that would be like a slap in their face to wake them up and be like 'you affect people and you don't even know.'"

Some boy, earlier in the day, had bumped into Lori and knocked her books out of her hands and instead of helping her pick them up or even apologizing he laughed at her then left, leaving her on her knees gathering her books.

"His laugh was so dismissive, like a tossing back of his head," she said. "As if he just tossed back his head."

She stopped and there was a silence, which she soon filled with her own laugh, a big loud laugh, an uninhibited laugh—she flung her face up and her hair bounced around on her back.

"You should write a poem about that," Isabel said.

"What would that do?"

"Make you feel better."

"I already feel better," Lori said. "I would wanna do something—not just write a poem, but do something, slug him, make that kid feel how I felt."

"Man, if a poem could do that," Perry said.

"Why can't a poem do that?" Gabriel said.

"Because it's just a poem," Ned said.

"And who'd read it anyways," Lori said.

"You don't write poems for other people to read, or—*Jesus fuck*," Ned said, "to change something."

"Why not?"

"'Cause you just don't," Ned said. "Powerful people don't read poetry—or write it. Dr. Fitzpatrick certainly doesn't. Or that kid who knocked your books down. Only pussyfuckers like us do. And we are the weak, the powerless, the insignificant. We do it to make ourselves feel better. That's it."

"Then why are you here?" Isabel said.

"I didn't say I didn't like poetry."

"He's just stating his opinion," Drew said.

"You're right I'm sorry," Isabel said. "But I disagree. I think poetry could definitely change things. And Ned, your pieces say just as much?"

"They're just words."

"Still."

"They don't mean anything."

"How can you say that?"

"Easy."

"I think poetry can change things," Sammy said.

"How?"

"I like what Lori said," Gabriel said. "About making that kid feel how she felt."

"Yeah," Isabel said, "poetry explains how we feel to people who otherwise wouldn't know."

"Wouldn't understand."

"Wouldn't care."

"Wouldn't read it." Ned turned away.

"Then we should make them read it."

"How?"

"How 'bout we write poems on posterboards?" Lori said. "Hang them around school."

"Why not just fill the walls with graffiti?" Ned said. "The powerless having their piece."

"We can't do graffiti," Isabel said.

"Why not?"

"'Cause we're a school club."

They all turned to Mr. Abrams: "Can we?"

*Is there something different about you,
something you like that others may not?
Explain. Would you change it?*

Third night in a row I couldn't sleep. At four in the morning my phone rang from an 'unknown' number and when I answered nobody was there. After work I arrived home to a mailbox with not one but two credit card offers for Gabriel. Sometime ago, off on one of his adventures, he directed his mail to my apartment and I'll probably keep getting his mail after *I'm* dead. It's like fingernails growing in the coffin.

Even though I kept to it, my routine sank into something altogether different: my sleep disjointed, my shower cold, my subway rides filled with memories, work a distraction.

I could feel Gabriel in my body—there's physical sensation attached to memory and sometimes there's just physical sensation with no memory. I'll feel a creaking in my bones and know something must be up with Gabriel. One time he returned from one of his journeys and even unannounced I knew it was him creaking up the stairs, hovering outside my door before he knocked. That whole week after the New Mexican state trooper called to say they found

Gabriel's abandoned car, I sensed Gabriel as if he were pausing outside my door. Between us a familiarity, a comfort, a shared history existed. We clung to the same memories—we sprang forth from the same matter. Once when we were boys we squished together through a subway turnstile because we only had enough for one fare, and a Transit Authority cop saw us and started after us. A train roaring through the tunnel into the station, we grabbed at each other and raced down the concrete steps, Gabriel in excitement letting out a howl echoing through the underground as we made it to the platform and onto the train right as the doors were closing.

That lurching action of the 'L' train had been imprinted onto us like an affecting youthful dream. It set Gabriel in motion from which he could not stop, yet for me it represented a stagnation. Or at best a comfort. We took the 'L' to school when we were young and it took me to work when I was older. The motion of the train alone can jar loose images, emotions, memories. The train lurches, my elbow smacks the back of a seat, and I feel the pain and anger and the love too and maybe the jealously I harbor in regards to Gabriel's adventures as if that resentment was brought on by my own stifling sense of responsibility.

My pocket was buzzing. I pulled out my phone and saw my mother was calling again.

"Hello," I said as I climbed the stairs from the subway into the light of the street. "Everything's great. Yeah, uhm, yeah, how are you—"

Her conversation mundane, I could tell she hadn't heard of Gabriel's latest—the New Mexican state trooper hadn't called her too.

I sat on a step beneath the arch of a building's entrance. "Mom, yesterday I got a call from a New Mexican State Trooper …"

"There's a certain place in our hearts where our truths reside." Gabriel stood in the middle of his classroom. "We need to find this place, we need to feel it, know it, be driven through with its spirit. What we feel there may go against all that is around us—all that our friends say or that which our heroes spew or what our parents and teachers and bosses insist. Don't be driven from your truth. Out there all these pressures may be lies and we'll realize that if we can press our palms to our hearts, and listen. We have to stand up for what we believe. For if we don't, if we won't, it'll lose its power. The light will dim. Never be afraid to speak your truth, to live what you truly believe—never fear being who you are. Never."

In Gabriel's classroom after school for the next few days the poets scrawled their poems in multiple colors on boards and hung them all over the school in open areas like the halls as well as more covert places like bathroom stalls and conference rooms and in the backs of bookshelves in the library. They taped them on the ceilings of classrooms and on the floors in the corridors. They wrote poems on index cards and stashed them between the pages of random books in the library and in the toilet paper rolls in the bathrooms. They stuck them with gum under chairs. They crumpled them in random students' backpacks. They slipped them through cracks into lockers. They left them sticking out of the coin returns of the soda machines. They wrote them and abandoned them on computer screens throughout the school.

    And then they waited.

    For what? For something. A response. An acknowledgement. Even a whisper or a rumor or a mention somewhere, anywhere, but nothing. To their knowledge, no one ever saw them or read them, much less were affected by one of their stealth poems.

One early morning as Gabriel entered the school building, he saw a security guard tearing one up off the floor and he had others crunched under his arm.

"There's not a single one left," Sammy said in the next Poets' Circle.

Gabriel suffered a tinge of disappointment at the removal of their posterboard poems, for their excitement and expectation had filled Gabriel with admiration—they desired to push their poems into the world and they concocted a plan and set it in motion. Gabriel should have anticipated the group's setback. They stumbled into his classroom crestfallen. Even Gabriel thought their poetry assault would elicit a reaction. He didn't know what. But nothing?

"How do we get people to read our poems?" Lori asked, already defeated, and then to herself, "How do we get people to read our po—"

"With a baseball bat," Ned said.

Isabel had been plotting: "Why don't we ambush them with poetry?"

"What do you mean?"

"Step in front of someone and present a poem."

"Walk right up and scream it in their *face*," Drew said. "Verbal graffiti."

"Where?"

"Just in the hall."

"Not at school, please," Lori said.

Drew leapt up on a desk making dramatic motions with his hands—and then he froze, staring out like a mystic: "We can set up on a street corner and just start rapping."

"Put a hat out for spare change."

"A poetry burst out."

"Awesome."

"Really?"

"Yes."

"What are we planning?" Lori was nervous.

"We'll go to the plaza—"

"Or any busy corner."

"Awesome."

"Really?"

"When?"

*W*ell before the end of second period, Gabriel's third period gathered in the hallway outside his door. Someone pulled the door open just to disrupt the class. The door drifted closed. And then again the door flew open as if by magic.

Though the bell had yet to ring, Gabriel released his second period class. As he walked back to his desk he noticed someone had dropped a pencil in his water bottle.

An excitement swept in with the students. Something had happened. Maybe another fight. Maybe a bomb scare. Gabriel had no energy for intrigue. Tired and stressed, he sat at his desk needing a big gulp of water, but a slimy pencil bobbed in his bottle.

Crystal, a sweet girl who sat closest to the teacher's desk, turned to Gabriel: "Oh Mr. Abrams, you won't believe what Nathan said to Ms. Harbough."

Gabriel knew he should care, because what happened in Ms. Harbough's class often carried over into Gabriel's.

"I can't say what he said—" Crystal buzzed like a bee. "Can I? Can I say it, is it okay, is it 'in context?'"

"He called her a 'gay fag dyke bitch cunt,'" Carl said.

"Carl! Please."

"But that's what he said."

"That may be but—"

"What am I supposed to do—lie?"

"You want him to lie," Jorge said.

"We just want you to know why Nathan's not coming to class."

"Yeah," Rodney said, "he called her a 'dyke fag bitch.'"

Gabriel schlepped back to his desk, fished the pencil out of his water bottle, and took a deep drink.

"N—."

The room filled with noise and activity as students continued to trickle in.

And then again: "N—." The despicable N-word sprang up into the air.

Shocked and now angry, Gabriel looked around—he did in fact hear what he thought he heard. Carl lounged back in a chair on one leg, and he said it again this time while looking right at Gabriel who had taken a position in front of him, scowling down at him.

"That is entirely inappropriate."

"What?"

"That word."

"Why?"

"It's racist."

"No, it's not."

"Yes, it is."

"I'm black. It's not racist if you're black."

Carl was a red-headed white kid.

"It's degrading no matter who says it, and I don't ever want to hear it in this classroom again."

In Gabriel's short career, Carl was the scariest. Even more so than Archie, who could do harm to another, but mostly Archie was doomed himself. Carl, not an immediate threat to himself, was an impending menace. He was an emerging big man on campus, star of the freshmen football team. He sat next to Clarissa, the strong-willed tomboy, and Gabriel overheard Carl saying awful things to her—asking her what her favorite position was, inviting her to wear his jockstrap.

Gabriel tried to talk to Carl after class, but Carl in protest twisted his arms over his chest—it was useless—he wouldn't even open his eyes.

A couple days later: "Clarissa, how many guys came in your face last night?"

From across the room Gabriel thought he heard it—he marched towards Carl.

"What'd you say?"

"Nothing."

"What'd you say?"

"Nothing."

Gabriel glared.

After class he asked Clarissa how she felt about the way Carl spoke to her.

And she said, "You don't hear half the stuff I say to him."

To Gabriel this was a dire situation. Carl—handsome, intelligent, athletic—was heading for trouble. Gabriel imagined the future headline: NMU RACIST FOOTBALL STAR ACUSSED OF MULTIPLE RAPES.

A teacher can start a chain reaction. Carl would listen to Clarissa as he would never to Mr. Abrams.

"If anywhere inside of you doesn't like what he says," Gabriel said to Clarissa, "you should tell him to stop. If not for your sake, then for another woman who's not as strong as you. You allowing Carl to say these things—he may think it's okay to say it to someone else. And worse."

"Maybe," she said, not looking at Gabriel at all.

Gabriel filled out a discipline referral form for Carl and for the first time he turned it in to the principal's office, though he never heard any response.

"Quiet please, quiet." The following day Gabriel was trying to cut through the turmoil, trying to start his third period class. "Let's be quiet now."

"You be quiet!"

"Excuse me?"

Bad behavior spreads faster than good. It wasn't Carl and it wasn't Jorge or Nathan; it was Robertson, who Gabriel couldn't see. All he saw was a clump of black hair behind a giant cellphone and a gloved hand holding it. With the edge of his index finger Gabriel eased the phone to the side.

"Excuse me," Gabriel said.

"I didn't say anything."

"See me after class."

"I didn't do anything," Robertson said.

"Tell me after class."

"I'm not staying."

"Yes, you are."

"No, I'm not."

"Yes, you are."

The endless downward spiral.

"And put your phone away."

After class Robertson, of course, walked right out.

First Gabriel ate lunch so as not to be fueled by his anger. And then he called Robertson's mother. Robertson was becoming disruptive and disrespectful and Gabriel hoped an easy phone call might cut it off before it got worse. Gabriel also thought to ask why Robertson insisted on wearing those gray gloves every day. The phone rang and rang past the point when voicemail should have picked up and then a sterile recorded voice informed Gabriel that for this number no voicemail had been set up.

A second later Gabriel's classroom phone rang.

"You called me!" the voice on the line said and it was not a question.

"Mrs. Sandoval?"

"It's *Ms.* Sandoval."

"Ms. Sandoval, hi. This is Gabriel Abrams, I'm Robertson's English teacher here at Los Pinos High."

"Is everything alright?"

"Well, I'm having a bit of a problem with your son."

"Oh please don't write him up."

"He's been acting disrespectfully towards—"

"Please don't write him up."

"I wanted to talk to you about—"

"We've been having a rough time. We're in the middle of a move and it's been hard on Robertson and he's been sick."

"Well Ms. Sandoval, his behavior is disruptive and—"

"Please don't write him up."

"I need his behavior to improve."

"It will I promise. He's he's struggling, we're struggling. And he's been sick."

"Can you speak with him tonight?"

"Yes, of course, just please don't write him up."

*D*rew's poem sailed along until he stopped—"This is like where the poem really starts to rock."

"Just keep going, Drew," Isabel said.

"But I want you to know what's happening."

"We do."

"Yeah Drew, you don't have to explain it."

"Do it again—straight through, it's great, don't stop."

"Alright alright."

Gabriel could reach out into the air and caress the excitement. That week leading to the Saturday when they would enact their Poetry Burst Out on the street corner, the poets met in Gabriel's classroom every day after school. The meetings had velocity. The poets rushed with an intensity, leafing through piles of poems and journals, searching for the best, and then performing them with gusto. They concentrated on helping to highlight nuances and strengths in each other's work. With a gentle touch Isabel could give criticism that didn't land like criticism. When she told Drew to read his poem without his flow-killing side comments he took the critique as it was meant, not that criticism could disrupt his confidence.

Drew started again. He performed his poem straight through and then gazed out at everyone with his cunning smile and said:

"We're gonna rock it."

And then after Sammy shouted one of his poems:

"Sammy you're the bomb," Drew said. "You can't miss."

And when Isabel told Lori not to hide her face and Lori lifted her head, Drew wailed:

"My God, you're beautiful."

After the meeting Isabel lingered, positioning herself in front of Gabriel.

"This is it."

That was all she said. And she had whispered it, holding an explosion of euphoria beneath her tight lips, her cheeks budding red and round. She ached and Gabriel felt it.

On Wednesday Drew wasn't there. The poets spent much of the time working on Perry's *Tiny* poem, which had grown to epic proportion both in theme and length. He stood at the front of the classroom re-reading the same section, trying to hit the right beat.

Ned sat back without comment and, after Perry, Lori tried to do a poem but wouldn't lift her head.

"Come on Lori," Isabel said. "Remember you're beautiful. Don't hide your face."

She scowled—"He just said that to ... I don't know, I don't wanna read."

The meeting lurched towards an anti-climactic conclusion. The reality of presenting their poems in public had sunk in and dampened their fire.

As if to salvage those last moments, Isabel said, "I found the perfect place. It's right on the street, tons of people, and it's—"

"You found the place?"

"Yeah."

"The actual place?"

"Yeah."

"Where we'll do our poems?"

"In public?"

"Tons of people?"

A panicked silence gripped the room. And then into that gap Lori said—

"Why, why should—just to make fools of ourselves?"

The comment slugged into Gabriel's gut and Isabel didn't right away answer and that empty space left bare took its toll, sapping the room of its confidence. Isabel glanced across the distance at Gabriel.

And then at the meeting on Thursday:

"Don't we need a permit?"

"Can't you get arrested?"

"That'd be awful for my transcript."

Terror flashed across Isabel's face. She stood alone in the middle.

"What are you guys talking about? This is ... this is what we've, it's ... I don't under—"

Isabel's mouth hung open, her eyes becoming wrinkled forms through which she stared. "You guys ..." She glanced around but no one would look at her. She slid into a chair.

"Can't we just do it here?" Lori said.

In a burst Isabel shoved her book bag off the desk and it slammed to the tile floor and everyone looked, but now Isabel stared down into her lap, her book bag dead on the floor at her feet.

Slumping in the desk, she unleashed a long self-imposed silence.

And then she scrapped her chair back, grabbed her bag off the floor, and left the room.

Adjusting his black T-shirt over his big belly, Perry got up and peeked out the door after her. He looked back in the room, strain in his face. Tiffany pointed through the window and the group gathered around to observe Isabel outside standing on the edge of the sidewalk, the ocean of the empty parking lot before her.

From the window they watched Isabel find her posture and take a slow, confident breath like a cliff-diver drinking in her faith.

Isabel, filled with an assertive presence and a deep commitment, began to recite a poem that no one in the classroom could hear, yet they witnessed her arching gestures, her intensity, her passion—her virtuosity. Turned away and off in the distance she was presenting one of her masterpieces to the barren parking lot.

After they watched Isabel vanish into the ripples of the horizon, the students made their way back to their desks, collected their goods, headed for the door.

"That's it?" Gabriel said.

Near the exit they all slumped together, peeking back over their shoulders.

"Do you have no feeling?" Gabriel said. "Did you not just see what I saw? Where's your heart? Where's your spines for that matter? Sit down. All of you, come back in here and sit down."

They slunk back in and sat in chairs, holding their bags in their laps. Gabriel prowled the room.

"This is your life. You can either let it be a pile of mud around you or you can get up and do something. Being nervous is not an excuse—*ever*. The most accomplished actors are always nervous before they go onstage, but it never stops them. Fear stops people you've never heard of. You know why? Ask yourself this: will you live courageously or will you suffer silently, anonymously, vacantly, never able to break through your shell to see what you could become? You guys have worked so hard and you're so ready. And Isabel, our leader, I ... I don't know about you but out that window in the parking lot I just witnessed something profound."

Four-thirty in the afternoon and the school was quiet. The poets had left and, in his classroom exhausted and sitting behind a pile of papers, Gabriel had no intention of leaning forward and grading them. His head was back, his eyes fixed on some random water-damaged spot in the ceiling. The soft green chair held him like a cloud; Gabriel's chair was way more comfortable than his students' chairs.

Without Gabriel having noticed, someone had slipped into his room. Gabriel's eyes fluttered. He looked up. Just inside the doorway, a student from his creative writing class lingered, looking—as if reaching through a shadow. Gabriel sat up and motioned for him to come in.

He crept across the classroom avoiding the desks.

From a plastic chair, this deserted student gazed up at Gabriel as if Gabriel could help. Gabriel looked into his eyes and saw a sea of blue and didn't feel a need to look away. Like this they sat in a bubble, unthinking, as if floating. Gabriel's brain stopped cranking through its normal clutches. He lost track of the minutes. Laughter waltzed in through an empty window before scurrying away. It felt as if this student, Peter Wallace, with all his might was reaching out, and Gabriel from the other side of the world also reached out and with the weight in their eyes they connected—fleetingly. A wellspring of calm opened in a moment outside of life when two looked and saw each other. Precious moments outside of the normal everyday seem so rare. A child playing in the leaves in the fall. A man on a rock in a hotspring. The sun balanced on the horizon at sunset. Sometimes a moment is all we need—a blessed moment when someone looks at us as if they care, a moment when we look and see someone is looking back.

Drowning out a hesitant smile, sweat appeared on Peter's face like a gauze cloth, as if painted, there glistening. He looked away.

He sat there with his eyes cast down towards the floor.

He said nothing.

For five minutes.

But there was no tension.

Peter swallowed in a deep breath. And then he let it go. He got up and shuffled to the door where he hovered. Without looking at Gabriel and through lips that did not move, he thanked him, then slipped out leaving the door ajar.

Gabriel took in his own deep breath and let it out. He leaned forward in his chair, gazing out the crack in the door. He felt a heat in the top of his shoulders just beneath his skin—tears begged to burn. Before today Gabriel had barely noticed Peter. He was like a creeping ghost and ghosts in these halls are often only seen when the blood is already spilling.

*O*n that final Friday afternoon before the momentous Saturday, Perry, Sammy, and Lori slipped into the classroom and unwound a homemade banner. In a spatter of color the painted bed sheet screamed: 'Poetry Burst Out!' They posed beneath it, grinning.
"Yes," Isabel said upon seeing it. "Yes."

Isabel was already there when Gabriel arrived.
The poets gathered on the plaza. They waited for Ned, but he never showed. Gabriel must have been more nervous than they were, for he wanted them so badly to succeed. As they crept to their chosen corner, they were an anxious bunch.
Beneath a large ornate doorway Perry and Sammy unfurled the 'Poetry Burst Out!' banner. They would present their poems beneath it, yet ... who would go first? Isabel had planned to go last, and nobody was volunteering. People on the streets went about their business, shopping, talking, hurrying to their cars. Isabel directed everyone into a semicircle forming an impromptu stage with Perry and Sammy in back holding the banner askew (due to Perry's height). But still nobody wanted to go. Gabriel was about—
"I'll do it," Sammy said. "Hold this."
He passed the corner of the banner to Gabriel. Sammy pulled his baseball cap from his head and, hoping for donations, dropped it on the pavement in front of him. He stretched his lips up off his braces, he pointed to Drew who started thumping out a rhythm on

his bongo drums, and he burst into poetry. A man across the street stopped to watch the spectacle, for Sammy was screaming.

With a little momentum, they traded turns with each poet presenting his or her words with passion, yet they could not attract a crowd. A few pedestrians turned their heads as they passed. A person or two across the street would pause to watch but only for a second. The poets tried to keep up the enthusiasm but with each passing poem and the mounting ambivalence of their potential audience it got harder. They made the best out of the situation. When a poet would finish a poem they would all applaud and shout out encouragements as if the poet were a batter who had just swung and missed.

When he knew his turn was drawing near, Gabriel sensed his fingers tingling. Were his hands trembling? Was he sweating? He wanted to act as poised as possible. He stepped into the center of the group. He had memorized his poem and when he performed it he tried to capture the eye of a passerby. A car alarm interrupted and in that moment Gabriel smelt freshly baked bread.

"I'm going to start over."

And then Gabriel presented his poem straight through with charisma, playing to the groups of people blocks away.

When he finished he felt refreshed. He felt present and powerful. He tried not to smile too widely, but he couldn't help himself.

Everybody had presented except Isabel. She stepped out in front and took a deep breath, finding her place, taking her moment, and then turning that indiscriminate spot into an amphitheater. She burst forth with her words and emotions, transporting herself and the members of the circle into the stratosphere. They had all heard the poems before, but she brought it to a higher intensity. A man stopped in front of her to witness. He dropped a Kennedy fifty-cent piece into the hat and walked on.

When Isabel finished, the poets applauded, but their enthusiasm quickly faded. Isabel's performance couldn't restrain their feelings of defeat.

In the end no one spoke. They shook each other's hands and nodded. Tried to smile.

Sammy scooped the coins out of his hat and counted them.

"Seventy-six cents."

"That's like nine cents each."

You're alone, marooned on an island. A bottle rolls in with the tide. There's a note. What does it say? Write a response.

Gabriel felt exhausted all the time, stumbling around like a broken electric guitar string reverberating with less and less strength. He couldn't catch up on his sleep; he couldn't keep up with the indignation in his classroom, because every day—new traumas, new problems, new lesson plans. No time to breathe. No time to reflect. No time to solve anything today that happened yesterday. A teacher can sleep all summer and return to the classroom rested and ready to go, but by lunchtime she'll be exhausted all over again. And a teacher can't fake it for a day or a class or even for five minutes. If a teacher had a restless night or has debilitating personal problems, it doesn't matter. No sleepwalking. At all moments in front of a class a teacher needs to be vigilant—she needs to be *on*. It's like standing in front of a giant, crashing waterfall. With all those raging personalities pressing, you can't close your eyes and not look. You can't not be affected, you can't not get wet. In a classroom full of teenagers there's just too much happening.

Gabriel had asked his three English classes to write one complete sentence. Out of the eighty-one students who were present, seven had written proper sentences. These were freshmen in high school. More than ninety percent wrote fragments or run-ons or some splash of words that didn't add up to a sentence. And the students were frustrated—

"This is stupid."

"Why do we have to do this?"

"I'm not gonna do this."

Gabriel wrote 'they complained' on the board.

"Can anybody," Gabriel said, "give me a simple two-word sentence? A subject and a verb."

Gabriel had no idea how to teach grammar. He knew not what a gerund was or even all the names of the parts of speech, yet he could write flawlessly. He knew the rules instinctively. Gabriel concluded that he learned proper grammar through reading. With books a reader becomes familiar with correct grammar—not in the mind, but in the bones. Though to write well one didn't need to know all the grammatical jargon, the standardized tests that the students took every other month included this information, and the Language Arts teacher was tasked with relaying this information, therefore Gabriel needed to know what a gerund was.

He spent an entire weekend memorizing grammar. At least when his students asked why they had to learn it, Gabriel had a specific answer: They had full careers of test-taking in front of them.

"How about a verb?" Gabriel prodded.

He gazed around the room. Nothing.

"Come on—a verb, give me a verb."

"Stupid."

"That's not a verb. Verbs are action, movement. I'm talking, talking. To talk. He talked. 'Talk,' that's a verb." Gabriel marched across the room. "Walking walking, I walk. 'Walk' is a verb."

"This is stupid."

"You think?"

"Yeah, I think."

"Good, right, good—'think'—you're thinking, good. 'Think' is a verb." He wrote 'I think' on the board.

The door blasted open and there stood Alejandro with one sagged shoulder weighted by an awkward gym bag. Through the room Alejandro greeted his friends—

"Patrick—What up? Alberto—S'up? China—How ya doin'? Lenny—*que pasa que pasa*? What up, dog? Good, gotcha Snap!"

When Alejandro arrived at his seat, he noticed his teacher's trained glare on him.

"What up, fool?" Alejandro said to Mr. Abrams.

"Excuse me?"

"I said 'what up?' *Que pasa*?"

"Don't ever call me that."

"Call you what?"

"Fool."

"I didn't."

"You did."

"Why you always disrespecting me?" Alejandro said.

"*Me* disrespecting *you*? Are you kidding? You punk."

Some students were intolerable. Mouths spattering nonsense claiming to be all about respect, thinking the world's a salacious music video filled with half-naked vixens lusting after them, they paraded around acting like reprehensible clowns and when questioned they demand respect. The videos showed them this, proved it to be possible, even likely, the way it should be. Act like a cad and be treated like a statesman.

"Okay, where were we? A verb—yes, okay a verb ..."

𝓑etween classes the mess of students socializing in the halls suddenly started stampeding. Gabriel huddled in his doorway. It was like a mass exodus with students pouring towards the exit.

In a moment the halls were clear.

Except at the end of one a single student drifted, his arms spread as if they were wings.

"What's going on?" Gabriel asked.

"A fight, duh."

Taller than the rest Isabel could see over the throng of kids in the quad pressed around the two grappling students. Hands held phones, filming the spectacle, and even though Isabel would have preferred not to have cared, she could see into the center—she could see the combatants. The big one was the star center from the basketball team and the other was puny next to him, but he punched the big kid twice in the face and the big kid staggered. Just then Isabel saw that the little one was Ned from the Poets' Circle, who after delivering these two shocking blows ducked into the crowd. Isabel followed his progress as the crowd above got agitated as Ned pushed through below.

"Excuse me excuse me excuse me," Isabel said cutting through the mob heading towards the edge where Ned would emerge.

But he was quicker and he rushed into the school building and Isabel followed. Now trailing behind, she heard him laughing.

He did a quick one-eighty and ran right into her.

All riled up, Ned grinned his unhinged enthusiasm up at her. Students were now heading towards their classes and though moments ago Ned had been the center of their attention they ignored him or didn't recognize him. Isabel did. She felt the blows he had delivered as if she herself had delivered them, as if somehow they struck somewhere close to her target. She empathized with him, appreciated his rage.

"Are you alright?" she said.

Through the force of his zeal, Ned sneered, "I just don't give a fuck."

And then he turned and vanished into the flow of students.

*G*abriel unwrapped his tuna sandwich—a blessing to be alone in his classroom and to put something in his stomach besides anger, disappointment, disgust, frustration, annoyance. A student who Gabriel had never seen before pushed his way in. Gabriel could have yelled, "Get out!" but he didn't. The student handed him an envelope, then vanished.

The envelope had a big red 'URGENT' scratched across its face, and in pencil Gabriel's name and room number appeared as an afterthought at the bottom. The letter could either be a trifle or some monumental tragedy. In this community the 'URGENT' didn't differentiate. Gabriel enjoyed the modest curiosity overtaking him, so instead of tearing it open he leaned the envelope in the keys of his computer keyboard so the red 'URGENT' shouted out at him as he took another bite of his sandwich. He noticed that the letter was open, that it had never been sealed. He plucked it up. When he slipped out the four folded pages, he desired privacy—he'll lock his door, but when he went to his pocket his keys weren't there. He searched through all his pockets. He looked in his backpack, over his desk. When he pushed the letter back into its envelope the words 'suicidal ideation' leapt out at him, but he was too busy to notice. For his keys he scoured through the room—on the windowsill, in back of the computers, in the closet, behind the dictionaries, on the seat of every chair, and all over the floor. He tapped his pockets. Again he searched through his backpack and his desk, again he poked around the room, then back into his backpack. Gabriel stood at the front of his classroom. He clenched his fists in front of him, he could have screamed a thousand swears. He yanked open his door—maybe he had left his keys hanging from the door's lock. Not there. He left his room open as he raced down to his bike—maybe he had left them there.

He hurried to the bathroom—maybe there?

He stayed in the bathroom, in the mirror searching for calm. When the fifth period bell rang he rushed into his classroom, greeted by a wall of noise. Usually when Gabriel entered his creative writing class, his students found their seats, focusing to the front, eager for their teacher to lend them a thread of inspiration.

"Has anyone seen my keys?" No one responded or even sat down. "Take your seats."

No one obeyed.

Maybe more than he had ever in this class, Gabriel raised his voice—"TAKE YOUR SEATS!" He had no patience. "QUIET! I want everybody to write about a time when they felt aggressive or angry or somehow disturbed. Get your pencils out, get your notebooks open. Write. Right now. What makes you angry? When have you been so aggravated your head exploded sending your dentures into your sister's lap?"

The class broke out laughing, and Gabriel stifled a smile.

"Ready set go."

And there was silence. And then pencils began to scratch across paper.

Gabriel strolled around the room, down the aisles, between the desks, behind the students with his eyes closed. He did his slow circles for twenty minutes until students began to rest their pencils on their pages. Gabriel asked if anyone wanted to read. Six hands shot up into the air. The students in this class were the ones who Gabriel related to, and not just because they were creative, but because they gave him a chance as a teacher. The first student read a poem about eating dinner while mourning her cat that had died.

The next piece might have been a run-of-the-mill teenage rejection essay if it weren't littered with concise similes: "My eyes looked into his deep blue spheres like hooks being cast into the depths of a frozen lake." It might also have been a common teenage treatise if it hadn't been written by a boy about another boy—and written so openly and read so courageously by Peter, who could be so timid sometimes.

Peter Wallace was a good-looking kid even though a veil of acne fought to displace his sculpted features. His most salient trait was his effeminate manner. Many gay students in high school creep below the radar, hiding their homosexuality. Peter dismissed this notion. He could seem a contradiction, sometimes filled with confidence and other times not so much. He wrote with a bold directness, yet he walked with his head cocked low as if trying to dispel attention. In creative writing class, even though he was quiet when not reading, students, especially the girls, seemed to be enchanted by him.

The final bell rang, the doors flew open, and the crammed building bustled with student activity. Two and a half minutes later the building sat empty, the students having made their speedy exit. Every day this repeated itself like a riot of ants suddenly sucked up by a vacuum cleaner.

Gabriel sat at his desk. Out from his chest and through his mouth a sigh unleashed itself like a strained balloon finally giving up its air. In his chair he stretched his arms and sunk into a crooked mess and groaned. When he returned to a normal position, he saw the 'URGENT' envelope sticking out from under a pile of notebooks. He pulled it into his fingers.

But the PA system boomed:

"EVERYBODY MUST LEAVE THE CAMPUS IMMEDIATELY. ALL MEETINGS, ALL SPORTS PRACTICES—ALL AFTERSCHOOL ACTIVITIES—CANCELLED. PLEASE LEAVE THE CAMPUS IMMEDIATELY."

Gabriel sat for a moment. Hmm? He guessed that meant he had to leave. And then he remembered his keys. Aah. He started to rummage through his desk (again) when the fire alarm went off.

AAAARRRR AAAARRRR AAAARRRR AAAARRRR!

Frantically he shuffled through his drawers and made a mess turning over everything on his desk. He stopped and clenched his whole body. His keys were stolen, he knew it.

"Shit."

AAAARRRR AAAARRRR AAAARRRR AAAARRRR!

Forced to leave his door unlocked, Gabriel headed for the exit. In the parking lot teachers gathered to discuss what could be going on. Gabriel walked past his bike as if it weren't his, for he didn't have the key to open his lock.

Gabriel's fatigue and anxiety dropped off his body in the wind as he walked away from the school, the AAAARRRR AAAARRRR AAAARRRR losing its luster the further away he got. He walked all the way home trying not to accuse every student who was ever rude to him of stealing his keys.

At home he stepped in through the front door almost tripping over the dog.

"Hello hello," Chloe said.

"Hello."

Gabriel stood in front of Holly as if they would hug.

"I'm making dinner if you want some? It's not quite ready. Another catastrophic day?"

"Yeah."

"Have a piece of chocolate—from Holland."

"Thanks."

"Can I have another piece, Mamma?"

"You've had enough."

"Not that enough."

In his room as Gabriel searched through his drawers he cursed his whole third period—first as a unit and then individually. He found a spare for each of his keys—his bike lock, his car, his front door—all but his classroom door.

He collapsed onto his bed. From his backpack he plucked the "URGENT' envelope. Los Pinos High School generated so much useless information. For all he knew the letter was a warning to all English teachers that at the end of *Romeo & Juliet* the title characters kill themselves. From the envelope, he pulled out the pages. Glancing over the first one, 'suicidal ideation' leapt out at him again. He turned to the next page and 'suicidal ideation' sprung up from that page too. These four pages were forms in which someone had checked all the appropriate boxes and written extensively in block handwriting in the larger boxes marked 'Comments'. Asterisks and underlining and sentences filled with successive capital letters littered the sheets. Gabriel flipped back to the first page. Written in the line marked 'Student's Name' was 'Peter Wallace'—the hesitant student, the courageous gay writer, the creeping ghost who had slipped into his classroom the week before to silently sit before him. The urgent contents of the envelope were a 'Section 504 Student Accommodation Plan' for Peter. Gabriel had no idea what a 'Section 504 Accommodation Plan' was, but he could guess what 'suicidal ideation' meant. Page after page would fill a reader with fear. "If Peter exhibits anger, depression, or suicidal ideation he MUST be ESCORTED to his school counselor or any school counselor or principal. ... Absences and tardies MUST be reported *IMMEDIATELY!* ... Needs protection from BULLYING or

HARASSMENT of any kind—this may exacerbate his suicidal ideation." Under the heading 'Certificate Of Distribution' thirteen boxes were checked: Parent, Language Arts Teacher, Mathematics Teacher, Science Teacher, History Teacher, Language Teacher, Administrator (in which three principals' names were filled in), and then in the space for 'Other'—Creative Writing Teacher, Counselor, Nurse, even the Librarian received this notification.

Distributed to all these people and in an unsealed envelope by a random student, Peter's Section 504 Accommodation Plan might as well have been broadcast over the PA system in the middle of lunch. Gabriel felt the gravity of the contents. Coupled with the trials so many adolescents endure, homosexuality is almost too much to bear in the cruel setting of a high school, where students can be so insecure and so mean, and in light of the fact that a gay person's allies—often other gay individuals—very well may hide their homosexuality and worse they may lash out at other people they target as gay to either better conceal their own homosexuality or to, in proxy, lash out against their own homosexuality. Or both.

Despite it all Gabriel still had to press forward preparing for another day. After dinner he retired to his room, and Holly waited for him to finish grading papers, figuring-out lesson plans, and shuffling through the clerical work that the administration forced upon their teachers and which Gabriel stared at for forty minutes before shoving aside. It must have been midnight when Holly heard him in the bathroom.

Through the door she whispered, "Movie?"

They sat on the couch in front of the TV, but both fell asleep soon after the movie began.

Gabriel woke in the middle of the night to find the two of them crunched together. His left arm was numb. Holly must have been uncomfortable too, but if he woke her up they would have to drag themselves to their separate rooms. He closed his eyes and felt her close and fell back asleep.

The next morning Gabriel's classroom door was locked.

"Do you realize now we have to change the lock on your door, Mr. Abrams? Do you know how much that costs, no?"

Even the secretaries enjoyed tearing into those who they deemed bad.

"I'll lend you the spare to your classroom, but you find that lost key, no? And return this one to me."

"Yes, ma'am, of course ma'am."

Gabriel would never find his lost key and he would never know why they kicked everybody out of the building the day before and he would never know all of the struggles his students endured even as they carried them into his classroom.

After creative writing Gabriel asked to speak with Peter. In the now empty room, Peter sat in a chair at the side of Gabriel's desk with his hands settled in his lap, though every thirty seconds or so he would squeeze them together.

Gabriel handed him the 'URGENT' envelope and Peter opened it and pulled out the sheets of paper. As he looked it over his facial expression did not change. He read the entire document, then stared at the last page for two or three minutes before looking up.

"When did you get this?" Peter asked.

"Yesterday."

The papers wobbled and Peter shuffled to the first page. His emotion, at last, broke across his face. Anger. Turning the front of the pages towards Gabriel, he pressed his pointing finger into the paper where the thirteen names of his teachers and counselors and principals were listed.

"All these peo—all these people got this?"

Gabriel nodded.

Peter lurched to his feet. He jerked away from Gabriel. He was crying. Gabriel could do nothing but witness Peter's mounting humiliation. Peter made for the door, and Gabriel snapped to his feet.

"Peter!"

Peter stopped—he actually stopped at Gabriel's voice. Right at the door Peter paused, swaying, almost hugging himself, showing Gabriel his back and nothing more, but Gabriel could see the four pages crunched in his fist.

"You're always welcome in here," Gabriel said.

Peter vanished out the door.

This happened on Wednesday and Peter was absent the rest of the week, which worried Gabriel but, if he inquired, he thought he might get Peter in trouble, so he kept his mouth shut and continued to worry.

At lunch on Monday Peter slid into Gabriel's classroom unnoticed.

"Hi," he said, lurking just inside the door.

In mid-bite, Gabriel looked up and saw him standing there. Peter looked good—he was smiling and Gabriel, feeling relieved, smiled too. He pushed his sandwich aside, wiped his mouth, and motioned for Peter to come in.

Peter leaned on a desk close to the teacher's.

"Are you alright?" Gabriel asked.

"Yeah ... yeah I'm good."

"You were absent on Thursday and Friday."

"I know. I'm just coming from the principal's office."

From his pocket Peter pulled the 504 form that he had left the classroom with the week before.

"Here. I didn't show it to them. I didn't mean to take it. I read it. A bunch of times."

Gabriel took the four pages that had been smoothed with great effort after being crumpled. Peter stood up and started to the door but stopped.

He said, "It's really hard to be me in this place, you know?"

Gabriel looked at him, wishing he could do more. "I bet."

The next few days in creative writing class Peter acted normal—always writing, sometimes reading, often interacting with his devoted admirers. And then on Friday after class, after the other students had left, Peter remained in his seat.

"My parents are making me see a counselor. Twice a week. Once alone and once with them."

"That sounds okay," Gabriel said.

"Yeah."

Peter glanced around the room before looking back at Gabriel.

"There's this boy I really like and all he does is insult me. Last night he sent me the meanest text saying he would never wanna be with me. He even called me a 'faggot bundle of sticks' and he's gay too."

"Unrequited love sucks."

"But what do you do?"

"Ah … maybe, ah, try to do other things, meet other people."

"But I love him."

"That's the challenge."

"But how?"

"I guess you have to agree with yourself to move on," Gabriel said. "And then move on. I know this, I've done this—"

"Really."

"—and I look okay. Right?"

"Yeah, I guess," Peter said. "But it's so hard at this school."

"Why?"

"It's just ... I don't know. I get hassled every day."

"How so?"

"I don't know. People call me gay-wad or whatever. Queer boy and worse. Every day."

"Every day?"

"The worst is right after school."

"Why don't you wait until everyone's gone? This place clears out pretty quickly."

"What would I do?"

"Hang out in here for fifteen minutes. Sometimes I'm not here, but usually I am. And the Poets' Circle. You should come to that, you definitely should. Why don't you?"

"I don't know." Peter glanced at his vintage watch. Then sat there for several more moments. "I'm late for counseling."

"You don't like counseling?"

"I don't know. It's ...well ... the counselor's our minister." He forced a smile which faded. "I gotta go."

Lacking the usual reverent moments leading up to the Poets' Circle, the ramshackle mood resembled the beginnings of a dreaded Language Arts class. The racket in the hall had dwindled yet the meeting didn't start. Being the first gathering since the failed Poetry Burst Out, no one seemed anxious to begin. Gabriel even stayed at his desk grading papers.

Isabel asked if anyone had a poem and only Perry raised his hand.

"A car backfired, the earth hissed, the president spat, and I went home ..."

Being the first cold autumn day, someone at central control had cranked up the heat to some ungodly temperature so all the students and teachers in their warm gear had to strip down to combat the blaze. Since it was the first day in a long time that the heat had been turned on, many little burning particles of dust that had collected in the vents through the summer spurted out into the classrooms. Gabriel had opened the door and one of the windows to create a breeze ushering out the unwelcomed atmosphere.

Nobody read a poem with any sense of urgency. Peter was there for the first time, but he had set himself off to the side. Lori raised her hand. She had a poem but couldn't find it amongst her things.

"Okay," Isabel said, "we should ..."

From his desk Gabriel glanced up, for Isabel had stopped mid-sentence. After school there was never any commotion in the hall, and if there was it wouldn't distract Isabel, yet she turned to look. And it wasn't much of a fuss. One of the secretaries from the office pointed an older man towards Gabriel's classroom. In the middle of a thought Isabel said no more. She collected her books and left with the man.

Two tall, silhouetted figures, Isabel and her father shrunk down the hall towards the exit.

Gabriel had stayed at his desk even after everyone had left the poetry meeting. He put his elbows on the surface and folded his hands in front of his face. Through his fingers he peeked out across the empty room. After Isabel had left with her father no one had much to say, Gabriel included, so all the poets left. During the short meeting three poems were read. Gabriel had offered none. In fact, he had sat at his desk grading papers. He was spent, unable to offer energy or enthusiasm. He had felt like this at other meetings, but Isabel would invite him into the circle and the poets would enliven him with their eagerness. Today everyone had gone through the motions—everyone except Gabriel who couldn't even muster that. Day after day after day wore on him, and now he felt annoyed with himself. Almost ashamed. He hadn't been able to do a thing for Archie and he probably couldn't do anything for Peter either, and, sitting at his desk, depressed, hiding behind the façade of grading papers, he had let the poets sink into their own morose.

Gabriel couldn't bear his classroom anymore.

At home he scooted through the house past Holly, who followed him. He didn't want her to see him in such a state and he could have blocked her out by closing his bedroom door, but he didn't. She peeked in at his back as he shuffled through yesterday's mail on his desk.

"What's the matter?" she asked.

"Nothing?"

"Are you sure?"

"Yeah."

She stared for another moment before going back to the kitchen.

Gabriel felt every last bit of the poets' disappointment.

He lowered himself onto his bed, and Holly returned to his doorway.

"We can feel your disgust all the way in the other room," she said. "You're certainly entitled, but ... can we talk about it?"

"What do you want me to say?"

"I don't know ... how about—what's the matter?"

"Just another sucky day."

"Sometimes it's nice to talk," Holly said. "Especially with someone who cares."

Gabriel looked up at her. He would have smiled if he could have. "I just well ... in the Poets' Circle I wish I ... they're all so sad about their supposed failure. I should have said something. It's so hard for them to take that first breath and begin to share their disappointment."

"It takes courage to show you're hurt," Holly said.

"I know, even when you know others hurt too, but once that first person starts, the healing begins. And I, the teacher, the mentor, the supposed mature one just sat there, when I should have said something, anything."

"I appreciate you saying it now."

"I should have alluded to their disappointment, yet when the moment arrived when they needed me to ease their woe—I crouched at my desk pretending to grade papers. I feel so incapable, and not just on this occasion. I'm supposed to be the adult, yet when Nathan or Alex or Jorge or Robertson or Alejandro or Lissa or any of them talk or talk back or chew gum or are late or knock something over or trip or blink or breathe, I shoot back with the same lack of control that I get from them."

"Oh Gabriel."

"Is teaching for me just another stupid idea?"

Gabriel felt unqualified, as if his very effort was defeating him. When he imagined being a teacher and when he taught in India it was all about grace, floating around the classroom, encouraging students who took what he taught into their hearts and blossomed before his eyes, but he couldn't do anything if his students wouldn't listen or sit down or care. When he had decided to become a teacher his entire life made sense. He was so sure that everything he had done, everywhere he had gone had led him right to the front of his classroom, yet now as a fiasco, as a person unable to fulfill that potential, unable to rise up into that role, he felt empty—scrapped and scabbed and useless as if he had trained his whole life to swim across the ocean and there he was drowning in the bay. Some people are meant to affect this world while others wander without direction, dreaming of being important, yet made of common sand.

*Describe a specific incident in
your life that has made you who
you are today. Don't know?
Make one up.*

"So, what do you guys do?"

"We're teachers."

"Teachers! Yuck."

Leave it to a hot, drunk chick in a bar to speak plainly.

"Are you serious?" Gabriel said—not offended, but amazed. "About what?"

"Teachers."

"Oh God yes—" flew out the woman's mouth. "Thirty thousand dollars a year. No thanks. Five-year-olds. No thanks."

"Well actually—"

"Pleease, long summer holidays and you work till—what?—three?"

This was Gabriel's attempt to make friends with his colleague, Mr. Detrick, and they met at a bar and got accosted. Gabriel had to call to relay the conversation with this woman to me, and it would have been told through a cackle of sarcastic laughter if it weren't for the events of the rest of his evening. And also if it weren't for my own emotional state.

Gabriel and I hadn't spoken in more than a week. He had called; I just hadn't answered. I didn't want to see anyone or talk to anyone or think about anything but my own sorry self. When I'm depressed I want to be alone so as not to infect anyone with my wretched state. If I'm alone I'm alright. Gabriel had known me for his entire twenty-seven years on this planet, so he understood; he wasn't offended. But he was rude—calling in the middle of the night.

I should have turned off my phone. I was scrunched up in my bed, eyes jammed shut when that factory-delegated ringtone—"bing BING bing"—chimed out. And then after it stopped it started ringing again.

So I answered it.

And there was my brother's voice going a million miles a minute—

"I have to get a mobile pump I can't believe I don't have one it's like my third flat this week—"

I could have hung up right then.

"I swear it was Jorge—I couldn't believe it—as soon as he saw me he turned but his buddy didn't—and I just had a meeting with his mother and he cried—he cried!"

"Are you drunk?" I asked.

"For like the first two months we had no parent meetings and then suddenly like five in a row. And Mark they suck."

"Gabriel, it's two in the morning."

"I know but I got to tell you this—I got a flat."

It's easy to blame the whole world. Riding home, cruising down West Alameda, feeling the wonderful cold midnight wind wash into his inebriated eyeballs, Gabriel felt his bike's steering wobble and before he knew it his front tire was flat. He stopped and cursed the air. First he blamed the goat head in his tire and then God for not providing a cover of snow under which to bury those thorny little devils and then that drunk woman at the bar and the principal at school and all those nasty students and their clueless parents.

The second major student/parent meeting that Gabriel had to attend was for Jorge, the obnoxious, flap-eared student in his third period class. Jorge said not one word during the meeting. A problem in all his classes, this poor kid was heading for trouble.

"Even his wrong answers were the same," Ms. Harbough said to Mrs. Gutierrez, Jorge's mother.

"They're probably copying off him," Mrs. Gutierrez said.

"They all passed—Jorge didn't."

The next teacher spoke of Jorge's continued disrespectful behavior.

"This can't be so," Mrs. Gutierrez said.

The freshmen principal showed a stack of disciplinary reports, most were gang-related—flashing gang signs, wearing gang colors, fighting, racism, and intimidation.

The blood drained from Jorge's mother's face. Her bottom lip faltered before she managed—

"Jorge's always been a good boy."

Just then, startling everyone, Jorge let out a colossal sob. Everyone sitting around the large oval table snapped towards him. And then, all of a sudden, Jorge was bawling, a flood of tears washing down his cheeks, and now his mother was crying too.

For the rest of the meeting Jorge and his mother sat next to each other both weeping, yet they never looked up, they never touched; the inches that separated them could have been an entire continent.

When the opportunity came for Gabriel to speak, he felt awful. Gabriel had waited for this moment, anxious to inform Jorge's mother of Jorge's transgressions. But now, at this juncture, it seemed entirely inappropriate to pile more of the same on top of Jorge and his mom.

"Much of what has been said," Gabriel began, "I've encountered with Jorge in my own classroom. I need it to stop. But also I want to say that Jorge's really sharp. He has a way of seeing things—he has a great skill at synthesizing situations."

Mrs. Gutierrez peeked up at Gabriel, and Jorge's counselor, Ms. Churchill, smiled.

Gabriel heard them behind him as he pushed his bike, with its flat tire, over the path. There are no clearly defined bad sections in Santa Fe like in other cities, in bigger cities, but past midnight on a Friday night this path above the dried-out Santa Fe River could be considered the dodgy part of town.

Gabriel's pace quickened. He peeked around to judge the threat. About ten paces back, creeping along in the shadows, three guys were hanging in Gabriel's wake. Gabriel's heart beat faster. He was ready to run. And he was fast. If he dropped his bike he could outrun anyone, especially with his adrenaline pumping. But he didn't want to abandon his bike.

"Remember when we were little and your bike got stolen," Gabriel said as I lay in bed pressing my phone to my ear. "You chased that guy riding off on your bike for like ten blocks. With those guys behind me I kept thinking about that—how you so much wanted your bike, I just couldn't drop mine and run. I just kept thinking of you."

Other people's stories always get a little more interesting when you yourself make a sudden cameo. I hadn't remembered that story. I was maybe ten and we had left our bikes leaning against a wall when we went into Walgreens. Through the plate-glass window I saw this kid jump on my bike. I raced out of the store and chased the bike thief for what seemed like miles.

"I just kept thinking of you, Mark, and remembering how you so badly wanted your bike. It made me—"

My phone went dead.

At first I had been annoyed that Gabriel had called so late going on and on about himself, yet I had been drawn into his babbling. But I didn't scramble to plug in my phone to call him right back. I lay there in bed remembering how I had chased that bike thief until, exhausted, I collapsed into a parked car. I swear, right when I stopped, the kid looked back and smiled as he coasted away on my bike.

Sometimes a big personality (like Gabriel's) can overwhelm my depression, even snap me out of it. I don't know. I see no pattern even though depression has been the one constant of my life. A mystery that springs as if from a puff of smoke—oh depression, you spindly black widow. Sometimes, when depressed, I sit trying to figure out from where it came, but I have no clue, and it scares me, it strands me, it hurts like a broken leg in my heart, and the only thing that eases the anguish is being underneath my covers, scrunched in a ball with my eyes crammed closed. Thoughts of black. Thoughts of mutilation. Images of hangings. I don't want anyone to know—I know they will and they'll worry. But it's more than that: I'm embarrassed ... I'm ashamed. I'll stink up every room I'm in, I'll call in sick—I need to sink alone into my own oblivion. I'm debilitated. I'm inept. And at the bottom of my bed, I'm lower than I was when first afflicted, because now I've been depressed for X amount of days, weeks. Sometimes it seems as if it'll go on forever. And sometimes a breeze can make me feel better. Sometimes worse. Sometimes a joke or an insult or a thought or a sound in the night can make me feel better. Sometimes a hamburger. Sometimes an acknowledgement. Sometimes my brother.

When I plugged in my phone, it rang right away. I wondered how long Gabriel had kept talking before he realized I was no longer there. When I answered, Gabriel spoke slower with a much different tone.

"What's up, brother," he said. "I haven't heard from you in a long time?"

"Yeah, well, you know … I've been busy."

"Busy, huh?"

"Yeah."

"Just call and swear at me if you like," Gabriel said. "If it'll make you feel better."

Gabriel paused, giving me a space to say something, but I didn't.

When no one says anything over the phone, that silence can be uncomfortable. This was not the case at this moment. We both laid there in our beds holding the phones to our ears, not saying anything, but absorbing each other. It felt good. I sensed Gabriel open and clear and very much aware of me on the other end of the line.

In our silence over the phone I smiled.

"So what happened?" I asked and Gabriel seamlessly slipped back into his story.

"You wouldn't believe it, Mark, it was him."

With those three guys close behind, Gabriel had pushed his injured bike off the sidewalk, making a sharp cut across the dark street. If they followed him, then he knew they were after him. As he made his way over the medium strip, Gabriel peeked back and sure enough they were cutting across the street too. Gabriel looked right at the short kid in the middle and the short kid looked right at Gabriel. They saw each other—they knew each other.

"I couldn't believe it," Gabriel said, "I could not believe it."

It was Jorge, and as soon as Jorge saw his teacher he stopped like a little bird slammed into a picture window. And then just as suddenly he twisted around in the other direction, hurrying away, grabbing at his buddy's shirt which snapped out of his fingers. The big one continued to follow Gabriel, who had hesitated on the far sidewalk. At this point Gabriel couldn't run, the collision already destined. From the back of his waistband Gabriel took his U-lock into his fist. He didn't swing it or brandish it in any way; he clenched it at his side and the big kid having seen it stopped—but still real close to Gabriel. Headlights flashed down the road. From the corners of his dark eyes and beneath a hairy blanket of a unibrow, the kid peered towards Gabriel's face and then he twitched his head up as if in some too-cool greeting. He smirked—and that was it—the kid turned and hurried away to catch up with his friends.

"My heart was thumping—I mean I was scared but with my blood spiriting through my body I felt the pulsing as if my life had been torn open—it was awesome."

If it had been me I would have been terrified, but Gabriel, man Gabriel, he on the other hand encountered his life with such a galvanized thrill. I love him.

Peter slunk into Gabriel's creative writing class with a huge red gash across his cheek and nose.

"Peter!"

Students gathered.

"What happened?"

"What happened?"

"Are you alright?"

"Yeah, maybe," he moaned.

The way Peter dragged his body, the way he collapsed into his seat, the way he sighed with anguish, he was eliciting attention.

"Really, I'm okay."

Peter sucked in a large breath through his teeth, and then he let it out as if trying to steady himself.

"Peter," Gabriel said, "maybe you should go to the nurse, or home. You don't have to stay."

"No, I want to, and I've already been to the doctor. It happened yesterday."

"What? What happened?" a student chimed back in and the class pressed closer.

"It was a hate crime," Peter finally said.

With the class' full attention, Peter told his story. After school the day before, two students had chased Peter, calling him 'faggot' and 'gay-wad' and when they couldn't catch him they threw rocks at him and right when Peter had turned back to see, a flying brick, just missing his skull, ripped across his nose. When the students saw what they had done they ran, leaving Peter clawing at his wound.

"I'm okay, though, I'm okay."

But his fellow students were concerned—

"Do you know who they were?"

"No."

"Are you gonna do something?"

"No."

"You should—this is wrong."

"Are you sure you're alright?"

"Can we do something?"

"What can we do?"

"I just wanna write something," Peter said.

Gabriel wrangled his students into their seats and asked them to write about something they hated and to try to determine if their angst was warranted.

After class Gabriel asked Peter to stay.

"Why don't you have a bandage on your nose?"

Peter peeked up at Gabriel, and smiled.

"'Cause a bandage looks stupid." And then his expression became altogether serious. "And I want people to see."

How can life not affect a breathing bleeding human when it's right there in your face?

After Gabriel's awkward conversation with Robertson's mother during which she begged him not to write up her son, Robertson, with his huge phone gripped in his gloved fist, came to Gabriel before class and apologized. It was a short apology but seemed sincere, his shoulders heavy and rounded with contrition, the fat of his body settling around his waist. But it didn't last long. Whatever had convinced Robertson to apologize lacked the force to alter his conduct for any significant duration, and soon Gabriel felt compelled to call his mother again, but when he dialed her number a recording informed him that the phone was temporarily unavailable.

The next morning Gabriel spotted Robertson alone in the hall. Gabriel snuck up so as not to be avoided.

"Morning."

"Morning."

Robertson's eyes were slits. Visible crusted sleep clung to the corners. He seemed a walking zombie, too tired to have any sort of attitude. He was wearing only one of his ever-present gloves—covering his right hand.

"I tried to call your mother, but there's no service."

"I know."

"Is there a new number?"

"No."

Robertson's face tensed, lines cut through his expression, and for an instant Gabriel witnessed Robertson's torment. His disarmingly handsome face teetered atop a misshapen body—skinny on top and bottom but huge around the middle. Robertson pushed himself against the wall, using Gabriel as a shield to hide from a couple students gathering down the hall.

"Me and my mom are moving. The sixth time this year."

It sounded like coach-surfing.

"I'm sorry, Robertson."

With liquid eyes, Robertson looked back at Gabriel. A tear rolled out and Robertson mopped it up.

As a teacher, one moment a student is cursing your soul, pins in your heart, and then the next that very same student needs—begs for—your empathy. Gabriel struggled with this dichotomy.

Gabriel sat there exhausted. Ms. Harbough was speaking, but was saying nothing about Nathan's horrendous behavior; she said nothing in reference to the homophobic rant Nathan had spit out at her the week before. Gabriel's stomach turned over. To this meeting he had hurried to arrive on time. He hadn't eaten. At 7:15 in the morning Nathan and his mother and Mr. Detrick, Ms. Harbough, Mrs. Harper, and Gabriel gathered in Mr. Detrick's classroom. Student desks were pushed together in a mock round table. Gabriel knew he would soon have to speak, yet he felt awkward and didn't trust himself to be graceful. He was in no mood for euphemisms.

"If Nathan applies himself," Ms. Harbough was saying, "I don't see why he wouldn't do well in my class."

Everybody smiled their polite smiles at Ms. Harbough, and she looked at Gabriel, and everyone turned their attention to him.

Gabriel needed water—even just a drop to run down his throat. He tried to swallow.

"Nathan's behavior in my classroom is unacceptable," Gabriel said. "He doesn't know how to act or doesn't want to act in an appropriate way."

Nathan slammed back in his chair and forced out a hiss.

"Most days," Gabriel continued, "he comes into my classroom and immediately starts demanding attention, disrupting—"

"I hate you!" Nathan shouted.

Stunned, Gabriel said, "Nathan—"

But Nathan persisted—"The whole class hates you. You're the worst teacher I ever had. I've learned nothing—nobody has, and everyone hates you." To his mother, "*Todos los estudiantes odian a el.*"

Nathan's mouth ground shut and he twisted his body up into a knot.

Gabriel managed to swallow down the glob that had formed in his throat, and with Nathan's words hanging in the air like thinning lines of stale smoke, Gabriel reached deep within himself as if searching for a prayer—

"In this life, Nathan, we encounter many obstacles, that if we can surmount, make us better people. Throughout your life you're going to encounter people who you don't like—but still have to deal with. How we react to these situations makes us who we are."

Gabriel paused. He sounded so stiff—and that stiffness stuck in him. Nathan was turned away, looking out the window.

To Nathan's mother, Mr. Detrick said, "*Intendio?*"

"*Que?*"

"*Usted intendio?*"

"*No.*"

"*En pecito?*"

"*No.*"

Mr. Detrick gathered himself as if to say something more in Spanish. Students clustered in the hall. The academic building tightened with noise. The meeting lost its focus.

"Can I go?" Nathan said.

"*Yo no se q'pasa en la clase de este hombre pero,*" Nathan's mother said. "*Yo tengo q escuchar a mi hijo. Inecesito escuchar a mi hijo.*"

Gabriel leaned forward to say something to her, but—

"*Tengo que ilme al trabajo.*" She got up, thanked Mr. Detrick, and left.

Gabriel remained in his seat. The other teachers were gone. Mr. Detrick moved towards his door, shooed a few students away, and closed it, leaving the two of them alone.

Gabriel had a question, yet he couldn't grasp it. His face went through a myriad of expressions trying to formulate it into words.

As if he understood, Mr. Detrick spoke: "We're teachers, Gabriel. This is a job. Students aren't supposed to like us ... but they're not supposed to hate us either."

"I know."

"You have to ask yourself how it became so personal?"

Gabriel struggled through his classes. Nathan didn't show up for third period. Neither did Jorge. Gabriel's brain was wet gook, his feet—lead balls, and he rolled along like a wooden doll. He was horrified at everything he saw, and a numbness seeped up from the floor like a radiant frost.

Of course it was personal. Everything's personal. Teaching is an intimate profession.

During his free period Gabriel found Ms. Bimble in the teachers' lounge measuring out a brew of her famous latte. Her gaze rolled over a shattered Gabriel.

"Looks like someone could use a latte," she offered.

"Please."

Gabriel let the coffee sit in his mouth before swallowing it down. Ms. Bimble's bitterness towards her students robbed her of her passion, yet still that sweetness lingered and when Gabriel needed consoling all her teacherly love rose to the surface. Gabriel paid her the respect her students no longer did, and she soaked it up.

As they pumped themselves full of caffeine, she encouraged him to complain and he did but not about the administration or the parents or even the students. He fretted over how he felt—and he felt defeated. In becoming a teacher, Gabriel thought he was uniquely qualified to connect with students who other teachers—the schoolmarmy-type—could never. And here he was unable to deal with the exact type of troubled student who he had hoped to help the most.

"Mr. Abrams, you can't care so much," Ms. Bimble said.

"What?"

"Teachers can't care."

These words sliced Gabriel open.

"For your own sanity, Mr. Abrams. If a teacher invests his emotions and his sense of self in the success of his students—or even in the equilibrium of his classroom, he'll go berserk. If in a year a teacher affects one student—just one, one single student who goes on to have a good life, who maybe otherwise wouldn't have, aren't you a success? You changed someone's life. But it's the other hundred and thirty-nine who take up all your time and drive you to shreds."

Gabriel hung there like a thick branch starting to give beneath the weight of the collecting snow. "How can I not care? I teach because I care. Why would anybody even become a teacher if they didn't care?"

"Point taken," Ms. Bimble said. "But to be a successful teacher you have to check that at the door."

"They'll know, they'll sense it."

"I'm talking about your own well-being, Mr. Abrams. You have to look out for yourself, or you'll fail. Somewhere down the road you will collapse."

"But how does one just not care?"

"Shit. You have to work at it."

"It seems self-defeating."

"It's reality."

"I'm sorry, Ms. Bimble, I just ..."

"You'd better start figuring it out."

"No. I won't. I can't, I just ... I can't—I can't just not care."

Ms. Bimble held her yellow smiling mug aloft. She went to take a sip yet didn't. She found the tabletop and put her mug down.

"Mr. Abrams, I've been teaching for as long as you've been alive. I admire your passion, but don't disregard my wisdom in a rush to save the world."

"I wasn't accusing you."

"My skin is thick. I'm powered by caffeine. And maybe I'm a bit past ..."

She reached out for her mug and eased back in her chair.

"I just hope good things for you, Mr. Abrams. Good things."

She finished her latte in one big final sip, and for a long time she glared deep into the mug's bottom.

After school Gabriel pushed his bicycle into the backyard, leaned it against the shed, and headed for the house. When he touched the door handle he let go, went back around to the yard. There, sitting beneath the pine tree on the rickety old bench with its peeled paint, was Holly, her dog curled at her feet.

"You alright?" Gabriel asked.

"Yeah."

"You sure?"

"A-huh."

Raw and uncomplicated, Gabriel's heart invited those he encountered into its warmth. He cared for people, even random weirdos, more than anyone I've ever known and asking him not to care was futile, almost an afront—it ran against his very nature.

The bench creaked as Gabriel sat down next to Holly. She may have been crying. He wanted to comfort her, so he rested his hand on the back of her shoulder, though he would have preferred to curl his whole arm around her. Holly looked up at him, tried to smile.

"Thanks," she said.

"Where's Chloe?"

"At a friend's. We're so close every month. It's just so close."

"Can I help?"

"You're sweet."

"So close to what?"

Holly laughed. And then—"We couldn't live in the woods forever."

"I'm glad you live here. I've never lived with a landlady before."

"Even if you have an address, even if you own a house, pay a mortgage, drive a car ... It's unbelievable what sort of power unhappy people can have over you. I never imagined until I was vulnerable, until it wasn't just me."

"What happened?"

She closed her eyes, started talking before opening them. "A fire before bed. Waking up to the sound of the creek. We loved living in the woods. Roasting marshmallows. I never thought—and still don't—that I was being a bad mother. I dedicate myself to my daughter. How many mothers in our society still do that? I don't know. More I hope. My plan was for our future."

"Your plan?"

"We knew we couldn't live in this house when we bought it. We needed the rent to pay the mortgage. It was an asset for our future. I could've paid it off in six years. That was the plan. We'd move in and by then Chloe would be a teenager and we wouldn't be total freaks to her friends."

"What happened?"

"It's not that we don't like living here with you, we do, very much." She took in a breath, held it, let it out. She looked at Gabriel, looked away. "In the summer when we still lived in the woods, a cop pulled over in front of us when we were hitchhiking into town—and he wasn't offering us a ride."

"What did he want?"

"He wanted to hassle us, he wanted to know if our car broke down, he wanted to know why we didn't have a car, why we were hitchhiking, where we lived. He threatened to call Child Protective Services. Told me I was an unfit mother, told me he could have my daughter taken from me."

"What did you do?"

"Bought a car."

"Did it help?"

"It sure was convenient. But over the weeks the cop kept following us, he figured out we were camping and I tried to lie, I gave him our address—your address—told him we lived here so he wouldn't hassle us, but he kept showing up at our campsite. Every cop car I saw I swore was him. And then after we moved in here he came to the door, saying he just wanted to make sure I was alright—and then, the fucker, he asked me out. Can you believe that?"

"What did you say?"

"I said no, tried to be polite, he scared me. But the next day he called."

"How did he get your number?"

"That first time he stopped us."

"That's gotta be illegal."

"I know."

"Did he call again?"

"A bunch of times."

"What did you say?"

"I said I was married."

Gabriel chuckled. "To who?"

Holly chuckled. "To you. I guess. I didn't tell him who. But he hasn't called since. But I saw him—or some cop car—driving slowly past our house today."

"What a bummer."

"I know, it's like a horror movie."

She laughed to herself, and when Gabriel laughed she touched his arm. She set her hand on his shoulder like he had done for her. Then she tucked her hands back in her own lap.

"I won't invite into my life those who judge me and have some creepy power over me. Never again."

Holly leaned over and laid her head to rest on Gabriel's shoulder. She bent her head up to see in Gabriel's eyes. And when she looked away she reached her hand into his. A warmth filled all the way round Gabriel's body. He felt her fiery fingers in his palms, between his knuckles. He closed his eyes, hyperaware of his every reaction—his chest undulating, his toes rubbing, his pores as if they were beating. Holly turned back and looked into Gabriel's eyes, looked deliberately. Gabriel thought they might kiss—he didn't mean to, he jerked.

And Holly stiffened. She pulled her hand back.

Neither looked.

"Let me help you," Gabriel said.

"No."

"You can pay me back."

"No."

"Please."

I often ask myself 'what-if' questions. What if I didn't take that job right out of college? What if I had studied art instead of finance? What if I watched less TV or threw my phone in the lake? What if I sat at that desk instead of this one? What if I took a left instead of a right? What if I paused in this spot for an extra six seconds—would my life be different?

Of course, the questions could go on forever.

What if I hadn't gotten so angry at Gabriel when he quit the job I had gotten him at Oberville? Would he not have vanished that first time? Would he be here now? What if I had been less critical of his distinctive force? Would things be different? Would I be different? Would I be more satisfied with my life?

Our lives are made of billions of little decisions we commit to every day. If you make a bold decision today maybe tomorrow you'll make another bold one and then another until you're living a bold life, but one audacious act does not make an audacious life. Momentum must be gained. But there must be that beginning—that impetus—the initial decision that starts it all. One courageous step could be the first in the right direction.

I was about to go into my mom's building when my phone rang from a 505 area code. I had to answer it—it was New Mexico calling. Right off she said my name—"Mark!"—not asking who it was or even if in fact it was me.

"Mark, you have to come," Holly said.

Inlaid in her voice was an intimacy that made me uncomfortable—even through the phone. She acted as if she knew me—at least as if what she said had some higher relevance that I could not rebuff, but how could I in one day decide to take off work and drive all the way from Chicago down to New Mexico?

"We need as many people as possible," she said. "If he's alive we'll find him. Please, come, Mark please. ..."

Standing on the street in Chicago, I was cold. I was grumbling too. Why should I disrupt my life to drive more than a thousand miles to search for my errant brother? Why did he get to be the adventurous one?

My mom stepped up close to my face.

"Are you sure you want me to answer these questions?"

I was taken aback by her sudden directness. A quiet woman, she's strong but not forceful, more like a rock than a fist. In her kitchen, she was making us tea, and I, instead of communicating with words, was letting off steam and words came out. Beneath my shoulders burned, and I was stunned at what I had been saying.

"Mark, you're an emotional man," she said. "You reflect on things. Not everybody is like that. Your brother ... " Holding a tea bag she glanced over at me, she struggled to swallow. "He's different. Gabriel's different. That's what you want to know?"

She synthesized my rant down to a poignant sum, for somehow seeing Gabriel for what he was could help me resolve who I am. Sitting in a quagmire of other people's opinions and demands,

I too want to live and not be stuck on some track designed and controlled by others who find it convenient for me to shuffle along like a drone.

"Who knows where to begin," my mom said. "Maybe at the beginning." She smiled again, but it was a tough smile for her. She gazed down at nothing in particular, probably thinking—definitely thinking. "Our society dictates quite a lot."

"Yeah they do."

"When you were born I was very young, and—society in my time required new mothers to be a certain way that went against our intuition."

"Yeah?"

Her lips started to move, steam shot out of the teapot; in fact, the water had been boiling for some time. She moved to the stove and clicked off the burner, pausing, still thinking.

"I tried hard to make it up," she said, "if not to you than for your brother."

"What do you mean?"

"Breastfeeding, for one."

"It makes that much difference?"

"It did to me."

This conversation—with my mother!—should have made me uncomfortable. I knew mothers of a certain era were pressured to be a bit standoffish towards their babies, but I hadn't realized that the infant Gabriel had been treated any differently than the infant me, that Gabriel had been breastfed and I hadn't. I wondered if, because I lacked that initial attention, I had some primal urge to stay close to home as opposed to Gabriel who had traveled so much. And is that a good thing? Which? I remember once when we were little, we were in a department store and my mom and I lost Gabriel. It seemed like for a long time and I became frightened. In the end Gabriel was lost probably for less than three minutes, and when we found him he was dragging around a hanger with a lady's purple shirt on it—not concerned at all. But me? After we found him I continued to be afraid. Even that night. While lying in bed the more I thought of those short few moments the more anxious I grew. Under my covers, each breath became an ordeal. Why was I obsessing on Gabriel being lost? Why did his wellbeing so affect me? If I could have forced myself to stop being consumed by it, I might have stopped feeling it, but I couldn't. I let the fear get a firm grip on me. It was as if from that point on, that's the way my life was. Fear fed on itself. The more fear I felt, the more fearful I became, and the more paralyzed I was.

Gabriel on the other hand had always been lackadaisical while my life seemed weighted with rocks. Fear is the eeriest force. It can stop a train. It certainly can prevent one from starting. Fear of failure. Fear of embarrassment. Fear of injury. Fear of death. Fear of being alone, fear of getting sick, fear of germs, fear of judgment. I have never taken chances, always guiding myself down the safest lane. I've never been out of the United States, I've lived in the same city I grew up in, I've had the same job since I graduated from college. Or had.

I hated my job and I stayed there for years. How many other people are like that? Fear kept me from finding something I love to do. Fear kept me from even looking. Fear kept me from experiencing my life. Fear kept me from being Santa Claus.

"You can't blame your brother because he made such a good Santa," my mom said.

"I know, I'm not."

But I was.

Yes, I wanted to be Santa. I know it was years ago, but still … I could easily blame Gabriel for his aggressiveness. During the holidays my mom had arranged for us to do a charitable event for children and when we found out that the temple had a Santa suit, Gabriel stepped forward. He'd do it—he'd be Santa. And I was angry. And I've been angry at him since, because he was too assertive. I wanted to be Santa and Gabriel stepped right up without leaving me the moment to stick out my chest and volunteer. He acted without thinking, without needing to think. It always seemed like that, and it made me even angrier because he was the younger brother and he was supposed to follow me, but he just kept stepping forward, pushing me back, shoving me out of the spotlight, so he could soak it in.

But the truth is, even though I was genuinely angry with him, I was secretly glad that he always stepped forward, because I was scared. Yes, I was scared, I was nervous, I was timid, and whenever Gabriel stepped in front of me and faced the bullet—I didn't have to. And he always did it with such a flair, with such a sense of heightened drama.

"Sometimes we have a right to be angry."

"It's true," my mother said, "but taking it to work, taking it home, harboring it in your heart for a decade ..." My mother made a face—tightening her lips, arching her eyebrows—as if agreeing how obvious it was: "Anger's corrosive."

We both sat there sipping our tea. I had never had tea with my mother before.

"Your father's back in town."

"Yeah?"

"He rented a small apartment in Rogers Park," she said.

"How do you know?"

"Nancy Dixon keeps in touch with him."

"I can't just take a week off from work."

"Not even for this?" She almost whispered, "For your brother?"

My mother stared at me for a long time without dropping her eyes, and I looked deep into them. Her dark brown eyes sat inside her round sockets with such seriousness. First they became glossy, and then sodden, filling with tears that rolled out across her cheeks. But she wasn't sobbing or heaving or making any sound at all. We kept looking at each other, and my eyes must also have filled with tears.

Not used to being physically affectionate with my mother, I staggered as if rising up out of quicksand—the struggle was there, but so was the euphoria of breaking free. Our grief unmasked, we hugged for a long time clinging to hope. My mother whispered in my ear: "You have to go. You have to go to New Mexico. Quit your job and go."

*If you knew the world
would end tomorrow
what would you do today?*

"TEACHERS! STUDENTS! STAFF! WE ARE IN A FULL LOCKDOWN! I REPEAT: FULL LOCKDOWN! CLEAR THE HALLS! CLEAR THE COURTYARD! ERRANT STUDENTS REPORT TO THE NEAREST CLASSROOM WHERE YOU ALL SHALL REMAIN UNTIL FURTHER INSTRUCTION. I REPEAT: FULL LOCKDOWN! CLEAR THE HALLS! REMAIN IN YOUR CLASSROOMS! DISREGARD ALL BELLS!"

With *Cannery Row* open in his hand, Gabriel hesitated, the room now silent yet choked with pressure. First the pregnant pause, then the excitement, anticipation, and speculation, students yanked out their cellphones.

"WE ARE IN FULL LOCKDOWN—THAT MEANS NO CELLPHONE USE! I REPEAT: NO CELLPHONES!"

And then over the same public address system the entire campus heard ruffling frantic commotion before the line clicked dead.

He had to—Gabriel tried to bring the class back around to *Cannery Row*, but they were full of questions—

"What's happening?"

"Why can't we use our phones?"

"How long do we have to stay here?"

Gabriel was full of the same questions. And more—

Are we in danger?

Do we lock the door?

Should we keep reading?

Gabriel moved to the classroom door, took out his keys, and locked it.

"How long do we have to stay here?"

"I have to go to the bathroom."

"I'm hungry."

The bell that would end second period rang, but nobody moved; the halls remained empty. Near the end of third period, three police cars and a fire truck pulled up and the students saw from the window before Gabriel drew them back. When the lunch period started to tick away, thus cutting into the students' (and the teachers') free time, attitudes darkened.

"When do we get outa here?"

"I need some air."

"I gotta piss."

Gabriel had given up trying to focus his students. He let them mess around on the computers, do their homework from other classes, talk amongst themselves. Gabriel pulled out a bunch of markers and invited them to draw. Gabriel sketched a picture of a screaming student atop a desk with a fist in the air, broken-spined textbooks scattered across the floor. The students loved it.

Paper airplanes sailed through the air and they needed a toilet. Gabriel hung some fabric he'd found, creating a private space in a corner—or more precisely: a bathroom. A plastic milk carton with its top cut off served as the toilet. It was the best he could do. After someone peed, they'd pour the warm urine out the window. They loved that too.

They played hangman.

They played charades.

They played truth or dare.

A student announced that she was getting a text. Could she read it? Everyone in the room pleaded with Gabriel to let her, which was peculiar considering that they all had been peeking at their phones the whole time. What they wanted was to talk openly about what was happening. Desperate for information, Gabriel acquiesced and suddenly everyone's phones were out.

Apparently a girl—a junior—was about to shoot up the school. Gabriel's students started talking about what they would do. Steven bragged how he would throw a desk into her path and tackle her. Others told of secret places they would hide. They became less speculative when the conversation turned to what had happened yesterday. It was the first Gabriel had heard.

So much exaggeration and misinformation can come from students. Yet sometimes, forming into a network and culling half-truths, students can disseminate the most factual information available.

As far as the reason for the lockdown, their explanation proved overblown, but in the matter of Ms. Bimble they were right on target.

Every day between periods masses of students gathered around the banisters of the academic building to hang over into the open air of the atrium that dropped three stories down. From the first and second floors, students lurched out over towards the basement, calling to friends, throwing paper balls. Often Gabriel saw students leaning out so far he was sure they would fall, that someone someday would fall, but there were so many students and

Gabriel walked around in a constant state of exhaustion from dispensing discipline in his own classroom, he didn't have it in him to be modifying the behavior of the crush of students in the halls. Not so for Ms. Bimble. She claimed it as her responsibility.

The day before the lockdown, between periods, Ms. Bimble glimpsed a kid cruising through the halls on a skateboard. She hurried around the atrium in the opposite direction and when their paths met they practically collided, the skateboard crashing against the wall upside-down, it's wheels spinning. Ms. Bimble, in plain sight of the students hanging in the atrium, snatched the skateboard up off the ground.

"You can pick it up after school from Mr. Reade."

"But it's not mine."

"I don't care," Ms. Bimble had said and a collective 'aaahhhhh' rose up from the crowd of students.

Under their scrutiny, Ms. Bimble began her long march to the stairs and down to the basement where the freshmen principal Mr. Reade's offices were. As she treaded towards the stairs the chorus rose up: the 'aaahhhhs' turned to 'ooooooos' and the 'oooooos' became 'rrrrrrrrrrs'. By the time she started her descent students were screaming.

"It's not yours!"

"Give it back!"

"Give him his skate!"

The voices emerged from individuals lost in the horde.

"You can't ride it."

"You're too old!"

"You old bag!"

Anonymous courage reared up from the cover of the crowd, yet in the face of this onslaught Ms. Bimble soldiered on.

"You bitch!"

"You fucking whore!"

"You dirty fucking whore!"

She made it to the bottom of the stairs and all the students above, hanging over the railings for two floors up, were screaming and swearing and now throwing trash down onto her. Trying to ignore it, she crawled as if through six feet of mud.

A wet glob smacked her at the hairline. She stopped as waste paper rained down. She touched her forehead. She looked at her fingers, which were stuck together in someone's coughed up discharge. They were spitting on her. Her stomach twisted and lurched up into her throat. She gagged. This was it. This was the collapse. The final insult. She could no longer stand. Destroyed, her insides shrieked and wept, this stoic woman who hadn't cried in a decade. Her head creaked upward looking into the motion of debris falling and the blur of wrenched faces screaming.

"You y-y-oou …" Her voice wobbled and shook and cracked. As if pleading towards God, she held her crusted fingers up towards the spiraling mob above. "You have no idea, you have no idea … "

But her voice was drowned out by the riot of student indignation.

Nancy Bimble tucked her head into her chest and dragged herself into the principal's office. She gave the skateboard to Mr. Reade's secretary, then locked herself in a teachers' bathroom. In her absence, her second period students trashed her classroom.

Somewhere towards the end of fourth period, after four confined hours of the lockdown, students began to notice by peeking out the windows that other students were leaving school. Gabriel's students begged him to let them go too.

Mr. Reade knocked on Gabriel's door and Gabriel unlocked it. Mr. Reade told everyone to gather their stuff and quickly and quietly leave campus, Gabriel included. Peppered with questions,

Mr. Reade refused to answer, telling them to hurry and then he moved on to Mr. Detrick's classroom next door.

The following day, as if being knocked off the front page by something even more sensational, the Bimble affair had been trumped by the lockdown. No one was talking about Ms. Bimble, who had quit. Everyone was dishing about the student who had supposedly planned to shoot up the school. As it turned out the student had posted to social media and then deleted a troubling image—but someone had captured a screenshot and it was all over online. She had posed for a selfie in front of her parents' crowded gun cabinet and someone else had commented, 'Columbine!' which referenced the school shooting that's recognized as the impetus of the present horror show of mass student violence. That word coupled with an unsmiling student in a selfie in front of a cabinet filled with automatic weapons and reams of ammunition created a robust administrative response.

And the next week there was another lockdown. This time a janitor discovered a bomb in the science building. After clearing that part of campus, they locked-down the rest of the school and brought in the bomb squad that discovered—not a bomb—but a box of broken discarded computers on which someone in thick black magic marker had written: "BOOM!"

Fifty-five, sixty, sixty-five miles an hour—hurtling south down highway 55, I was feeling the bulk of loosely held together hunks of metal that was my ancient Toyota Camry shaking beneath me like a go-cart about to burst apart under the stress of too much speed. My car wouldn't go faster. Anyone who's driven a dilapidated car a long way knows some cars simply refuse to comply no matter how hard you shove the pedal into the floor. As other cars shot past I took an uphill like an elderly rhinoceros. I swear I could have run faster than my car was going. Up ahead at the top of the hill, a figure appeared in the ripples on the side of the road. Hitchhikers are dangerous, parents tell their kids. Society disapproves of hitchhiking, and Hollywood plays it up. A hitchhiker will smile to get you to pull over, but as soon as the car is back cruising down the interstate that same smiling hitchhiker now sitting beside you will slip out his foot-long 'fishing knife'. It's not such a stretch to ford the gap between Hollywood horror flick and a murderer sitting next to you, so when our mothers say don't pick up hitchhikers, we obey. Statistically speaking, the fear is real, because if you never pick up a hitchhiker you'll never get killed by a hitchhiker.

But the tables turn—at least empathetically—when we discover that a friend or a son or our brother has taken to hitchhiking. When Gabriel started, or at least when I became aware of his exploits, every hitchhiker I passed I thought of Gabriel. I would wonder if he was as benevolent as my brother, simply needing a ride and offering in exchange a little curious conversation. I'd wonder if on the other side of the country or on the other side of the globe a car shuttled past shunning my brother on the edge of some freeway fearing he could be a bad guy. It's just a ride, Gabriel would smile, standing in the wind, his thumb leveled in the direction he hoped to go. It must be quite a naked feeling standing in the wake of a hundred zooming cars.

Does my car protect me? I certainly would be terrified to hitchhike, to be out in the road with nothing. Waiting to be picked up by … by what? The odds seem even worse for the hitchhiker— out there waiting to be picked up by … by whom? Someone else's mother? A charitable Christian. The Interstate Strangler. It's the hitchhiker who's vulnerable, for his goal *is* to be in a stranger's car. The only thing going for the hitchhiker would be if in fact he were a murderer. Then if the guy who picked him up also happened to be a murderer, they would be on equal footing, and the hitcher at least would have a fighting chance.

So if you are not a murderer it takes a lot of courage to be a hitchhiker. I hadn't seen Gabriel in this light. I assumed he was an idiot, an idealist who figured anyone who would pick him up couldn't mean him harm. Maybe this was part of his entitlement issue. Or maybe he was right.

I never hitchhiked. Not once. I've had the same job—or *had* the same job—for almost ten years. I wasn't unhappy, but I wasn't happy either. That seems worse than being something else—anything else almost. I think in this snug society we crave for something to happen to shatter the status quo of our existence. By the end we are ground down to nothing anyway.

As my car reached the top of the knoll, it was struggling and sputtering and going so slow the hitchhiker must have thought for sure I was going to stop and pick him up. I thought I would stop and pick him up. I almost had to pick him up. Usually a driver experiences the guilt of not stopping for a split-second. I had an eternity. Puttering by I was forced to look at him, really look at him, and just the looking heightens the possibility of stopping. He was a hardy older man wearing a Yankees hat and a round graying beard. As I drew up towards him, he peeked through my windshield right at me and smiled. From his eyes, crows' feet blessed the sides of his face. My car, over the knoll, pointed down and away I went.

Forty-five, fifty-five, sixty-five, seventy-five, eighty-five, ninety miles an hour, my car was going faster than it could on its own. That much speed can rattle your sanity. The car began to quiver. No wonder so many of us are guided by fear. This is how we travel every day—in quivering tin cans. Driving this fast should scare the shit out of us, but instead we do it every day, we're used to it, we don't think about it. Airplanes too. I can't imagine a more precarious predicament than to be strapped in a long tight metal tube shooting through ten thousand feet of open space. Yet we do this every day. Not just for daredevils, it's commonplace. We're terrified of death, yet we shoot ourselves out of cannons daily.

The sun, still just a hint in the dark sky, left the few early morning coffee customers in shadow. I knew it was her even amongst the others. Very tall with a long fluid stride, Isabel stepped out the door, walked down the path, and smiled at me as I stood beside my car.

"Hello Mr. Abrams," she said.

She bore a fierceness apparent in that first instant that I could not have appreciated on the phone before meeting her. She had a velocity about her. She stepped right up to me, reached out her hand, and shook mine, looking me in the eye the whole time.

"This is my friend Tiffany," Isabel said.

I hadn't even noticed Tiffany behind Isabel, and Tiffany couldn't have been more different. Much shorter and with blond hair, she reached out her fingers to shake my hand as her eyes glanced past me. She quickly climbed into the back, and Isabel slid into the passenger seat.

We drove without speaking except for the single syllable directions Isabel gave to get us out of Santa Fe. Once on the highway I appreciated the speed, for I had grown aware of our silence. All I could think to say was how much Gabriel respected Isabel. I thought about this for a while, finally deciding that I should say it—that the sentiment was appropriate—even if I'd been sitting there thinking about it and now the words would feel forced.

"Gabriel respects you so much."

Isabel's smile appeared like a flicker of sun and then serious again.

"I love Mr. Abrams."

She said, 'Mr. Abrams,' while I had said, 'Gabriel'.

There was a long pause, and I could feel her studying my face, sitting in the passenger seat beside me. I peeked over and she blushed, but she didn't look away. I had to glance back at the road.

"I knew how much trouble Mr. Abrams was having in his other classes, but still ... It sounds so small, so many adults say they want to help but make demands that aren't helpful at all."

Enunciating, Isabel spoke to me—not turning away or mumbling like so many teenagers. With her words, with the impassioned tone of her voice, with her searching eyes, she reached out to me.

"I tried to, well, I mean ... oh gosh I was always so glad to be in his classroom. Mr. Abrams, Mr. Abrams was—"

"You have to call me Mark."

"Your brother is like no one else in my whole life. And now ..."

Her face tensed—almost froze—and then it slid down into her taught fingers. She peeked back at me. Maybe she hadn't realized what she was saying and the rush of emotion surprised her—it surprised me and I struggled to swallow. Looking at the side of my face, she seemed to be ... I felt as if she were searching for my emotion, trying to determine how I was feeling, maybe trying to connect on what we were doing, where we were going. My face filled with sensation as if it were an over-stretched balloon; no more could I look at her. I glared at the feeble snowflakes cruising past the windshield, I squeezed the steering wheel struggling to keep hold of myself, to keep the car on the road, I clenched my jaw, and I could tell I was breathing loudly through my nose. I was embarrassed. My eyes started to sting and I was blinking and the snow was flying past and my palms were sweating on the steering wheel.

"Are you alright?" Isabel asked.

"Yeah."

"Should we pull over?"

"Yeah."

I forced the clicker and slowed the car to the shoulder. Once stopped I stumbled and fidgeted. I pushed both my hands through my hair. Inches from us cars zoomed past at eighty miles an hour.

"I'm sorry," Isabel said.

"No, no. I'm sorry. I didn't mean to, I mean I didn't—"

"It's okay."

I might have recoiled, but I looked at her, I looked into her, I peered into her face, and she was open. Isabel's eyes were very dark; they were green. I hadn't noticed. I took refuge there, for they were looking in my eyes as if—not examining or searching anymore—they were giving, they were sharing, they too were full of grief. A comfort settled between us. For me this was unprecedented, for I'm protective and hard to know, I guess. I could have been humiliated. Isabel smiled, and I tried to smile too. After hugging my mother—really for the first time as a man—something had happened. A barrier fell. I'm more accessible—or I can be accessible instead of the opposite. At least now, here, in this car, with Isabel. I took a breath and looked through the windshield. I peeked at Isabel who then glanced into the back seat at Tiffany, who had been so quiet I had forgotten about her and realizing she was sitting behind me I got all uncomfortable again. I pressed the gas and turned the wheel. I eased us back onto the road, and, as we built up speed, a Jeep shuddered past and Isabel waved, but no one in the car saw.

"That was Lori and Perry," Isabel said.

"Probably Sammy too," Tiffany said.

We were all heading out to the caves where a formal search with the New Mexico Search and Rescue was to begin at nine.

Often in awe of Isabel, Gabriel marveled at how she seemed to do the perfect thing at the precise moment, even when that perfect thing seemed arbitrary. In any other situation I would have been mortified at myself in that car having a panic attack and probably wouldn't have been able to recover. Maybe because we were feeling in reference to the same thing we had a deeper knowing in that moment. Whatever happened, she made me feel comfortable in an instant when I could have leapt out the window.

I wanted to pay her a compliment, I wanted to express my appreciation of who she was or tell her of the connection I felt. I wanted to say something now that we were back on the road, but as I sat there thinking of what I could say Tiffany shifted around behind me and Isabel began to speak.

"Every day, I swear, every day Mr. Abrams would come into the classroom, stand at the front and spread his arms and pronounce, 'Welcome to the Machine.' It was the funniest thing, it was always the funniest thing. No one knew what he meant … or he never explained what he meant, but we all knew. I started to picture Los Pinos High as this giant machine with all these churning gears and wheels and this grid like a massive cookie cutter stamping out fifty students at a time, all marching out with the same dull expressions and in the same gray clothes. 'Welcome to the Machine!' I can see him now."

She laughed. I laughed too. And then we were silent for several miles.

"Gabriel admired you," I said. "How you could do the right thing at the right moment, enliven a room."

"What do you mean?"

I could have mentioned as an example how she had just made me feel safe on the side of the road, but I didn't want to talk about that.

Sometimes Isabel would stand up at the right moment—or sit down at just the exact instant in order to cede the floor to a hesitant poet who might need a little disguised prodding. I didn't offer this as an example either, for it was more of a subtle instinct she applied in delicate instances and hardly robust enough an example to illustrate my point.

I did think of something that may have served as a better example: that time when the poets' enthusiasm wavered thus jeopardizing the Poetry Burst Out, Isabel walked out of the classroom and performed her forlorn piece to an empty parking lot while everyone in the classroom gathered around the window to watch. From where did that come? A non sequitur, yet perfect, it worked. At a desperate juncture it reinvigorated the poets.

"Oh yeah," Isabel said, finally, in reply. "It wasn't really like that at all."

She sat there in the passenger seat for a long time without speaking; something was brewing up inside of her. She glared down into her lap.

"He put a fork in my bed."

"What?" I said.

"It's stupid."

"What did he do?"

"He put a fork in my bed."

"Gabriel?"

"No, my stepbrother."

Now Isabel was staring at me; I could feel her intensity.

"All through dinner my stepbrother Matthew stole moments when only I would see," she said. "He'd look at me and then he'd look at his fist so I'd see his fork squeezed in it, his knuckles bulging white, grinning like some schoolboy squishing ants."

As best I could I looked at her as I drove. She turned back to herself, took a steady breath. And then:

"The fork scared me. More than the rest. It's like a poem can take a mundane object and give it an altogether different meaning. When I went and said that poem outside in the parking lot it was all about that—the fork. And it wasn't even really a poem." Isabel turned in her seat and stared back at Tiffany. "I didn't know anybody was watching me. I was so embarrassed when I found that out."

Gabriel hadn't counted how many times he'd been summoned to the principal's office. He felt like a problem student, growing nervous as he stepped up to the door, not knowing what he had done this time. Dr. Fitzpatrick ordered him in. The two chairs in front of the desk were occupied—one by Robertson and the other by a hunched-over woman who Gabriel assumed to be Robertson's mother. She seemed worn, but couldn't have been old. Robertson leaned away, though his mother turned her head to watch Gabriel's stilted steps into the room.

Dr. Fitzpatrick glanced towards the door at Gabriel. She took a breath as if to speak yet paused. Gabriel's eyes drifted upward to look above Dr. Fitzpatrick's head at a small cheap American flag stuck out of the wall on a rod with a painted gold tip.

"The Sandovals have lodged a complaint against you," Dr. Fitzpatrick said.

The words only confirmed the scene. Gabriel looked at Robertson who wasn't wearing his usual gray gloves. Gabriel peeked around Robertson's round body, trying to glimpse his hands but Robertson, under Gabriel's scrutiny, shoved his hands deeper into his lap.

"Would you mind waiting outside?" Dr. Fitzpatrick said.

Gabriel sat in a chair outside the office. Through the door Gabriel heard mumbles but no words. The secretary at her desk kept peeking up at him. Gabriel tried to remember some past encounter with Robertson that would justify a complaint. There were so many, but all, from Gabriel's perspective, warranted Gabriel lodging a complaint against Robertson—not the other way around.

Since Robertson's moment when for a split second he let down his guard and admitted that he and his mother were without a place to live, his attitude only got worse. In the classroom Robertson became downright rude. At his desk he would sit with a blank slate for a face. He would pull out his massive phone and stare into it, huffing and refusing to put it away when Gabriel asked.

"Whatcha gonna do about it?" Robertson would say.

And worse. He would comment on the way Gabriel smelt or tell him only 'codgers' ride bikes. Usually when they squabbled over Robertson's cellphone, Robertson would drop it in his lap beneath his desk, still working it, and Gabriel would have to claim victory and move on, but one day Robertson wouldn't even respond to Gabriel, just sitting there scrolling up and up on the screen with his fingers. Without fanfare, Gabriel sat at his desk, filled out a discipline referral form, and walked it down to Mr. Reade's office, requesting Robertson be removed from his class. Robertson was shocked when security arrived, but he exited without further commotion, leaving behind on the desk a mess of half-eaten chips. Later Gabriel discovered from Mr. Detrick that Mr. Reade had released Robertson without addressing any of the issues or doling out any sort of punishment. The next day Robertson was back in Gabriel's class working his phone.

One morning Gabriel entered his classroom and found a crumpled sleeping bag shoved beneath the overhead projector cart, a couple nearby dictionaries as a pillow. The makeshift bed was still warm. Like a sinkhole, Gabriel's chest collapsed. He recalled all the insensitive remarks he had made in frustration to Robertson.

Gabriel hung Robertson's sleeping bag from the overhead projector hoping that Robertson would come forward and confide in him. In class that day Robertson was worse than ever as if rebelling against the sight of his sleeping bag. On repeated occasions Gabriel tried to talk to him, but Robertson refused in the rudest of ways, shunning and turning away. After school Gabriel tucked the sleeping bag in the closet. Every morning he checked to see if it was still there. Night after night Gabriel lingered in his own bed wondering, worrying: where was Robertson sleeping? Then one morning in his classroom he was sure the sleeping bag—though still in the closet—had shifted its position. Gabriel felt it and it may have been warm. For several days after that the sleeping bag was returned to the closet but always—and now Gabriel was sure—to a different configuration. Also in a corner of the cupboard a jug of water had been shoved, and over the days Gabriel watched the water level rise and fall. He wanted so much to help but anything overt was met with such disdain from Robertson. At Albertson's, the supermarket, Gabriel bought two coupons that looked and worked like credit cards and he left them on a desk after school, and in the morning they were gone. Gabriel thought it must have been Robertson who had stolen his keys.

And then one morning the sleeping bag was gone. And Robertson's behavior got worse. And Gabriel struggled to be patient. He talked to a school counselor who claimed to know of Robertson's troubles, yet insisted they were doing everything they could.

It's funny how we can concoct stories in our heads and with enduring conviction believe that they're true when really they're flimsy notions of preconception. No matter how sure Gabriel was—the sleeping bag in his classroom was not Robertson's.

Dr. Fitzpatrick's office door opened and Robertson and his mother walked out. Robertson never looked back, but his mother, following her son down the hall, stole a glance at Gabriel.

"Mr. Abrams."

Gabriel was being called into the office.

Dr. Fitzpatrick lifted a piece of paper off her desk and stretched out her arm motioning for Gabriel to take it.

The top read: "Problem with Mr. Abrams".

Holding the page, Gabriel was standing near the desk. He peeked up and Dr. Fitzpatrick offered him a seat. He sat in the chair Robertson had been sitting in, and it was still warm. Beneath the principal's scrutiny, Gabriel was going to have to read the Sandovals' complaint.

It began: "Mr. Abrams should be in trouble. Mr. Abrams called my son a bitch. Mr. Abrams should not be fit to be a teaching."

Written in shaky cursive, the paragraph was filled with all sorts of errors. Maybe to soften the blow, Gabriel's mind began correcting them. Not wanting to look up, he took refuge in the grammatical mistakes. The letter was signed, "Joan Sandoval."

Still Gabriel didn't look up.

He was being accused of calling Robertson a 'bitch'. Gabriel remembered the encounter to which the letter seemed to be referring. A few weeks ago during his prep period, Robertson and Jorge came to his classroom demanding a better grade for an assignment they both had turned in a week late. They claimed that their IEPs (Independent Education Plans) allowed them to turn their schoolwork in late. This seemed ridiculous, yet with them they had their IEPs, which did seem to verify their claim. Gabriel had told them that he would have to look into it. They left and returned ten minutes later with Ms. Peters—their school counselor. She said that, yes, in fact by law Gabriel had to allow them more time to complete their assignments because it was in their IEPs, which are legal documents. How could this be? It seemed unfair to other students and a disservice to Jorge and Robertson who were being taught that they were exempt from basic rules of life. For a job interview you can't show up a week late and expect employment. Gabriel proposed that if they needed more time with their work, Robertson and Jorge had to request an extension at least two days before the due date and not on the day it was due and certainly not a week later. This seemed reasonable, and Ms. Peters agreed, but Robertson snapped.

"You are such a ... you think you're above the law. I don't have to listen to you—you and your B.O. oh my God, you—"

He spoke with such a sneer, a greenish gas may have exited his mouth. Gabriel, embarrassed, asked Ms. Peters and Jorge to leave the room. Yes, Gabriel was mad, so anything he said to Robertson in that private moment was imbued with that emotion. He asked Robertson where he got the idea he could talk to him like that. Robertson's body twisted away from Gabriel, but Gabriel kept talking. He told him it didn't matter who Gabriel was or who Robertson was—he was a student and Gabriel was a teacher and that was enough reason why he cannot speak to him like that. Robertson just started to laugh, turning and laughing right in Gabriel's face.

According to Joan Sandoval's complaint, somewhere in that private encounter, Gabriel had called Robertson a 'bitch.'

Dr. Fitzpatrick ruffled around in her chair. It had been too long for Gabriel to be reading the short paragraph that was the complaint. So he looked up. He felt guilty just having to defend himself, just being in this flower chair beneath Dr. Fitzpatrick's judgment.

"This is not true." Emotion pressed into Gabriel's throat. "I would never say that, never to a student. I know I've—"

Dr. Fitzpatrick started writing something.

"—gotten mad, but I would never swear at a student or do anything intentionally to harm anyone. I did not call Robertson a 'bitch.' If in a different environment I were to call someone something comparable, it certainly wouldn't be that. It's not my language, it's not what I would say."

Pen in hand Dr. Fitzpatrick was now gazing at him, and Gabriel gazed back.

"This is going to have to go into your file."

It wasn't that she seemed uncaring—it was worse. She was abrasive, she was cold. Unconcerned with the truth, Dr. Fitzpatrick didn't ask any questions or give him the same amount of time as she had the Sandovals.

Almost comical, the phone rang and she answered it. She covered the mouthpiece and said, "I have to take this."

She was concluding their meeting. Bitch. He couldn't believe it; she was ending it just like that.

Dr. Fitzpatrick had him all wrapped up and guilty.

And maybe he was.

Bitch.

Oh my, Gabriel kept thinking it.

Bitch.

He couldn't get it out of his head.

Bitch.

Now he thought it was funny.

"Bitch," he said—this time going right along with it.

Gabriel couldn't help stumbling around calling everybody a 'bitch'. Well, not exactly, but in his head he did, and it wasn't completely involuntary, for Gabriel had succumbed to his unconscious which had grabbed onto the word and insisted. He might not regularly use that word, yet now he rebelled against the accusation. The too-slow guy in the grocery line was a 'bitch,' the lady in the SUV was a 'bitch,' the woman with the cigarette, the bank teller who couldn't count. Maybe this wasn't appropriate or teacherly or even very wise, for dear lord if in front of someone the word 'bitch' slipped out of his mouth as an actual sound. Maybe in a meeting with a principal. Maybe in class. Maybe with Robertson. Gabriel knew the hazards, but he was on the bandwagon. He couldn't stop. His brain was like an errant dog unable to quit yapping—scratch that: his brain was like an errant bitch refusing to quit bitching like the little bitch it was.

Maybe he had to work it out of his system.

Gnarly, nasty, bitch-ridden Gabriel had barreled through the door, all lips and air and attitude. At the kitchen table Chloe was licking and affixing gold stars to her homework. Despite everything, Gabriel was jovial—gnarly, yes, but jovial.

He eased past Holly—the backs of their hands touched. Powered by a stream of silliness, Gabriel tripped forward, not swearing, but hurling around emotion and energy and insight:

"It's amazing teachers can even breathe at all," he said. "Not in pennies, they should be paid in mansions. Yachts. Islands. In countries: Ms. Bimble, I present thee ... Luxembourg. How wrong it's the students carrying Gucci purses getting the discounts at the movies. How about teacher discounts! Students—forget it. Why don't teachers go Columbine? You never hear of that—do you? We might—one day."

He moved like a leopard stalking. Gabriel had perfected his slow stroll around the classroom. With each step, his front foot hovered above the floor before settling onto the heel and rolling down to the toe, step after quiet step. Instead of being in one place, he was in many—not a unit, but a constant, spreading himself around the room. The purpose of his slow stroll, and thus the characteristic of it as well, depended on what class he was teaching. In the morning with his freshmen he was the enforcer, coercing students into behaving with his close proximity. If a student started to whisper Gabriel would make his way around the room towards the disturbance before it grew. In his creative writing class he was a hovering asset, suddenly there with an answer, a little inspiration, a detail that could send the student off in her own creative direction.

When they finished writing Gabriel asked and everybody in his creative writing class claimed to know what metaphors and similes were, yet when it came to defining them the room went silent. Isabel raised her hand. She had a nice sense about her. She raised her hand because no one else would.

"A simile is a comparison using 'like' or 'as' while a metaphor just gets rid of them all together."

Perfect.

"My water bottle is red like blood. Simile," Gabriel said. "My water bottle is as red as a fire truck. Simile. My water bottle is a screaming fire engine racing down the road discharging water into the blaze of my parched throat. Metaphors." Gabriel took a sip.

Gabriel set each student to compose a list of the most important things in their lives. Five minutes later he asked them to form their lists into a string of metaphors and similes. Make it a rap song, make it a poem, make it a paragraph.

"Make it your own."

The class had agreed on ten minutes, yet as Gabriel slowly strolled around the room he realized it had already been fifteen. It was all but quiet save the pencils scribbling across paper and the occasional guttural grunt that steamed off the creative juices flowing. Fully absorbed Gabriel's creative writing students soaked themselves into their notebooks like blood gushing into bandages. After twenty minutes a few students put their pencils down and stretched their arms. When most had stopped writing, Gabriel urged the others to finish up.

And then: "Okay good. Who'd like to share?"

More polite than nervous, nobody volunteered—then five hands went up eager to share: Isabel with her profoundness, Janice with her trite love metaphors, Max and his rims, Peter and his thinly disguised homoerotic similes and metaphors and witticisms. And then a quiet student, Teresa, cleared her throat and read a fairy tale in which a girl with an orange ponytail travels through her life talking but nobody ever hears, as if her lips moved but sound never came. When she finished nobody said anything.

As if to explain she said, "It's all a metaphor."

A stroke of genius!

"Yes yes yes," Gabriel said leaping around the room. "Exactly—it's exactly that. Excellent Teresa excellent. It's an extended metaphor. And you can all do that. You can write a story where the characters stand in for something larger. Like one character can represent everyone at this school. Entire books can be like that. Like wrapping a pill in peanut butter—"

A commotion in the hall distracted Gabriel. His door swung open. Everyone turned to look. One of the assistant principals, Mr. Forgerty, stepped inside and glared across the room at Gabriel. Just outside the door stood two of the security staff's largest officers.

"Mr. Abrams," Mr. Forgerty said, "may we speak with you in the hall."

It was not a question—Mr. Forgerty's voice wrenched with pressure—it was a command.

But Gabriel hesitated.

"Mr. Abrams."

Mr. Forgerty motioned for Mr. Smith, another teacher, to enter and he headed for the front of the classroom. In the doorway one of the security men imposed his presence. In the hall the other security officer's radio crackled.

"What's going on?" a student asked.

Mr. Forgerty didn't answer. Instead: "Mr. Abrams."

"What's going on?" the student asked again.

"It's okay," Gabriel said.

The students began to rustle around in their seats.

"Mr. Abrams, we need you to come with us."

"Right now?" a student asked.

And another—"We're in the middle of class."

"It's okay," Gabriel said.

And Mr. Forgety said, "Mr. Smith will take over—"

"We don't want Mr. Smith."

"I'm sure he'll do fine—"

"—And I'm sure he won't—"

"Hey!" Gabriel had to say to quell his student's mounting insolence.

The security officer in the doorway stepped into the room and the other officer took his place in the doorway. Isabel raised her hand.

"Mr. Abrams," the security officer said, "you need to come with us now."

Tension flowed into Gabriel's chest. At first he was worried about his class being disrupted and then about his students appearing disrespectful, but the security officer had made his way into the room and now hovered right in front of Gabriel.

"Mr. Abrams!" Mr. Forgerty commanded one last time.

At the edge of the doorway Gabriel peeked back at his students. Mr. Forgerty ushered the group down the hall. The security men, now flanked on either side of Gabriel, wrapped their hands around his arms.

*Write a screaming headline.
What are the details? How
are you involved?*

Isabel was running, her sneakers tapping over the hard dark street, the sound hollow and hurried, running from her house, running from her life, running from a fork in her bed.

"He was so sweet to me leading up to the wedding."

After Matthew's mother and Isabel's father decided to marry they all four gathered together to build a blended family. They had dinner and went to movies, attended the air show. Considering Matthew was the basketball star at Los Pinos High, Isabel had known of him before meeting him. Lori's brother was one of his friends.

The September wedding was idyllic. The folks in attendance dressed for the occasion. Isabel and Matthew served as maid-of-honor and best man, wearing a ball gown and tuxedo, respectively. Isabel arranged wildflowers into wreaths. Her father had cried.

The following weekend Isabel and her father moved into Matthew and his mother's house. From the rented truck to the house, they carried boxes and speakers and books and suitcases.

Together, Isabel and Matthew lugged a loveseat. It wasn't big, but it was heavy, and Isabel, facing backwards, tried to navigate up the two steps at the front door. The weight of the sofa jarred her into the doorframe and sent her tumbling to the ground, the sofa on top of her. As Isabel writhed to free herself, Matthew, trapping her, balanced the loveseat in place—a grin etched up into his cheeks. He had done it on purpose.

Isabel pushed and squirmed her way free. She scrambled. She cut through the house, out the kitchen door, and into the small backyard. A high concrete wall fenced her in. She stuttered and prowled like a trapped mouse.

"There you are." Her father found her. "Is everything alright?"

"Yeah, fine."

The new wife stepped out the door.

"Is everything alright?"

She glanced at her husband, and Isabel could hardly stand it.

"Fine," Isabel said. "Fine," she said to her father. "I just, I just jammed my wrist."

"Here let me see, maybe a little ice—Susan, some ice."

That quickly Isabel's life collapsed into a series of dodges and forced smiles and long hours barricaded in her bedroom. Matthew played the angelic stepson and stepbrother when observed by others all the while acting clandestinely cruel to Isabel.

"I crept through school pleading to God I wouldn't run into him," Isabel had told me, sitting next to me in my car. "Seeing him down the hall was like being hit by a wave of needles."

At school Mathew didn't punch her or pinch her or pull her hair, though he would try to intimidate her by glaring and laughing or blowing her a kiss from across the quad. At home he was physical. He would sneak up on her and punch her in the thigh or, slithering up behind with spit on his finger, he would stick that finger in her ear and jump back, screaming, "Wetwilly! Wetwilly!"

Far worse than the dead-legs, the wetwillies were so invasive.

Isabel had to expect that anytime she walked through the front door of her new home she would be confronted and disturbed by Matthew.

Though a star basketball player, Matthew was small—a foot shorter than Isabel, but his aggression and agility made him one of the most valuable players on the team. Yet at the same time, Matthew was fully aware of his diminutive stature and over-compensated with his mouth, with his actions, and with his hostility. Maybe he couldn't stand being towered over by Isabel. She had a regality about her that she could not repress.

The classroom became Isabel's safe haven. At the beginning of the year, she had asked Gabriel to sponsor the poetry club when her blended family seemed like a fairytale—after the wedding but before Matthew drove the sofa over on top of her. She had imagined the poetry group would meet at lunch for forty minutes a week and lightly read their poems, applaud with their fingertips on the plump parts of their palms. Isabel hadn't experienced a privileged childhood, but she never had pressing adversity that maimed her every instant. When Matthew's nature revealed itself, Isabel's reality burst, and with it the mild character and the limited scope of the poetry club. Isabel needed a counterbalance, and it took an entire existence of excellence at school to offset Matthew's virulence, and the glory and success of the poetry group became intertwined with her survival.

Could you even call them rumors?

After Gabriel had been escorted from his classroom by security guards, stories were repeated and embellished with each new teller adding his own twist as well as his own authority. But doesn't even a rumor need a tinge of truth?

Mr. Abrams had plundered the school treasury. Was that it? He was a notorious embezzler—no a terrorist. That's it. He was in the witness protection program (real name: Goldberg Gambini). Mr. Abrams had threatened to kill the principal, set the school on fire, burn down the town.

Any teacher would lament: why can't these students be as creative and proactive with their schoolwork?

Six monster cops had stormed into Mr. Abrams' classroom. In front of his students and without a word they had leapt upon Mr. Abrams, punching and kicking him into a straitjacket and then dragging him out with a jet-black hood over his head. It took six more cops to stuff him into the squad car and six more to get him out at the station. When he refused to talk, they broke his legs.

When he did finally return to the classroom, the first question—

"Where's your crutches, Mr. Abrams?"

Truth is, it was a mostly quiet affair. With Gabriel pressed between them, the two security men marched to the principal's office where they ushered Gabriel in but did not enter, for inside were two standing Santa Fe police officers whose uniforms were crisp as wood. The door had been shut behind Gabriel and the stench of fresh paint in Dr. Fitzpatrick's office lingered, the walls bare and bright white. The younger of the two officers leaned forward.

"You are not being arrested."

"Not being arrested for what?" Gabriel asked.

"You are being detained for questioning—"

"Detained?"

"Detained at your employer's request."

And there she was, Dr. Fitzpatrick, lurking behind her desk.

"You are not being arrested, Mr. Abrams," she said. "But please sit down."

She was polite. She stepped around her desk with her fists clenched behind her back. Pulling a chair into position for Gabriel, she leveled a stare into his chest. Gabriel didn't want to sit.

The cop stepped up to Gabriel and patted Gabriel's pockets, reached around and ran his hand along Gabriel's waistline.

Holding his elbows away from his body for the cop, Gabriel asked, "What is this about?"

"Please sit down, Mr. Abrams."

"What is this about?"

"Sir, we're going to have to ask you to sit down." The young officer placed his hand on his holstered pistol.

Gabriel bent into the chair and peeked up at these three dark figures looming above. They shuffled around into their prearranged configuration.

Gabriel had lived rowdy but not criminal. Throwing mudballs at cars, writing rebellious crap on bathroom walls, fighting, stealing, lying—that was it from small, medium, to the present. In his life Gabriel had smoked marijuana and eaten mushrooms and drank plenty of alcohol. Was he going to hell for it? Maybe living in the woods or riding his bike or pulling a bag of cookies from a grocery store's dumpster proved unbecoming of a Los Pinos High School teacher. Was he going to hell for that? It's true, Gabriel had done different things, made choices outside of society's norms which can piss-off a plethora of people who lack the audacity even though at night those same people dream in those exact colors. That's me, I admit it. The pull of society's expectations silences plenty of inner voices. The truth is Gabriel didn't like to smoke or drink or steal or lie. He much preferred himself clear and clean, balanced and healthy, and if you exclude his sometimes-provocative ideas and often arousing choices, deep down Gabriel was pretty well the curious, studious-type. He just had different notions of what was right and how best to live his life. Was he going to hell? Maybe in America.

Dr. Fitzpatrick faded into the background and the young cop began asking Gabriel a glut of arbitrary questions, starting with—

"Where are you from?"

Earth, Gabriel felt like saying and it almost rolled out, but for the first time in his life when confronted, something loomed larger than his angst. And that was his students. While sitting in that chair, Gabriel wondered what was going on in his class. The bell hadn't rung, school was still in session, and Gabriel's creative writing students were in his room yet Gabriel was not.

"Are your parents alive? Do you have any other family? Why did you move to Santa Fe?" the young cop peppered Gabriel as the older cop took notes in a little notebook with a half pencil.

Gabriel had been polite, his answers short, yet his emotions pushed through his restrained demeanor.

"What is this about?" Gabriel asked.

"Do you like being a teacher?" the cop continued, "Why did you become a teacher? Do you like your students? Where did you meet your girlfriend? Do you like your girlfriend's daughter?"

His girlfriend?

It was as if these people were trying to knock him off balance, to scare him. He had no idea why he was there, they weren't telling him, he hated cops, he hated their authority, he hated the power they yielded and the sometimes not so subtle ways in which they exercised it. And the subtle ways too. Like in this moment by not telling him the purpose of this interrogation.

"Why am I here?"

"We want to ask you a few questions."

"I answered a few questions."

"We want to ask you a few more."

"I want to know why I'm here."

"Can we continue?" the cop pressed.

Piercing with resolve, Gabriel glared at the cop: "Why am I here?"

The cop stared back, then looked away. He glanced at his partner and then across the room at Dr. Fitzpatrick. The bell that ended the school day sounded off and commotion like rumbling thunder rose up outside of the office. The young cop puffed out his chest and to Gabriel he spoke with great enunciation.

"We have reason to believe you're planning a Columbine-like assault on Los Pinos High School."

Excuse me?"

That was all Gabriel could say.

"Excuse me?"

He was in near shock. Not like a body shock when all perception goes askew—he could see just fine—more like a mental shock caused from utter disbelief. This dementia was not issuing from the inside but pushing in from the outside.

"Excuse me?"

"Do I need to repeat myself?" the cop said.

"Yes, by God, you do."

"Mr. Abrams, we have reason to believe you're planning a Columbine-like assault on Los Pinos High School."

"Excuse me?"

"Sir, I'm going to have to ask you to stop saying that."

"Excuse me?"

"Sir!"

"What possible evidence do you have to support such an accusation? I'm a teacher. I'm trying to ... I would never think of such a despicable act. Teaching's like a seed, we plant an idea and then hope. We have no bombs or guns. Our explosions are marked by the speed of a growing tree. You must know this Dr. Fitzpatrick."

"Maybe if teachers spoke normal," the young cop snarled, "kids might like school."

"What evidence do you have?"

Dr. Fitzpatrick stepped in.

"Mr. Abrams, remember you are not being arrested."

"But I am certainly being accused—so what evidence do you have?"

The older cop's cellphone rang and he slumped into a corner to mumble a conversation.

The truth was they had no evidence. They had no cache of guns. No homemade bombs. They found in his breast pocket no blueprints of the campus with his killing route penciled in. Really all they had was a panicked principal. As far as evidence: they had nothing. This was a witch-hunt.

I imagine when Dr. Fitzpatrick and the cops finally released him, Gabriel went straight home, collapsed into his futon and said fuck about a million times. All his former swearing—his 'shits' and 'assholes' and even his 'bitches'—lost significance in the gloom of these fucks. As he said them over and over as the hours like elastic stretched past they changed meaning. First he was in shock and the word repeated involuntarily like hail bouncing off a windshield—fuck fuck fuck fuck fuck. Later the word slowed ... and elongated, stretching itself out. Fuuuuuuuuuuuuuuuck—the 'u' sounding off in disbelief. The word had become a question. And then, when the icy darkness had made itself comfortable in the night, the line of fucks transformed themselves into a mantra, repeated like bursts from a machine gun, full of rage, exclaimed with a clenched fist: fuckfuckfuck fuckfuckfuck.

Out at the caves a ranger had warned Gabriel not to crawl through the caverns alone, because if something happened his chance of survival dropped off significantly. The ranger related a story of a family in the 1970s that went into a cave and never came out. A week later all they found was their wood-paneled station wagon still in the parking lot with its bent Iowa plates. But they were a family, Gabriel had mentioned in light of the ranger's warning about not going in alone. It was just to make a point, the ranger had said. The more people the less risk. If a rock roof caves in, a survivor might be able to lead rescuers back to the spot where his buddy lay trapped. Without a witness there's no thread.

Gabriel hadn't heeded the ranger's advice. But now, deep into the frozen night, between the word illustrating his shifting moods, Gabriel could have remembered the ranger's warning: "All they found was their wood-paneled station wagon."

Considering Gabriel's history of desertion, it wasn't such a leap to imagine that he would shrewdly plan and cunningly execute his getaway, for he was being pushed out by his job that was caving in on him from every angle—students, administrators, parents. The police! It grew worse every day. Gabriel had been dragged down; he was worn out. As a teacher you don't just give your time, you give your life, and in so doing the teaching, the students, the administration, the bureaucracy, the onslaught takes your energy, your self-respect, your hopefulness, your idealism, your sanity, leaving you with a mess of a mind and a cracked bowl of a spirit leaking bile. Look at older teachers—bitter, angry, disillusioned—all of them. Gabriel saw this. He saw how the students responded. With disdain, they scratched through the halls, sprawled out in the classrooms, tore up textbooks and teachers and curriculums. At best, they encountered their schoolwork with reluctance, if they cared at all. And the apathy of society in regard to teachers wasn't unfathomable, after all society is made up of former high schoolers. Gabriel had been torn down; he was burnt out. And now the police?

So, yes, running wasn't such an offensive option. He had done it before. Adventure-seeking, he'd called it. Searching for that precise place where all settles into perfection. Those who don't seek never find, he would explain so as to excuse his actions.

He probably stayed up all night thinking about ditching his job, his repeated fuck fuck fucks becoming more and more assured. He probably stayed up all night planning and in so doing realized there wasn't much planning to do. He'd go to an isolated section where the caves were extensive and uncharted. He'd camp there that night and then, leaving his car, he'd trek out during the day trying to look as much like an inconspicuous hiker as possible.

Gabriel used to read stories of intrigue. He was interested in spies and bank robbers and assassins from the biblical courts. He wanted to know their devices, their concoctions, their secrets. He used to send away for pamphlets from *Looponics*. Best methods of torture. How to extract revenge. How to steal someone's identity. I remember this one called the *Heavy Duty Identity*. It explained how to become someone else while shedding your present legal self. I don't think Gabriel ever expected to fabricate a new identity, or to torture a prisoner, or to ruin someone's credit—he was just curious. Couple this type of reading with his extensive travel and I'm sure he thought he could pull it off. He's such a personable guy. During his journeys he hung out with all sorts of characters—monks, hobos, barons, felons. I don't think he was especially tough. What he was was fearless and real without being too stupid and naïve. He had a lot of experience. He knew when to pull back. But also he was curious and open. He wanted to know different sorts of people.

Gabriel would have had to get into Mexico without having his identity recorded by the authorities. He knew he could do that by walking over the bridge that spanned the Rio Grande. And then he'd head to Mexico City where he would stay in some fleabag joint while searching out the lower element who could secure him some Australian's stolen passport. That would be his biggest expense. Then after perfecting his Australian accent he'd be free to head to the beaches of Asia where his dwindling U.S. dollars would stretch further.

*O*ne night after dinner Isabel found herself abandoned at the table alone. Her father and stepmother were in the kitchen, and she didn't know where Matthew went. Considering a specific gesture she could do when she performed a certain line in one of her poems, she twirled her wrist and raised her arm, saying the line over to herself in her head when Matthew snuck up behind her and wrapped his arm around her neck in a vicious chokehold.

He didn't say anything. But he squeezed.

Isabel couldn't breathe. Couldn't scream.

Her hands rose up to his forearm around her throat and held on as if she were being silently suspended by her neck above an abyss.

When he finally let go Isabel's first breath entered the room as a shriek.

All night Isabel laid in bed stunned. The next day at school too. She went through the motions in her classes—she smiled, she small-talked, but she wasn't there. All through the day she could feel her breath—or rather the absence of her breath as if it were stuck in her throat, inaccessible like a half-swallowed stone. She spent the day in mid-shriek, stalled in that most terrifying moment of Matthew's powerful arm wrapped around her neck, strangling her.

In creative writing class she didn't want to write, didn't think she could, yet as she sat there while the others worked she manages a title—*The Aftermath of a Really Bad Car Wreck*. She stared at her page for a long time. She had never been in a car accident, but she couldn't write about what was happening to her, but still it felt good to write out the title even as she scratched out six of the eight words. And then she wrote the poem, almost sweating, and then she stopped and read it. She liked it. As Mr. Abrams wandered the room, he leaned over her shoulder and she ever so slightly re-positioned her journal for him to read her poem.

<u>*The Aftermath*</u>

long after the ambulances
and sirens and gawkers have gone
the crushed-in heap
of what was once a Lexus
sits abandoned half in a ditch

so much metal and broken glass
taking up so much space
before the mess is cleaned
before the heap has been towed
before the sun has risen

Barely a word made audible, "I love that," Mr. Abrams said.

When Isabel arrived home that afternoon she entered without thought or feeling. She was surprised to find her father home, for he worked nights and usually didn't have two days off in a row.

"My darling, hello," he said with a smile so big.

Isabel's resolve solidified. She couldn't tell her father what Matthew had done, for the very foundation of his new life would crumble, the entire blended family would be affected, yet if Isabel kept it to herself then only she would suffer.

At the dinner table she poked at her food. Matthew had been trying to get her attention by focusing his silent force on her. When she finally looked he glanced at his hand: his white-knuckled fist strangled a fork inside his fingers. Isabel's body jerked. He barely had to do anything to assert his power over her. This was the fork that Isabel would refer to in my car a month later.

After dinner on her way to her bedroom she passed through the living room where Matthew sat. He never looked up over his phone, yet Isabel felt his heat, felt him knowing she was there.

When she went to bed, she crawled beneath the covers and something stuck her in her thigh. Frozen terror returned in all its immediacy. She struggled for air. Isabel never cried but when Matthew would sneak up on her and punch her, the shock and sharp pain could press tears into the corners of her eyes. Full-on she cried now. Out from her bed she threw the fork so hard it could have stuck in the far wall. She buried herself in her bed. Didn't want to move, she didn't want to breath. She wanted to vanish. The wood floor creaked outside her door. And then there was no noise there for a while as someone lingered. Isabel held her breath. And then the floor creaked again and moved away.

She whipped back her covers, she had to move. Her hands were shaking, she had to go. She shook empty her piggybank. Into the front hall closet she dug out her father's sleeping bag and slipped out the front door.

Once clear of the house, she ran.

Hurrying down the street with the sleeping bag tucked beneath her arm, Isabel, with an indeterminate objective, traveled the backstreets, keeping to the shadows. She hoped her father wouldn't peek in her room to say goodnight to an empty bed.

She marched as if the movement was her destination. She stomped all the way into town, stopped for nothing, then curved around and walked back out of town. She wandered through neighborhoods in which she had never been—huge adobe houses and walls and gates in front of driveways. After a couple of hours her legs began to ache and the cold began to penetrate. She had to sit down, maybe lie down. She didn't have enough money for a motel. Would they even give a room to a teenager? She was too embarrassed to call a friend. It was cold, and an image stuck in her head. Last year she had gone on a hike with Tiffany and Tiffany's mother and it was so cold then too. They had seen tucked into the armpit beneath a bridge what right away Isabel knew was the bed of some long-gone homeless man. The image of the makeshift abandoned bed would make a great poem. In her mind as she walked she turned over phrases: '... old blankets swept with dirt and time ... old blankets swept with dirt and sand by time crusted in the crooks beneath bridges ...'

She wandered along the path above the Santa Fe River. She peeked around before skulking down into the shrubbery. Halfway down the hill she stashed herself deep beneath several thick bushes, breaking branches as she rolled out her sleeping bag and smooshed herself inside. It wasn't quite winter, but she froze half-awake all night. Hearing a noise, she thought someone was approaching—it could have been her own breath. She felt around for a heavy stick and held it with both fists in her sleeping bag.

Wide-awake when it was still so dark, she knew it was morning—or as close to morning as possible. She felt out of time, and the darkness lingered for eternity.

Throughout the school day her exhaustion followed like melancholy. She brushed her teeth with her finger and tried to straighten her hair, tried to smile, tried to act normal. She couldn't quite swallow the feeling that tonight she should just go home. But she couldn't bring herself to do it—she wouldn't. She had been able to endure Matthew's abuse, but the fork in her bed, the chokehold changed everything. She was scared. She was scared.

At the poetry club's gathering after school she conducted the meeting with poise. All day she had strained to hide her misery, fooling even herself—that's how she was able to go on. But when Ned burst in late with his ripped shirt and disheveled hair, Isabel saw in him herself. She couldn't help but to keep glancing at him. She knew she didn't look as he did, but with his arrival her mask fractured into veins. Others wanted to read, but she wanted Ned to stand up and find a route out for his angst—she needed him to express what she herself buried—she knew whatever he said, whatever words he used, was sure to describe how she felt. Simmering even before he stepped to the front, he began:

Dr. Fitzpatrick is a cunt
Dr. Fitzpatrick is a cunt ...

Isabel wasn't shocked —she yearned for the words for they struck so rough and wrong. Concerned, Mr. Abrams glanced at her. Earlier when I first related this scene, all Gabriel was thinking was that he had needed to stop Ned from cursing the principal, but to Isabel this was everything Gabriel had inspired in them—the raw search for candor and authenticity. Ned's words, though posed in the gangster rap-style, always expressed his life at that moment—something Isabel could not do for herself. She needed to feel his sharp words, see his rage, she needed to watch him express himself, she needed to be reminded of effectiveness and purpose and the importance of her own potency. The poets were all so angry at so much and they strove to express that anger both as an attempt to name it and to exorcize it, but Isabel lacked the courage to share—much less write—what was happening to her now. She could only skirt around it, while Ned in his gurgled fury spit forth an exactness Isabel desired. Yes, Ned's right hand made that stereotypical circular rappers' motion but the distress was all his own. Laced with his urgent anguish, Ned's poem made Isabel feel less sorry for herself, it made her feel rebellious, it reminded her of the spirit of Mr. Abrams' illuminations. It made her want to do something—not necessarily bludgeon Matthew, but she did not rule that out.

And then in six words Ned discredited all the enthusiasm, all the momentum he had inspired.

"Only pussyfuckers like us write poetry," he had said.

Right after the cop had accused him of planning an assault on the school, Gabriel's stomach lurched. His head may not have allowed him to remember what he had said at home, but his body knew.

This was how the interrogation actually ended: after receiving several calls on his cellphone, the older police officer made another quick call in the corner, then turned to his partner and gave him a knowing look. They pulled back. They thanked Gabriel and said they were done.

Dr. Fitzpatrick rushed to fill her mouth with words—"I ah uhm—you may be free to go, Mr. Abrams, but you are suspended until further notice."

Out the front door of the Student Services building Gabriel dropped into the dark and cold. The brisk new smell of frost froze inside his nostrils. A brown cotton ball-sized mouse bumbled across the vast desert of the empty courtyard. When Gabriel reached out to open the school building door it was locked. His coat was in there, in his classroom, so was his work and his backpack. His phone. He glanced around the empty campus. All the lights were out except Dr. Fitzpatrick's. He would not be going back there, so he prowled around the building.

Standing beneath his classroom window, he thought about climbing up and prying it open. That'd be great if he got caught. This time he'd surely be dragged out in handcuffs, and this time he'd be taken straight down to the station and tossed into a cell. The principal would get a call and she would jump for joy. She could fire this thorn, and she wouldn't have to face the professional embarrassment of having overreacted. She'd be hailed a hero, paraded in front of teacher safety conventions, and Gabriel, sitting in his cell, would lose the benefit of the doubt and be crucified in the press as the 'Columbine Teacher'.

No, Gabriel won't be breaking in tonight.

He felt flat and abandoned. Fractured webs of sadness creaked through his bones. He was trying so hard. Despite all his troubles in the classroom, on the best of days he glided. Even if he was just sowing seeds in students never to see their flowers, he knew deep inside something was happening. It takes a lot of faith to plant a seed, but that faith is grounded in more than just hope. We've all eaten fruit and we've all smelt flowers and we've all seen seeds— seemingly little nothings, but we make the connection. We know that a seed with a little water, a little soil, a little sun will grow. So when we plant a seed we have that expectation. It's more than faith. At the front of his classroom, Gabriel wasn't hurling rocks into an abyss—he saw the target and sensed the future.

On his bike without his jacket, Gabriel pushed his way home. He wanted so much to teach. Despite all the harshness, he knew he had something special to offer. There was rot in the soil. It started to rain. And the rain turned to snow.

When he got home he was soaked.

"What happened?" Holly was frantic. "I couldn't get a hold of you."

"My phone's locked in my classroom."

"What's going on? They wouldn't tell me."

"Who?"

"The police. They searched your room. And your car. They had a judge's order."

"Shit."

"I'm sorry I couldn't stop them."

"Thanks. Is Chloe okay?"

"I'm fine."

"She was still at school."

Holly reached her fingers up towards Gabriel's face. She brushed a strain of wet hair out of his eye. A pot of stew on the stove filled the house with warmth. Chloe and Gabriel shared a worried look.

Gabriel tripped over something in his room before he could find the light. All his drawers from his desk and his bureau had been pulled open and ruffled through. Heaps of papers and books were scattered across the floor as if a bear had crashed through his room.

Gabriel pulled his blanket up off the floor, wrapped himself in it, and dropped down onto his futon. He felt violated. He felt humiliated—he was humiliated. If he were allowed to return to work it would be even harder for him now. His authority had been undermined like a boat suddenly bottomless. Who would climb aboard now? Nobody. That's who. What student would listen to Gabriel's admonishments now? What student would follow him down the line of a brilliant lesson? He had worked so hard in his classroom to recover from his naïve beginning and now he was forced even deeper into his hole.

His bones ached as if they were hacking up tears.

Like no other stressful night, Gabriel fell asleep and slept the whole night through. He slept untouched like a wet shirt on a rock near a river in the sun. He dreamed of our father. Not of him in his physical body, but as a sound of his sweet mournful soul. But in the morning he didn't remember, for his head immediately filled with the previous day's events.

First and foremost, he cleaned up his room and cleared out his car. He still felt nauseous. Who was teaching his classes?

While Chloe ate breakfast Holly came out and stood in the street next to Gabriel beside his car. For a long time neither spoke. Beside each other, they settled as flowers leaning together.

Alone, Gabriel drove out to the caves and crawled through the murky caverns. When he got deep into one he sat on a rock and clicked off his flashlight. Utter darkness. It was chilly, but Gabriel had dressed well. The darkness felt like a toasty coat wrapped tight around him. The darkness, like warm water, washed over him.

He sat there for an hour. He wasn't crying or plotting or condemning anyone.

"I'm exhausted," he said to himself in the dark.

He was defeated, he was upset, yet he allowed that anger to rise up off of him like steam. There must be successful healthy effective veteran teachers out there—there must be, somewhere. Unicorns, mermaids—superheroes: they stand beneath crumbling structures with their sinewy arms and gritty fingers balanced on their hips looking, full of resolve, through the dust and debris. Gabriel wanted to be one. A lifelong teacher needs tremendous patience and not just in the obvious way when dealing with students, but in receiving its rewards as well. Gabriel had never before recognized teaching on the timeline of a seed growing into a tree, and it lent him more tolerance—for himself. It made him feel as if everything wasn't such a rush—a rush to become an expert teacher, a rush for his students to suddenly be brilliant. The patient pace of this timeline gave Gabriel a chance.

He sat there in the darkness satisfied.

Until he remembered he was suspended.

He screamed as loud as he could and then sat back and let it echo through the dark caverns and then dissipate into the distance.

He'd go back to work. Even if they barricaded him out of his classroom. He'd at least show up. Everything was against him, and the thought filled him with resolve. It inspired him. He was a teacher and he would teach. He appreciated the underdog—he liked being the underdog, especially when he knew he was right. Fuck everything else. Yes, fuck. He thought the swear. And then he said it right there in the dark. "Fuck." And then "bitch" for good measure. Somehow swearing had taken on a new dimension. No longer the flag of the jerk in his class, it had reassumed the virtue of the rebel. Dammit, he would reach out to his students. If society was going to abandon their children, Gabriel wouldn't; if Dr. Fitzpatrick and the cops and school security would try to prevent him from returning, he would at least knock up against them, show them a little spirit.

*Describe a moment when you had
to stand up for yourself. How did it
affect you? How did it affect others?
Would you do it again?*

Gabriel woke up with a little less courage. Having spent the first day of his suspension in the caves, on his second morning he waffled there in bed. He could sleep another five hours, and why not? He was suspended. What was the point of forcing his way back into his classroom? He inhaled a breath and as it eased out of him his bones settled back into his futon—but his eyes were blinking; they refused to close back to sleep. He heard Holly and Chloe in the kitchen. He thought about having been escorted from his classroom in front of his students. Obviously Dr. Fitzpatrick had no evidence because Gabriel wasn't in jail—as well as the small fact that Gabriel wasn't considering such a distinct breach of his moral contract with humanity. Now offended, he climbed out of bed without having decided to.

He lingered in the shower for a long time. Under the wet, warm flow, the barrier that had arose around his cognizant mind collapsed. Yes, a teacher could go Columbine, and he knew this wasn't the first time he had considered this. In a state of loony playfulness, he had arrived at this very same thought—a blasphemous thought indeed—but he had said it as a joke, as an insightful witticism, and to Holly and to no one else. No one else was even there, except Chloe.

In hopes of talking to Holly and Chloe he rushed out of the shower, got dressed, and went into the kitchen but they had already left. A warm pot of oatmeal waited on the stovetop. On the table Holly had left a brief note. "Definitely go," it said.

With the note Gabriel sat down at the kitchen table and let the steam from his bowl of oatmeal rise up into his face. No matter what he had said in a private moment, he had been wronged and he was angry. But that was no real reason to burst back into his classroom. Or was it? Gabriel wanted to be effective, wanted his idealism to work in real situations. If he just sat there would he in effect be accepting other rousing teachers being strong-armed out of the profession? Gabriel wondered if he had been targeted by Dr. Fitzpatrick.

His resolve strengthened and his courage returned with the realization of the importance of his actions. For those not spectacularly wealthy and powerful, our conduct can be the most authority we have to assert. Standing up for what we believe could be our life's work. And that's contagious.

Into the school building Gabriel passed one of the security guards who had escorted him out of his classroom two days before. On his classroom board he wrote the Do Now.

As he finished he turned around. In the doorway stood another security guard with keys in hand and a substitute teacher behind him.

"This is room 103, right?" the guard asked.

"It is," Gabriel said.

"And you're the regular teacher."

"I am."

"Hm?"

The guard and the substitute turned and exited and the door closed behind them.

The first students who entered stared at Gabriel. When others arrived they too stared in bewilderment, took their seats, remained quiet. Right as Gabriel directed his students' attention to the Do Now there was a knock on the door.

That same substitute crept in. A barely-upright old lady, she worked her way around the desks to Gabriel. She whispered, "I am so sorry to interrupt, but they told me I'm supposed to be here and you're to see the main principal."

Not quite the battalion Gabriel expected, he wasn't about to scream in protest in this poor woman's direction. It'd knock her over.

Gabriel asked her name.

"Mrs. Marks."

"Folks, this is Mrs. Marks, please be respectful to her while I'm away."

As he walked across the quad he felt positively cowardly. Marching into uncertainty he felt as if he had a hole in his chest, but because of his past encounters with danger Gabriel's bones held a memory of his courage. All the experiences in our lives, even if we can't articulate their sum, add up to something. They must.

Wracked with anxiety Gabriel kept putting one foot in front of the other until he arrived at Dr. Fitzpatrick's door. The secretary ushered him in, but there was no one there, so Gabriel took a seat. He struggled to decide on an appropriate attitude to take. He wanted to stand up for himself, demand evidence for her accusation, but he didn't want to be too aggressive and have the meeting digress into a dogfight. If so, he'd probably get arrested. Was she calling the cops now? Gabriel took a deep breath trying to summon his courage. Around the entire perimeter of the room, framed prints sat on the floor leaning against the wall waiting to be hung. Some were wrapped in brown paper, some were turned inward, a few Gabriel could see—a Renoir, a Picasso. Gabriel decided he had to be strong, not necessarily forceful, but strong, demanding the evidence and providing a positive rebuke. He didn't want to get fired, but it had to be alright if he did.

The door opened and with a pile of manila folders Dr. Fitzpatrick entered, turning to make sure the door was closed. She didn't look at Gabriel. After she set her stack of manila folders on a side table she sat in her chair, rested her elbows on the desk, and pressed her fingers together, staring off to the side. Gabriel took a quick deep quiet breath.

When she did turn forward, her eyes, not focusing, bounced around Gabriel.

"Your pay has not been docked," she said. "You understand the importance of a person who has the well-being of so many young people in her hands. Sometimes—all the time really—she has to be prudent." Dr. Fitzpatrick spoke with great effort. "If you like you can take a few days off ... with pay, and they won't be counted against your sick days."

"What?"

"You can take a few days off."

"What do you mean?"

"Take a few days off."

"I'm suspended."

"Uhm, no, you're not."

"Not anymore?"

"You never were."

"Yes, I was."

"Look Mr. Abrams, a person in my position needs to be prudent."

"Of course."

They looked at each other, Dr. Fitzpatrick's eyes settling on Gabriel for the first time.

"Why did you accuse me?" Gabriel asked.

"A person in my position needs to be—"

"Prudent. I understand. But what did I do to deserve to be taken from my classroom in front of my students and to be greeted in here by—*the police*?"

Gabriel felt Dr. Fitzpatrick's defensiveness; she was backpedaling.

"You were not arrested, you were not detained, I only wanted to ask ... we, look, I'm offering you a little time off to reenergize."

"Am I required to?"

"No. You're not."

"Then I won't. But I want to know what prompted your accusation." While careful to temper his anger, he pushed hard, wanting from her a clear admission. "Why was I taken from my classroom?"

"I'm not required to inform you. According to our lawyers."

"Your lawyers?"

"Yes."

"Am I in trouble?"

Dr. Fitzpatrick struggled to answer—"No." She leaned across her desk. "No, Mr. Abrams, you're not in trouble, not for this, but I'll be paying close attention."

"Fine. But why was I taken from my classroom?"

"You want to know? You really want to know? Your girlfriend's daughter told her teacher that you were 'about to go Columbine.' What do you think of that? Her principal called me frantic, barely able to contain himself—he wanted to call the police right then. Does that satisfy your curiosity, Mr. Abrams? Does it?"

"I feel as if you're mischaracterizing the situation."

"Maybe so, and maybe irreverence does have a place. But not in front of an eight-year-old, and not when including the word 'Columbine,' and certainly not when you're a teacher."

Gabriel hated it, but—Dr. Fitzpatrick was probably right. From across her desk they peeked up at each other, their clenched aggression having loosened. Dr. Fitzpatrick's eyes rounded as if for a moment acknowledging. An urge moved up into Gabriel's chest, and he eased in a breath.

"I'm sorry, I, I just—"

"Prudence, Mr. Abrams—*prudence*."

Even after catastrophic events, in the onslaught of a teacher's life, things return to normal pretty quickly. Gabriel had to move on. He had to placate the administrators and inform the parents and concoct more lessons and teach more classes and grade more papers and interact with a hundred and twenty needy students every single day. Gabriel continued to be overwhelmed. For a teacher, especially a new teacher, catastrophic events are a daily occurrence. He didn't have the time to dwell on what had happened or how it had happened or what the ramifications were now. He had to teach. He didn't have the convenience to ache. The word 'Columbine' causes the immediate disruption of all rational behavior, and he would never say it again, and he probably shouldn't have said it to begin with—he wished he hadn't said it, specifically because of how it may affect his homelife.

He had felt so comfortable with Holly and Chloe. Would he now have to be as guarded and tense at home as he was at work?

Frustrated and exhausted, Gabriel crept into the house and shuffled through the kitchen, first nearly tripping over the dog and then passing Holly and Chloe with a nod and that was it. Gabriel hadn't known what to say—afraid maybe of what he would say.

He paced his room, anxious and hoping they hadn't noticed that he had said nothing to them. He moved to his bedroom door that he had left ajar. He paused listening but couldn't hear them in the kitchen. Were they still there? He couldn't leave them with the bad taste of his non-greeting, but he was upset and wanted to sulk in his room alone, he wanted to push it aside, maybe forget it, move on, just be angry and then not.

When Holly knocked, they were so close to each other peeking through the clearing of the half-opened door.

"Are you alright?" she asked.

"Yeah."

"Are you sure?"

"Do you wanna come in?"

"Do you wanna come out?"

"Mom," Chloe called from the kitchen. "Mamma."

Gabriel didn't want to go out—not yet—he had to tell Holly.

"If there's something wrong—that's alright, I understand. But I have a daughter and I can't not deal."

"I just ..." Gabriel said. "It was Chloe."

"What was Chloe?"

"She said I was going to go Columbine or something."

"You're kidding. At her school?"

"Yeah."

"Why didn't they tell me? I'm her mother! The police came into our house and ..."

"I don't know," Gabriel said. "I just, you know—I'm upset."

"At Chloe?"

Gabriel wavered. "Well ..."

"She's eight."

"I know."

"I'm sure she didn't do it maliciously."

"I know."

"Gabriel, she's eight—"

"Mom!"

"You need talk to her," Holly said.

"And say what?"

"We don't have the luxury, Gabriel—they're kids, they're fragile, they know. You have to say something. She knows you're mad, but she doesn't know why."

"Yes, she does," Gabriel said.

He sat down on his bed and Holly glared at him.

"Gabriel, you need to talk to her right now."

"What should I say?"

"It doesn't matter."

"But I'm upset."

"Swallow it."

"It's not so easy."

"Yes, it is."

"Okay," Gabriel said, yet still not moving.

"Mamma!"

"You wanna be cool, Gabriel—here it is, be cool."

Chloe came in sporting a green feather boa wrapped around her neck. She pranced in front of Gabriel.

"Look, I'm sophisticated."

Chloe enunciated that last word with such care, and Gabriel looked at her—looked at her hard, trying to see, trying to muster up the courage, the compassion, the maturity. But it wasn't there. Yes, she was cute and endearing, but Gabriel was afflicted. He glanced at Holly, who stood stiff at the door with her arms crossed.

Gabriel inhaled and then exhaled a loud and perceptive breath. He reached for his coolness.

"Where'd you get it?" Gabriel asked.

"Mamma got it for me at Goodwill."

"It's pretty."

"Thank you."

"Remember the other night," Gabriel said, "when I was saying a whole bunch of loud things?"

Chloe stopped prancing. She looked away, refused to answer.

"What's going on?" Holly asked her daughter.

"Nothing," Chloe said.

"Nothing?"

"I don't know," Chloe said, then took three quick steps, and vanished out the door.

"Chloe!" Holly shouted after her. "Come back here."

Holly went after her and Gabriel followed.

"Chloe, you're not in trouble."

"Yes I am," she said hurrying through the living room disappearing into their bedroom.

Grabbing her sleeve, Gabriel stopped Holly.

"Let me," he said.

Holly stopped and Gabriel followed Chloe, but as he passed Holly seized his hand, forcing him to pause so she could look at him—they pushed out small smiles at each other—and then she raised his hand up letting his fingers slide from her grasp as he continued to follow Chloe.

Gabriel knocked on the doorjamb. "I'm coming in Chloe, okay?"

"I'm sleeping."

"Can I sit down? I'm not mad at you, you know."

"You're not?"

"No."

"You should be."

"Why?"

"'Cause," Chloe said, "'cause ... I didn't mean to. I said it, not really anything. And then Ms. Scott took me to the principal's office."

"It's okay. Are you in trouble at school?" Gabriel asked.

"No. Are you?"

Gabriel giggled. "Not really."

"That's good."

"Why didn't you tell your mom?"

"'Cause she really likes you."

Gabriel peeked up at Holly leaning in the doorway.

That night after Chloe fell asleep, Gabriel and Holly stood by the stove. Their lips touched so softly for the first time.

As the cold night invaded first her toes and fingers then her arms and legs and almost into her heart, Isabel crunched there in her sleeping bag above the Santa Fe River beneath those same damn bushes. To occupy her brain, to help her fall asleep, to keep her warm, she composed a mess of poems in her head. She tried to mine the moment the way Ned did, creating spontaneous verse about the eeriness of the dark night, or about the branches that looked like crooked fingers, or about the waterless river below.

In the morning she was cast out into the simmering stew of Los Pinos High—people everywhere and exhaustion a wet towel in her head. Whenever she spoke, her hand lingered in front of her mouth—she hadn't brushed her teeth in two days.

That afternoon she went to the public library and, forgetting her problems, she worked on her homework for hours. When she finished she sat thinking, not where she would sleep, but about Ned and how he had implied that poetry has no real worth. How effective could poetry be? Poetry was just words and words aren't action. And did Ned even believe his own words?

People write poetry to express themselves, and young people often come to poetry because they have profound complex complicated feelings that they don't know what to do with. That is what makes poetry such a useful teaching tool. Poetry can attract students who otherwise sit bottled up in the backs of classrooms and who refuse to speak to their parents or friends or counselors or anyone who occupies space in their lives. Poetry can prompt students to articulate things they would never say in any other context, and these are things they often must convey yet have no forum in which to say them. Boiling up inside, their thoughts and feelings, their words and ideas are of the utmost importance resounding with their deepest emotional resonance. Imagine cramming that down into your belly. Poems can also be a heap of gibberish, but the act of writing can be empowering. Writing poetry can give a student a sense of purpose as well as a feeling of authority that he never knew was available to him. Their journals in which they write are both nonintimidating and a source of power. They can sort out their fears or construct their anger or express their dreams in a safe place and feel able and enlivened. When students share their poems either by presenting them or by allowing another to read them or even when writing next to each other, they connect. They recognize someone else experiences similar sensitivities, and they realize that communicating their cavernous emotions is possible. They don't have to suffer alone. They collect confidence while participating, so they may be more apt to share themselves with others and live more engaged and genuine lives. So many of their days are marked by shallow encounters, unfair consequences, and pointless assignments. The poetry club wanted more. Isabel wanted more. We all want more.

In a small box by the computers the librarians had left old card catalogue cards to be used as scratch paper. Isabel collected a bunch. On one orange card she wrote a few lines that she thought of as a single perfect wisp of her brush. It reminded her of the verse Mr. Abrams created. She wrote twelve poems, one for each of the twelve dictionaries on the reference shelf, then she filed each one in each dictionary under 'poem'.

She went back to her table and lost herself in her book, *Things Fall Apart*. She hadn't considered sleeping there. Only at the last minute when the public library closed and she had to go, yet had nowhere to go, did she press herself beneath the table on the seats of several chairs, her head twisted and her ear pressed against the underside of the tabletop. She remained as the rows of lights flicked off, as the noise receded, as the night meandered.

When Isabel woke up it was light outside and she heard no noise in the library. She snuck out from under the table and peeked at the clock. Five past nine! Her French class had already started and the library was still closed. Isabel crawled back under the table hoping the library opened at ten and not eleven. Or twelve!

She heard some commotion and waited another fifteen painful minutes to crawl out. She put her hair in a ponytail and without looking she hurried to the exit and raced out into the morning.

Sleep-deprived. Paranoid she'd run into Matthew at school. Hoping her father sensed nothing and her friends couldn't tell either. Concerned every night where she would sleep, Isabel was on edge. She kept her coat on all day so no one would notice that she was wearing the same clothes. She showered as best she could in a sink. Yet during this time in the classroom she became even more poised. And it wasn't a façade, for she was working out what needed to be done to survive—even to thrive.

Still—Isabel's situation was worsening. She just didn't know where to sleep. The library was warm, but she couldn't miss her morning classes. Her hovel under the bush above the river was too cold and, if she let herself think about it, too exposed and dangerous, and she refused to ask Tiffany or Lori or Jennifer if she could sleep on their couch or under their beds because she was just too embarrassed. She didn't want her father to know either, so she had to at least make an appearance at home. Maybe today was his day off.

After school she walked home.

Nobody was there, so she stood under a steaming hot shower and brushed her teeth twice. Needing her presence to be known so her dad wouldn't suspect anything, she strolled through the empty house until she found the living room where she sunk down into the couch and, without meaning to, fell asleep.

She kept itching an itch on her nose that wouldn't go away. She opened her eyes to a giant looming Matthew. He was sitting on the coffee table right in front of her, lightly touching her nose. He smirked, got up, and left.

Isabel's father had to work that night and Matthew and his mother had already eaten out, so Isabel cooked herself some noodles with olive oil and garlic. She talked a bit with her stepmother who asked where she's been and casually Isabel told her she had a lot going on at school.

"Good for you," her smiling stepmother said and left the kitchen.

In her own room, before crawling into bed, Isabel dragged her bureau in front of her door as a barricade to keep him out. Under her covers she curled up into a ball and shrieked with joy. Her bed was her home.

Her door opened, but banged into the bureau. Only after that did the person knock. It woke Isabel from a deep sleep.

"Who is it?"

No answer.

"Who is it?"

The door started beating up against the bureau, and Isabel leapt out of bed, drove her shoulder into the bureau, and dug her toes into the carpet to keep the door from being forced opened. But she couldn't hold it. The bureau gave out, Isabel tumbled backwards, and the door flew open, the knob banging a hole through the drywall.

Matthew loomed above her.

"What do you want?" Isabel said from the floor.

"Nothing."

"Get out."

"Why."

"'Cause I said so."

"This used to be my weight room."

Isabel scrambled to her feet, backing away. "What do you want?"

Light from the hall bled into the dark room falling across the back third of Matthew's face.

"Don't think you're better than me," he said.

"I don't think I'm better than you."

"Fuck off." And then his tone softened. "We could do it, you know. It wouldn't be incest."

"Get out."

He laughed.

"Get out."

"Why?"

"Get out!" she yelled.

"Whatever you say," he said, chuckled, and left.

Isabel's heart was racing. She righted the bureau. She packed some essential clothes as well as her toothbrush. She made her bed, then escaped back out into the night.

*O*n Gabriel's first day back after his 'suspension,' when he stepped into his third period class—his worst class—awe hung in the air like a giant puff of smoke. All eyes followed him to the podium. Gabriel pointed to the Do Now, and the class dug out their papers and pencils and started to write. As Gabriel strolled around the room bodies shrunk away as if intimidated. Carl gave the thumbs up, Nathan avoided eye-contact, and even Jorge had a pencil. It took little thought to know what was going on: the class swam in admiration for their outlaw teacher with his newly secured shattered credentials. He'd been busted, beaten, broken, and now he was back, carrying his wounds beneath his shirt like a Glock. The class accomplished more on this day than on any other day. They wrote, they read, and they discussed with a hushed focus. They were into it, and in the softened velocity Gabriel stood back, a satisfied smile, not visible, but it was there beneath his lips, in his jaw, in his eyes.

But by day two, the smoke began to disperse. And by day three they were again restless and rude.

"This is stupid," Carl announced, pushing back in his chair, refusing to continue writing his Do Now.

"Let's just do it anyway," Gabriel coaxed, hoping to avoid a distraction.

"Stupid," Carl said.

Students peeked up.

"Come on, Carl."

"What?" he said. "This is so stupid."

"Yeah, why do we have to do this?" Rodney said.

"Come on, let's go, keep working."

"What does this have to do with English?"

"Come on, keep going, keep writing, you're doing great."

Carl leaned forward as if to write, then—"Stupid!"—he slammed down his pencil and it bounced onto the floor.

The few emasculated the many; now no one was writing.

Gabriel, having been floating atop the momentum of the previous two classes, crashed face-first into the dirt. He had almost expected them to follow along in the same constructive vein, but instead that expectation left Gabriel unprotected and the disturbance cracked him open leaving a flapping gaping hole where a serious wounding could enter. He covered himself up. He had had enough. Gabriel grieved that these students were disturbing the others who might actually accomplish something. The leaders of this class—or at least the miscreants who forced themselves into that role—were escorting the class into a pit. Fine, he thought, if you don't want to do anything—then sit there and keep your mouth shut. Let the others do their work. We don't need your insolence, your laziness, your insecurities infecting everyone and permeating the classroom like several rotten eggs.

Not at the actual stunts, Gabriel was tired of the useless crap that these same three or four students pulled over and over again every day. Gabriel calculated his anger. He had had enough. He took a deep breath. Yes, he had had enough.

Inside Dr. Fitzpatrick's office while being stared down by those two ugly cops, Gabriel had had an epiphany. Well, part of an epiphany at least, for right now in the middle of his classroom that epiphany was solidifying into action.

Gabriel had been dragged out of his classroom in front of his students, confronted by the police, subjected to humiliating questions, suspended, and then reinstated with barely an explanation and no apology. All year long he was exposed on a daily basis to disrespectful behavior by a bunch of goons who were forced into his classroom yet put not one ounce of energy into anything except harassing the teacher, hassling the other students, and disrupting the class. They were getting nothing out of school. Nothing. Most of them were failing, most of them planned to exit as soon as they hit sixteen, and most weren't even interested in trying. My God, they were required to be there, yet made it a total waste. And in the meantime they dragged the other students down with them, other students who very well may have opened to their teacher and gained something.

Menaced inside Dr. Fitzpatrick's office, Gabriel stopped caring. Well, that's not exactly true. Let me try to put this in the right words: Gabriel stopped feeling beholden to Dr. Fitzpatrick, to the school's confining rules, to the misguided parents, to the students who could care less. When society refuses to support a person giving everything, obligation drifts out into the wind. Gabriel had worked hard to operate inside the rules of the school even when they seemed arbitrary and counterproductive. Gabriel had supported Dr. Fitzpatrick in her efforts to turn the school around. Gabriel had tried to understand the parents who demanded special treatment for their ill-mannered children. Gabriel had tried to cultivate empathy for the students who insulted him. He tried to get through to them when they wanted nothing of the sort. Gabriel wanted to teach, yet he spent all his time banging heads with students who didn't care, with parents who treated teachers as idiots, and with administrators who no longer had a clue what it was like to be inside a classroom.

Gabriel was through with these distractions.

He let all the shackles drop from his waist and his wrists and his ankles. He would no longer be chained to all that hindered him, for he no longer cared if he would get in trouble, if he would get written up by an administrator, if a student who refused to do his work would concoct some lie labeling Gabriel some sort of amoral character. Gabriel no longer cared. If they were going to fire him—fire him. Fine. But Gabriel would go out swinging his fists and screaming for justice. He would teach the students who wanted to be taught.

"Anybody who doesn't want to be here—leave," Gabriel said. "Collect your stuff, get up, walk out that door, and don't come back."

Gabriel's third period class fell into silence. Not one person moved.

Then Carl let up a chuckle. "Are you serious?"

"Dead serious. If you don't want to be here, I don't want you here."

"But we have to be here."

"I don't care. There's people who want to learn and I'm tired of you taking that from them."

"Like who?"

"Yeah, nobody wants to be here."

"Good. Then clear out."

"But we'll get in trouble."

"That's your problem."

"You'll write us up?"

"No, I won't. If you want to come, come, if you don't, don't. If you can pass the final at the end, I'll give you a 'D.' But don't come if you don't want to be here."

"We can leave right now?"

"Yes, Carl, you can leave right now."

"And I don't have to come back?"

"Not if you don't want to."

"And you won't write me up?"

"That's right."

In disbelief Carl started laughing as he collected his books and headed for the door. His high-pitched cackle was powered by excitement.

At the door he paused, "Are you sure?"

"Positive."

Carl threw open the door and in the hallway he screamed "Yeeaaahhh!" as he faded away.

The other students just sat there, staring.

"Really?" Clarissa asked.

"Snap! I'm outa here," Rodney said, collecting his things, heading for the door.

Jorge had been silent for weeks. And he remained silent now as he hoisted his bag over his shoulder—a slight 'thank you' in his smile as he glanced at Gabriel as he walked out the door.

Before anyone else could leave, the bell rang. Everyone gathered their possessions, scrapped back their chairs, and left the room—everyone but Crystal. In the now empty classroom she remained in her seat.

"What you're doing is illegal, you know." She was one of the students who Gabriel knew would prosper in a classroom absent of the distractions. "You're gonna get in trouble. Everyone who left's gonna get in trouble. I'll probably even get in trouble."

*Think of a friend—now render him
into a cartoon superhero. What does
she wear? What are her superpowers?
What's his kryptonite?*

She grew silent, silent for many moments.

I glanced over, but she looked down into her lap. Her back curved over like a strip of paper thrown into a fire.

All the way out to the caves, Isabel sat up straight in the passenger seat of my car, often gesturing, always steady even as she told me of her struggles. Set back from the highway, long angular mountains stretched out before us. Emotional, yet still confident, Isabel spoke to me, turning to me, looking at me when I looked at her.

But now she sunk into her seat, her head bent forward, chin in her chest.

"Are you alright?" I asked.

She straightened at the sound of my voice. She peeked back at Tiffany. Turned and stared out her window.

"I was desperate," she said. "I'm so sorry."

She stretched back around to show me her face where lingered a suggestion of her wound.

And then she told me the true story of who had really stolen Gabriel's keys.

Cramped in her desk during Ms. James' third period, Isabel felt as if she were underwater; she couldn't hear what the teacher was saying, what the students were saying—everything was blurred. Exhaustion in excess as altering as any narcotic, she needed air. Under the guise of going to the bathroom, she wandered the halls. It was peaceful and she liked it. She experienced what the other students, the wayward ones, experience when they ask to use the bathroom and don't return for forty minutes. In the empty hall Isabel could breathe, she floated above the warm waters flowing through the corridors, she waved her arms through the liquid mass moving her forward. She waded downstream past Mr. Abrams' classroom and felt like going in but had no reason. She circled around an eddy and manufactured a motive.

As she tried to be quiet when she eased open the door, the roar of the room nearly knocked her over. Amidst the disorder Mr. Abrams was begging a student to sit down, but the student refused. Mr. Abrams was a stressed mess, and Isabel was shocked to see him in such a state.

Gabriel looked up at her. He gave up on his struggle and moved towards his desk and Isabel skirted the room to meet him there, but as she arrived that same kid started slapping the back of the head of another boy, and Gabriel shot over towards the aggression—

"Sit down! Now! Immediately!"

Isabel stood at his desk unable to watch. An incongruence leaked from Mr. Abrams—it was desperation. She barely recognized him. She looked down at the surface of his desk and saw his set of keys splayed out and glinting as if it were a tiny broken bird having fallen out of the sky. In her collapse not one single thought entered her head as she scooped up the keys and jammed them in her pocket. She glanced around the room full of its commotion, yet now to Isabel it all seemed distant and silent. She was a shadow amidst all the activity, all the disorder and chaos. It was as if everything was in slow-motion, and Isabel floated out of the room as if she had never been there. No one saw what she had done and no one saw her leave and maybe no one even saw her come.

As she swept through the halls and delivered herself back through Ms. James' door, everything had changed. She found her seat, but the silence in her head had been supplanted by noise: every word, every scrape of a chair over the floor, all the laughter, all the coughing and sneezing and hocking up of loogies shrieked into her ears as if she were in the middle of a construction site— the slamming and pounding and beeping. She had to hold her ears, she almost screamed, she needed again to leave and find refuge wandering the empty halls, but just then the banging of the bells erupted into her brain and the students threw back their chairs, pushed each other aside, stomped out of their desks, and crashed into the halls, and Isabel was caught up in their rush, her insides rupturing. She clung to her backpack as she was pushed and jostled and jabbed through the halls. Her hands were squeezing and they hurt and she glanced down and saw Mr. Abrams' keys poking out of her fist, digging into her flesh as her fingers wrapped red around them. She froze as all the commotion washed around her. She shoved her entire hand with the keys down into her backpack.

Suddenly she was forcing her way through the oncoming crowd. Even though it was the middle of the school day, she rammed open the door and leapt out into the daylight. She slipped around a corner and ... ran as fast as she could never looking back, never considering being seen or caught by school security. She kept running even though she was blocks away, she kept running even though she was a mile away, she kept running down Cerrillos even though she didn't know where she was going. When she stopped, she released everything, pushing her backpack to the pavement. Her hand was mangled from squeezing the set of keys.

In a classroom when something secretive or unseemly is happening often the teacher first senses it as a cold breeze before the storm. It is felt before it is recognized. Gabriel walked around in back of the chairs noticing that nobody was writing the Do Now. They were glancing at each other. Someone had to say something.

"Uhm," Alejandro began, calling attention to himself. "Uhm."

And that simple syllable burst the bubble—

"Do we get the same deal as third?"

"Do we have to come if we don't want?"

"Yeah, it's not fair."

"Yeah, it should be fair."

And there it was. Gabriel hadn't anticipated that what he had pronounced the day before in his difficult third period would visit him in his other freshmen classes. He should have known.

Although in a sensitive moment Gabriel had told his third period that they didn't have to attend, he had meant it. He'd be overjoyed if the disruptive students never returned. Yes, he had meant it, but he had meant it for his third period and no one else. He hadn't considered that word of what he had said would spread. He should have known.

He could have explained to his first and second periods that it applied only to his third, but that would seem unjust to them as it seemed incongruous to Gabriel. In addition to the students who ached to learn, most of the rest could be enthusiastic if given the chance yet were infected by the few who hated everything. For everyone's benefit, schools need to accommodate young people who have no interest in academics.

Archie would have profited from learning the three Rs before tumbling out into the street on his sixteenth birthday, but that didn't happen. The question is: how can a school assist a boy like Archie? If forced, Archie was not going to learn, but if attracted, if he looked at something—anything—in any classroom and thought, 'hmm?' That's an opening. If in addition to math class, Archie had other appealing options like business, music, psychology, auto mechanics, even a graffiti class—one of these selections may have piqued his interest which might have made him receptive in another subject which he had previously refused to look. That happens. Please don't cancel the art classes. Success in one segment of life can spread to another; confidence can't stay cooped up in one particular part of the brain.

Also, having a choice helps a student invest in his life. Adults too. People excel at different things. Imagine if we were all forced to do the exact same thing all day every day—and that thing happened to be what we sucked at most. We'd have a society filled with frustration. It's the same with kids. Making them do math and science all day long creates antisocial, angry cads out of some students who could have succeeded with a varied schedule. Let them choose other activities and they may do better in required classes.

A lot of unhappiness comes when we feel as if we have no jurisdiction over our own lives. I want to direct my energy in a way I relate to, in a way that is relevant to some bigger view I hold for myself and the world. And I'll work harder, because I'll care more. School needs to make sense to students, and by giving them options it may seem to them as if they're not just being pushed around.

Gabriel didn't debate this inside his head while standing in front of his class; he reacted to the present situation. He believed in what he had said to his third period, and if he believed it for them he believed it for all his students.

In front of that first period class, he had to act on instinct, and his instinct said yes this is the way it should be.

"If you don't want to be here—you may leave."

There—he said it.

Half his first period class got up and left, and two-thirds of his second period.

*H*as anyone seen my keys?"

Forming a lump in her front pants pocket, Mr. Abrams' keys poked into Isabel's thigh. Her insides constricted. Why had she returned to school? She should have just kept wandering up and down Cerrillos. She thought to rush from her creative writing class and race to the edge of an arroyo and hurl Mr. Abrams' keys as far from her as she could. Or maybe give them back and burst into tears. She shrunk down into her seat.

After school Isabel hurried down to the river where her sleeping bag was hidden beneath the bush. Most teachers have impressive sets of keys, but not Mr. Abrams. This one was his house key and this one his car key and this one his bike lock key, so this one had to be his classroom key. She worked it off the ring and then bent onto her knees and in the dirt she buried Mr. Abrams' keys, keeping the classroom key for herself.

It wasn't late enough for the front doors to have been locked. Isabel returned to school and snuck down an eerie and empty hallway. Across from Mr. Abrams' classroom she slipped into the girls' bathroom. She washed the dirt out from beneath her fingernails. With her clothes on and clinging to her balled up sleeping bag, she sat on a toilet in a stall. She read *Things Fall Apart* until she finished it and then she crept out into the dim hallway. It was already night. She eased the key into the lock of Mr. Abrams' door. And it opened. In a corner of the empty classroom she rolled out her sleeping bag and used several dictionaries as a pillow. Laying there she felt safe—and not just safe to be inside, but safe to be in Mr. Abrams' classroom. She wrapped her arms around herself and thought of her teacher. She liked the fact (but not in a vindictive way) that Mr. Abrams was having trouble with his freshmen, because to Isabel it made him seem normal. Well, not normal, but heroic. It made him seem more different. More real. She felt connected to him, for they were both struggling, and in the same place they found their success—that is to say, in creative writing and in the poetry group. That's what Isabel thought for herself and she imagined for Mr. Abrams.

Despite the hard tiled floor, she slept.

The little money Isabel had was running out, so she put herself on rations. She bought a loaf of bread and peanut butter and jelly, sardines. She took a knife from the school cafeteria, a carton of milk.

The next few nights she slept in Gabriel's classroom and by Friday she was rested but she'd have to find somewhere else to sleep for the weekend so as not to be locked up in the school building till Monday.

Friday night under the same table she slept in the public library. On Saturday she strolled around town, on a bench she made herself a couple sandwiches, opened a sardine tin and then returned to the library where she looked at art books until closing time when she slipped beneath her table and waited before rolling out her sleeping bag and falling fast asleep on the ground up against the wall.

Off in the distance a mechanized roar soothed her as she slept, but it grew louder and she rolled awake as the vacuum cleaner moved closer. The middle of the night and someone was vacuuming. Isabel hunched up under the table and scrunched herself and her sleeping bag as close against the wall as she could. Her heart was pounding and she was praying to Mother Mary. When it screamed up close, she could see the bulking industrial-sized silver head of the vacuum. But as soon as she saw it, it pulled away.

A "thank God" slipped through her lips.

But then the vacuum shot under the table bumping into Isabel's scrunched knees. The vacuuming lady bent, peeking her head below—then screamed and leapt back knocking off her own headphones. In a full fit Isabel struggled out of her sleeping bag, wrapped her arms around her belongings, and sprang through the library to the door, but when she pushed to get out it was locked. Trapped, her eyes darted, she stumbled in a circle, she tried again to push the door, she started back into the library when the cleaning lady ambled into the vestibule. Isabel froze and the lady glared at her as she stepped past, unfurling her keys. She unlocked the door and Isabel pushed her way out and ran down the block, her sleeping bag waving behind her in her wake.

All to itself the night seemed like a poem: dark and quiet with the far-off sound of some unseen motor. Through the streets Isabel stumbled. She wrapped her sleeping bag around her shoulders and hugged her book bag as if her heart were somehow inside. Everything could have been a poem. The hump of each street dwindled down into the next like water falling for five blocks, and at the bottom a blond dog padded past. A streetlight fluttered and blinked off. An old door hung by a hinge. How could poetry be powerless when Isabel felt so potent writing it and reciting it and reading it and hearing it, even just thinking about it while walking around in the night? How could Ned deny poetry when its effect on him was so obvious?

Should Isabel have recited a poem to the cleaning lady at the library? What would that have done? The cleaning lady didn't care. She wanted to finish her work probably and go home. What if Isabel had recited a poem to Matthew after he kicked his way into her room? A tinkle of revenge invaded Isabel's sodden feet. She would love Matthew to experience her fatigue, her hunger, her worry. How could she get him to hear one of her poems? Just walk right up and scream it at him, or better yet tie him to a stake and perform it with all her drama and passion and sorrow. He'd laugh at her—even tied up.

Some people need to be ambushed with poetry. That's what Isabel wanted to do. That's what the poetry club should do.

Stumbling around she didn't realize she had gone in a circle. She was back at the library. She turned and shuffled away. If she closed her eyes she'd probably end up back there again. Or at school. Or at home. Or at the end of her life. Everything was a circle—even life. Especially life. Dust to dust. That's a guarantee, but it's what we get to make up that matters. Maybe that's the poetry, Isabel thought. Birth is a fact, death a certainty, but what we do in between is a variable—it's the magic, the poetry.

Isabel made her way back down to the river and tucked herself under her bush, the ground now indented from all the nights beneath the weight of her body.

Isabel's nights had become an endurance test, her days sluggish rivers of mud. On Monday she sat in her morning classes unable to focus. She kept the key to Mr. Abrams' classroom in the plastic pocket for papers inside her three-ring binder. During every class she'd trace its form molding a permanent outline of the key on the outside of the pocket. She could remove the key and there in the plastic would remain that impression. Even the nights in Gabriel's classroom began to wear on Isabel's equilibrium.

She had no idea what time she had fallen asleep, but she knew what time she woke up—way too close to first period; in fact, so close it was Mr. Abrams opening his classroom door in the morning that woke her. Maneuvering his shoulders out of his backpack, Mr. Abrams was distracted. He wandered the other way around to his desk, oblivious of anyone else's presence in the room while Isabel, shielded by a line of desks, in a hurry slithered out of her sleeping bag and slipped out the slowly closing door, managing to grab her book bag but not her sleeping bag.

Isabel stressed all day. She was sure he hadn't seen her, or she hoped he hadn't, but how could he not have? As creative writing approached she thought to skip class but that would just prolong the inevitable. She needed to know if she was busted. Stalling in the hall till right as the tardy bell rang, she stepped in and hurried to her seat. Mr. Abrams had already begun class and didn't look at her. All seemed normal—until she spotted her sleeping bag hanging off the overhead projector stretching down almost to the floor.

"Like Mussolini hung upside-down by his toes."

That's what Isabel said to Tiffany and me in my car.

She struggled not to look at it, Gabriel never mentioned it, and Isabel couldn't claim it. At the end of class as she left the room she gave her sleeping bag one last painful look.

After relenting and extending his offer to let all his students choose whether to attend his class or not, Gabriel had to watch some of his best freshmen, along with the others, gather their books and shuffle out the door.

Yet in his first and second periods, once he had endured that bit of humiliation, the classes gained momentum. Small and active, they discussed the characters of *Cannery Row*. A student, in fact two students spoke up who had never said a word in front of the class before. But, in light of that, more than half the class was running around in the quad or ditching down an arroyo.

Only two showed up for Gabriel's third period—Crystal and Monica.

At this point—distressed—Gabriel realized he might be fucked.

He had challenged his third period. Maybe he figured they would rise to the occasion and realize what a blessing his class could be. Maybe Gabriel was bluffing, hoping no one would call him out and everybody would continue to come and thus be duped into thinking they chose to be there and thus be hoodwinked into acting up less. Gabriel was thickheaded not to figure word would spread, and he was reckless to suppose students given the choice would continue to attend. He wanted students to take possession of their lives, but also his deeds had ramifications.

After school Gabriel sat in his empty classroom but only for a few minutes did he enjoy any sort of peace. His classroom phone rang, and right after he hung up it rang again and the next morning he received another call. The first parent simply wanted to know if it was true. The second couldn't believe what she had heard and wanted Mr. Abrams to know that her son would be attending his English class no matter what. The morning caller was an irate father. He scolded Gabriel:

"If children had a choice we'd all be illiterate. I'm a personal friend of the superintendent—who I'll be calling next."

Not one student came for his first period, two for second, and only Crystal for third.

Yes, now it dawned on him: he was fucked.

After school Gabriel tried not to converse with anyone or see anybody or even have anybody see him. He gathered his things, slipped out of the building, and rolled home as winter brought night much earlier.

On the third day the only person who showed up for Gabriel's second period class was Dr. Fitzpatrick. She leaned against the computer table in the back with her arms crossed. For five minutes she stayed there as if waiting to see if any students would arrive while Gabriel slouched at his desk. She slowly shook her head and then left without saying a thing.

On Monday several students attended each of Gabriel's freshmen classes.

Who knew what trouble the others were up to?

Gabriel finished *Cannery Row* with the handful of brave students in each of his morning classes. Everyone thought carefully, spoke quietly, treaded lightly. A reverence rose up in the room. Each student expressed herself, bringing to class a certain sense of purpose that had before been absent. Over the next several days a few more students trickled back to class. Those present wanted to share their feelings, and even more impressively, they listened to the others when they spoke. Gabriel spent no time correcting student behavior; he didn't pace back and forth hovering around the backs of students so as to coax them into focusing on their work. He wasn't at once pulled in twenty-nine different directions. Gabriel sat in the circle of desks with the others, listening to the students with his full attention. Able to hear and consider and respond, Gabriel was more present and competent than he had ever been before in the classroom.

But, again, who knew where all the others were?

In the dark Isabel wandered the town without her sleeping bag, feeling alienated from Mr. Abrams. She thought to call Tiffany and confess everything, but really Isabel couldn't face anybody because she was so embarrassed by the very fact that she needed help. Making no decision about where to go, she discovered herself back within a block of school. She was doing circles again. She crept up to a door—locked. Sticking close to the wall she rounded the building to another door. Also locked. Should she go home? This was a disastrous thought in itself because at this point it was all too obvious that no one in her faux family even noticed that she was gone. She thought to consider her predicament as if it were a story she was hatching in creative writing. What would her gallant hero do? He could go into the woods and make a fire, but a fire might attract trouble. He could scale a hotel's wall and spend the night in their jacuzzi. Uhmm? He could go to a laundry mat and curl up in a dryer. And then it hit her: dryers often have external vents that deal out their heat. Her school bus passed a laundry mat, but she couldn't remember the vents. She marched all the way there, and the lights were on, though a big 'closed' sign hung askew in the glass door. Inside, a woman in a domestic uniform was working a row of dryers. Isabel crept around into the alley and sure enough there they were—twenty silver vents pointing down, light white bursts gushing out. She stepped beneath one as if entering the stream of a hot shower. The balmy gust warmed her all the way through. She sat down and almost cried. For what must have been an hour she soaked up all that heat. After this long, long journey she had found mercy. She bent her face upward and drank down the heated flurry as if it were the true blood of Jesus, the real body of Christ. She showered in the waterfalls of heaven, she basked in the heat of grace, but, as with all perfection, a balancing act is prone to teeter.

Light shined down at the end of the alley. Fifteen yards away a car had pulled around the corner and now sat there with its headlights staring. As everything had become to Isabel, it all could have been a poem: the warm air, the frozen yellow headlights, Isabel's limbs hardening with fear. Were they purposefully casting their lights on her? Then the car started to creep forward and Isabel sprung to her feet. Another poem could have been the juxtaposition of the slow crawl of the Chevy and the panicked jerks of Isabel's movements. Closer now the car stopped. Flicked off its lights. The doors creaked open, and Isabel started to back away as two figures climbed out.

"Hey," one of them said.

But she ran, she ran so fast, so far, until she walked and she walked so long, all night, until morning—poetry spiraling through her head: she'd point at a garbage bin and twist a poem around it, she'd gesture to the light emerging in the far-off sky and make a poem out of it, she'd glance down at her legs and thus arrived an ode to her feet taking on so much of her burden. Like this she propelled herself the whole night long, through the morning, and right up to the school building.

She shuffled like a zombie through the halls, thinking in generalizations and speaking in short stiff sentences that may or may not have made sense. Without her even noticing, her classes sailed past and she hadn't even thought of a poem. Besieged by her exhaustion in the confines of Los Pinos High, her poetry abandoned her. In fifth period in Mr. Abrams' classroom her sleeping bag was no longer hanging from the overhead projector and Mr. Abrams carried on as if nothing had happened and Isabel wrote about geese. After school she resumed her stumble through town. The sky grew pink then purple then dark without suggesting a poem.

She had walked the life out of her feet. In her moonless aimlessness Isabel found herself near to where her father worked. She no longer had the strength to shield him. He must now know. Right?

With her hands cupped to her eyes she leaned to the window in order to see into the dark gallery. She could make out a few of the larger-than-life bronze statues. She knocked. She had to knock again, and a figure loomed up towards the glass. When her father realized it was his daughter, he fumbled through his great ring of keys to unlock the door.

"To what do I owe this pleasure?" he said. "Come in come in. I was just having my lunch."

Without a comment in regards to the fact that it was almost midnight, he led her through the gallery towards the small security office in back. Isabel lingered to look at a painting in the shadow. A giant mess of color.

On the desk in the closet office, stacks of papers tilted like faltering skyscrapers. Three video monitors each showed a different gray and motionless view of the gallery. Yogurt, cookies, chips, and a small thermos sat on top of a flattened brown paper bag.

"Please," her father said, offering Isabel his lunch.

"That's alright."

"No, please do."

He handed her the thermos, and she drank down the thick warm soup. She ate most of the yogurt, some of the cookies, and all of the chips. Her father's security uniform was stiff, but he sat with his pants bunched up so Isabel could see his white socks. In silence he had watched her eat, but when she finished and a gap extended between them, her quiet father started jabbering. He told her about the slight shift in his work schedule, he told her how the last part-time security guard wasn't suited for the work, he told her that one day he and his new wife would go on a honeymoon. He went on and on as they strolled around the gallery, making his rounds until they ended up at the front door.

He unlocked the lock and gave her a hug.

Isabel left the gallery feeling peculiar. She had nowhere to go. Through the night she walked for a long time, she sat on a bus stop bench, and then she walked some more. Her father had never been talkative, yet he had been talking just to talk—maybe to cover any potential awkward pause. The stoplight was yellow and when it turned red Isabel stopped—froze—mid-stride in the middle of the street like a misplaced mannequin. There were no cars, there were no pedestrians, no stray dogs. Isabel felt as if her father knew but wouldn't bring himself to say. She looked up into the sky where a low thin layer of mist collected. Winter was coming. She felt as if the last strand had been severed, and now she dangled in the instant before she would fall. She got herself out of the street. She sat on a step in a vestibule of a storefront. Her mind was clear but her heart was broken. She may well remember her father doing nothing longer and feel it more profoundly than all the good he had done in raising her alone. There was an unavoidable weight to her father's apathy that Isabel was forced to bear.

In the morning Isabel was still walking. Anticipation for the Poetry Burst Out kept her from crumbling, but barely. Although upright, she was crawling, her heart now several hardened pebbles.

At school between periods she rounded a corner and rammed right into Matthew.

"Hey hey there sissie, where ya been?" he said snickering.

Isabel forced her knees to bend to get her legs to move to walk her feet away.

In our various relationships we can seem as if we're different people. Isabel, in Matthew's presence, felt like a weakened set of ticks and shudders, yet while running the Poets' Circle she was a commanding force. And she wasn't faking it. Somehow we have to incorporate our divergent traits into the best renderings of ourselves.

After school when Isabel entered Mr. Abrams' classroom for the lead up to the Poetry Burst Out, a swell of apprehension from the other poets washed over her: They were terrified to read their poems in public and would prefer to cancel the Poetry Burst Out. Abandoned, Isabel let the last bit of her energy leak out of her. Her predicament had defeated her. She was crushed. And then, in a burst, she rushed out of the room.

Alone at the edge of the school parking lot and in the eye of her storm Isabel eased a breath in before exploding emotion out. She delivered her spontaneous masterpiece to the empty parking lot. Every bit of bile in her gut filled up into her chest, bursting towards her mouth. Like a purged dam, she spilt herself out over the pavement. The first words that came described exactly everything in detail—Matthew's grimy arms around her throat, the poke of the dirty fork invading the warmth of her bed—and everything else followed like a sudden mass exodus. She voiced it all as if freeing herself. She felt as if she were Mr. Abrams' homeless man singing his golden sorrow, she felt as if she were Juliet bawling over Romeo's corpse, she felt as if she were Holden Caulfield or Okonkwo or a siren sending out her beautiful song of death. The convergence of many storms, she let it all out. She couldn't call it a poem or poetry or a performance, and she wouldn't have knowingly exhibited it in front of anyone. In fact when she exhausted her emotions, embarrassed in front of herself, she hurried away, casting her final syllables out into her wake.

This was from where this act came—not from some premeditated stroke of brilliance as Gabriel had thought, but from desperation and disappointment, and from the hope that the truth of expressing herself (even if only to herself) would ease the strain. It hadn't worked—or if it had it wasn't instantaneous. Her fingers cold, her toes cold, she dragged herself from the school parking lot.

Just like the Poetry Burst Out, the whole experience of torment at the hands of Matthew and the struggle through every night and every day never got resolved nor reached a climax where a conclusion could be drawn. She waited for the circle's completion. She wanted closure or insight or acceptance or maybe even a catastrophic ending—something that validated what she had experienced, but instead there was blah. Maybe the Poetry Burst Out could have filled that void, but that too was blah.

One afternoon after school during their poetry meeting, Isabel's father showed up outside Mr. Abrams' door and without a word Isabel left with him. They drove back to their new home and had a nearly silent dinner with Matthew and his mom. About Isabel's absence and Matthew's abuse nobody said anything, ever. Isabel felt nauseous. Despite this dodging of responsibility to address the matter, Isabel started to sleep again in her bed, and for a long time Matthew left her alone—he avoided her at school and ignored her at home. It was as if none of it had happened—as if her nightmare had all been a thought, a worst case scenario that never came to be. Only blah.

*Make up a new candy bar.
What's in it (rocks)? Design
the packaging. Will it sell?
Does it matter?*

Every poet had entered with quiet veneration. So when the door swung open and a student crashed in, everyone knew he was not a member of the Poets' Circle.

Over the previous month the group had been recovering from the disappointment of the Poetry Burst Out. Despite their weakened ambition, they couldn't help but to re-arrive at a place of substance. Peter, whose nose with its horrific-looking scab was in fact healing, had become an active member, reading his provocative poems and exhibiting his engaging problems. Ned forever pressed his discontent into the corners. And Lori of course had been done wrong and needed to vent. The group was anxious, in purgatory, waiting for the next opportunity. Isabel already felt stale.

There's a reason the phoenix rises up out of his own ashes—a good burning leaves a fertile soil. When the laughing Nathan stepped into the Poets' Circle he sunk into the cinders of a field that had been burnt to the ground. As if hit by a wave, Nathan noticed that this was not his world. All the poets stared at him as he searched the room for his English teacher who was sitting on a desk between two students.

He held up a few stapled pages: "I brought my *Theme Steinbeck* paper."

Nathan hadn't been in class that day, and he hadn't been the day before either. In fact, he hadn't been since the infamous day when Gabriel made his nobody-had-to-come-to-class pronouncement now more than a week past. Nathan was one of the students who had walked right out.

Heading to his desk, Gabriel motioned for Nathan to follow. Gabriel pulled out the large envelope marked—'3rd - To Be Graded,' and Nathan handed him his paper.

Had Gabriel misjudged Nathan? It can be hard to like someone who hates you, but when you're fourteen some of who you are isn't yet developed, and what is there, especially the prickly stuff, isn't necessarily who you'll become. Teenagers are a mess of hormones, and this was high school. Reality was skewed. Most students who didn't like Gabriel didn't like him because he was a teacher. It wasn't because of who Gabriel was as a person.

But it was different with Nathan, who in that parent/teacher meeting had flat out told Gabriel he hated him. It was personal, right?

How did it get so personal? Once, Nathan in response to the Do Now—'Why love thy neighbor?'—launched into a diatribe about his gay next-door neighbor. Taken aback Gabriel questioned him, and Jorge jumped in, defending Nathan's right not to have to live near a homosexual, yet neither could advance a convincing argument. Gabriel should have ended it when Nathan claimed he'd "rather live next to an ax murdering rapist." A chill had washed over Gabriel and he stepped to the center of the room and announced to the class that one in ten people in America are gay. Gabriel proceeded to count out loud the twenty students in the room that day. And then he suggested that if there were twenty people in the room then two of them, statistically, had to be gay. "Which two could that be?" he had said, eyes shifting suggestively back and forth between Nathan and Jorge.

How *did it* get to be so personal, Mr. Abrams?

When Gabriel took Nathan's *Theme Steinbeck* paper, Nathan's eyes weren't dripping with venom.

"How much are you gonna take off?" he asked.

"It's a week late, Nathan."

"But I did it."

"You did. How much do you think I should take off?"

Nathan shrugged his shoulders.

In this moment the courteous Nathan affected Gabriel. Gabriel took a long clean look at him.

Something behind them in the classroom was brewing.

Nathan's shoulders tensed. Gabriel peeked at the poets. They all sat stiff, looking at Peter, whose color had drained from his face—Peter's bleached features held tight round eyes that were boring holes in the back of Nathan's skull.

Nathan turned and looked but quickly twisted back. The entire room was now glaring at Nathan, and Nathan had no safety but in the conversation he was having with his teacher.

"Do you think I'll get a good grade?"

"You know better than I at this moment," Gabriel said, participating in the charade even as he came round the desk and stood at the front of the room. Gabriel's glower came to rest on Peter, for whom nothing existed except the groove his glare dug out in the air between him and Nathan.

"What's going on?" Gabriel asked Peter.

"Nothing."

"Do you know him?"

"No," Peter said, his fixed stare refusing to yield.

"Do you know him?" Gabriel asked Nathan.

"No," Nathan said, squirming.

"Isabel," Gabriel asked, "what's going on?"

"I don't know."

"Peter, Pe—PETER!" Gabriel forced Peter to break his stare. Peter's eyes refocused on Gabriel. "What are you doing?"

"He's the one who threw the brick at me."

"No, I didn't, I did not—I don't, I don't know what he's talking about."

Peter took a deep breath and as he exhaled his anger wafted out into the air away from him.

"It was him," Peter said.

"Is this true?"

"NO! ... no. No," Nathan said.

Sammy sprang to his feet. "You're the one who threw the brick at Peter's *face*?" Sammy shouted this, but when he came to the last word he gnarled it up, slowing it down, giving it all the inflection in the world. "His *face*!"

When Isabel stood up, everyone looked at her, and in that instant Nathan, with the back of his hand, wiped the moisture from his mouth. Isabel's stature and confidence commanded attention, but she was looking only at Gabriel, who glared across the room at her.

"May I?" she asked.

"May you what?"

"Proceed."

Gabriel should have redirected this clash into a private moment, yet with Isabel standing there asking, he felt compelled. He waved his open palm forward, giving Isabel the floor.

"Let's be fair, you guys. Okay?" Isabel said. "What's your name?"

Nathan didn't answer.

"What's your name?" she asked again.

He flashed his eyes at her. "Nathan," he said.

"Nathan, did you throw the brick at Peter?"

"No—of, I've—no. No."

"Are you sure?"

"Yes."

Nathan glanced around the room but focused on no one.

"Peter? Did Nathan throw the brick at you?"

"Yes."

"Are you sure?"

"Yes."

"How do you know?"

"I saw him. He called me a 'faggot' and he and his friend chased me and when I looked behind this brick came flying right at my face."

"Did you see him throw it?" Isabel continued.

"Yes."

"You've seen him since?"

"Yeah," Peter said.

"Why didn't you do anything?"

"Like what?"

"Tell a principal."

"I don't know. I didn't … I didn't wanna have to go to the principals. I didn't expect him to walk into the Poets' Circle."

"Is this true, Nathan?"

"No."

"I saw you! I saw you with your friend in the red Starter jacket."

"You were there but you didn't throw it?"

Nathan steadied his eyes into Isabel's torso—he wanted to admit this.

"You were there?" Isabel pressed. "Were you?"

"I don't have—you're not a principal."

"You're right. But were you there?"

"Why do you care?"

"I ..." Isabel paused, considering Nathan's question. And then, slowly—"Because it matters, because I wanna care."

Nathan glanced up at Isabel and Isabel's expression held no aggression.

"Were you, were you there?"

"Fine, I was, but I didn't throw the brick, I swear."

"Yes, you did," Peter said.

"Did you try to stop your friend from throwing it?"

"No."

Isabel glanced across the room at Gabriel who was now standing in the back, letting the scene unfold.

"You can sit down if you like." Isabel pulled out a chair, but Nathan wouldn't sit. "So what should we do now?" Isabel asked Nathan. She glanced around the room as if to ask the rest—no one answered.

"I have to be somewhere," Nathan said.

"I bet you do," Sammy said.

"In history today," Isabel continued, "Ms. James said that when the oppressed finally take over they perpetrate the same atrocities that they endured for so long. I don't believe it, I won't believe it. Do you think if you were principal, if suddenly you got to decide people's fate, that you would be just as unreasonable as Dr. Fitzpatrick?"

"No," said Drew.

"No!" said Ned.

And then a little softer—"I don't know," said Lori.

"What don't you know?"

"Well, first it's it's really not our business," Lori said. "And second maybe we should just tell Dr. Fitzpatrick."

"That bitch!"

"Sammy, please," Gabriel had to say.

"You're already guilty if you go to the Disciplinary Committee."

"With a wave of the hand he'll get thrown in juvie."

"Maybe he deserves it," Ned said.

"Maybe he doesn't."

"Well what does he deserve?"

"It's not our business."

"It's my business," Peter said.

Nathan sat down.

"It may be your business," Lori said, "but that doesn't mean you should be judge, jury, and executioner."

"Why not?" asked Ned.

"Because he might be too harsh."

"No I wouldn't."

"I think Peter should definitely decide," Perry said.

"Decide what?"

"Decide some punishment."

"I think we all should."

"Whether he threw the brick or not I think he deserves some …"

"Retribution."

"So do I."

"But what?"

"I don't know."

"How 'bout he decides what happens to him?" Perry said.

"Who?"

"Nathan."

"That's stupid."
"Is it?"
"Kind of."
"I think it's important that he agrees."
"On the punishment?"
"No—to let us decide."
"Why would he?"
"I don't know."
"Ask him."
"Would you?"

Nathan had been following the progress of his fate and now the light had landed on him. He made several motions as if to answer.

"It's either that or Dr. Fitzpatrick," Isabel said.

Gabriel had made his way to the side of the classroom. "It's important for us to say that we intend to be fair, that that's our ultimate objective."

"I don't want him to go to juvie," Peter said. "I just want him to know what he did really sucked."

"So do we agree? To do this?" Isabel asked. "Sammy?"
"Yes."
"Perry?"
"Yup."
"Ned?"
"Let's crucify him."
"Ned!"
"What? Fine. Whatever. He's small fish—I want the heart of the plutocracy."

Isabel went around the room and everybody agreed.

"Nathan, what about you?" she asked.
"What?"
"You can either let us decide or we can go to the principal."

"I don't wanna go to the principal."

"Is that a 'yes?'"

He nodded his head.

"Whether you threw the brick or not," Isabel said, "you deserve something. Do you agree?"

"No, well, I don't know."

"I saw him throw it," Peter said.

"What do you think should happen to you?" Isabel said.

"Why you asking me?" Nathan said.

"'Cause it's your life."

"We should make him write an essay about what he did," Lori said.

"How about a poem?" Perry said.

"He should be Peter's slave for a week," Sammy said.

"A year," Drew said.

"We should make him wear a sandwich sign that says, 'I'm a fag.'"

"Ned!" Gabriel said.

Ned receded, chuckling to himself.

"We should at least make him tell us who his friend in the Starter jacket is," Tiffany said.

"That's crap." Ned leaned forward again. "This school puts so much stock in ... what's the point? Call the principal."

"He's right."

"I agree."

"Maybe Nathan can convince him to come back."

"I have to go," Peter said. "I'm really sorry but I have to go."

"Me too."

"But we need to finish this," Isabel said.

"I know but I really have to go," Peter said.

"Me too."

A renegade group of students circumventing the principal's authority could seem like a direct affront to that principal's sensibility. If Dr. Fitzpatrick knew, she'd certainly be offended. Often out-of-touch people in power mete out punishment as punitive attempts to extract some sort of private revenge. Even Gabriel as a teacher had felt that bitter urge, but these are still children. When teenagers get in trouble, their sins don't need to be ripped from their sides, leaving permanent damage.

Even the most studious members of the Poets' Circle could feel forever misunderstood and always in trouble as if their lives were controlled by a million overbearing and irrelevant entities. It's a crushing impression to struggle into our adult lives and realize that all these dreary imperatives begin to supersede our childhood ideals and dreams and goals. As we grow up we don't stop wanting justice and freedom and fame and fortune, we just become overwhelmed with responsibility and societal demands. We don't sell-out, so to speak, we let go.

Young people may not see this even as they are being rolled into the fold, and they aren't wrong in assuming that everyone is against them and that they're forever misunderstood and always in trouble. Adults feel that too—it just doesn't matter so much anymore—we no longer have the time and energy to care. We're too busy working jobs, trying to feed, clothe, and shelter ourselves, and to feed, clothe, and shelter our kids, too busy trying not to make waves. Teachers like Ms. Bimble—teachers like Gabriel—who made it into their adult lives with a sense of their idealism intact, can get crushed. To do something different in this world, something against the flow, maybe something interesting and potentially spectacular and important, you have to not only decide to do it, but you have to be comfortable being an outsider; not supported by no one—worse—up against everyone. For his entire life, an anomaly will have to push against all who desire to corrupt him for their own profit, as well as against most everyone else because many who have conformed are threatened by he who hasn't; they're jealous of his experiences, of his freedom and opportunity, and they fear his wildness will pervert the status quo and thus disrupt their own small lives. It is an eternal fight and you the rebel with your finite amount of energy trying to live outside the box are up against forces with unlimited resources. Imagine the toughest fighter on the planet not facing one opponent one night, but the whole night through facing and defeating one combatant after another. You knock one out and a bigger guy steps into the ring and then another and another and the line of adversaries stretches up through the stands, out the door and around the block. As morning approaches you grow tired and the opponents start coming into the ring with tire irons and baseball bats, two and three at a time. Not only is it not a fair fight, it's a losing proposition—no matter how big and bad you are. But all you have to do is give in. Give up. And then you get a seventy-two-inch flat-screen TV and a thirty-year mortgage as you take your place in line becoming another drone waiting to help defeat the last proud lone wolf.

 Gabriel knew, partly because of his own hurtful academic career, that the pressure that crushes a spirit starts early. He sensed the urgency, the all-out importance of empowering kids when they're fresh and not yet battered and corrupted, for if young people get a taste of their own potency they may not be so apt to submit so easily. And the more who survive this soul-crushing machine the stronger we become. In this realization Gabriel fingered the true power of a good teacher. He could infect this sense of self in his students, and if he had an entire life of spreading this infection he very well in the end may prove more potent than the most influential pop star. All told an effective veteran teacher through the span of her career may very well yield more influence over society than the captains of industry, than the fists on the levers of government.

There's a reason why, when the tyrants take over, among those first dispatched are the teachers.

*W*ithdrawing its warmth, the sun fell towards night. By the pine tree Holly and Gabriel lay together on a skinny red-cushioned lawn couch huddled against the cold. In the backyard right outside the master bedroom they had stopped whispering and were talking in normal voices figuring Chloe in the bedroom had fallen asleep—when her plea sailed out through the open window:

"Mamma, I want some water."

"Chloe, you're big enough to get it yourself."

"Okay, thanks ma, super cool."

Holly and Gabriel squeezed each other silently laughing at Chloe's 'super cool'.

"She's so grown up, I suddenly have all this time."

"What're you gonna do?"

"I don't know—be ambitious. I guess it's ingrained."

"Law school?"

Holly laughed. "I want to be a public intellectual."

"How do you be a public intellectual?"

"I don't know—get a megaphone. I want to help new mothers—and not in an overbearing self-righteous way. Well, maybe a little self-righteous. And slightly overbearing."

Gabriel laughed; he basked in the smooth rumble of her voice. He could have laid and listened to her all night, studying the way her lush lips curved around each sound. As it is with lust, it wouldn't have mattered what she said—but that was what was so breathtaking—even her words enlivened him, reminding him of the possibility that people could be wonderful. Embodied in this woman was the universe. Gabriel's head had been so tucked into the world of Los Pinos High that maybe he had forgotten how amazing students can become.

*D*id Gabriel do the right thing in telling his students they could choose to come to his class or not? I don't know, but man did he have guts doing it. I would have languished forever in whatever mess I was stuck.

At times in our lives I viewed Gabriel's past rash behavior as a major fault, when maybe in reality many of his decisions and actions were enlightened. His instincts were intact—more so than mine. I second-guess everything.

There were times I would snap into anger because Gabriel was so cool and confident. It seems stupid, for I couldn't appreciate my brother in his very best moments and for the exact things for which I loved him most. Why? Maybe because I wasn't like him. Instead of being inspired, I was offended. Instead of basking in my love for him, I sulked—sunk into my own insecurities. I try not to hate myself for this above all other personal failings. I hope this feeling doesn't stay forever. How could I not have appreciated Gabriel's wonderfulness in the moments when he really shined? With some things you just can never go back, you can never correct, you can only leave them as they were—and move forward. I must try instead to remember in my life today his bold deeds, and be impressed and encouraged. Knowing when to love is a prized trait that far outshines jealousy and resentment. When you're old and you peek back you may wish you had let your love overrun your incessant groaning just a few more times than when you didn't.

Between classes Gabriel wasn't so certain. In his heart he knew letting his students choose must be right, but it was in his head where questions fermented, and not because of what was happening inside his classroom, but what was brewing outside his classroom. Word spread and people began to judge.

Teaching a small class with a growing dedication—teaching eager students contributing—felt like a blessing to Gabriel. While surrounded in his classroom by willing students, he thought of nothing—he was entirely present, but when the immediateness of teaching gave way to idleness, Gabriel's mind drifted to the vultures who must be circling outside his door. So as to avoid it, in the mornings he arrived as late as possible and in the afternoons he gathered his belongings and pushed himself into the rush of students washing towards the exits. Dr. Fitzpatrick never dropped by again, and as far as Gabriel knew she didn't summons him to her office, though he stopped checking his mailbox. All he ever found in that small wooden hole were demands on his time that would never benefit him or his students.

After Nathan stumbled into the Poets' Circle, the very next day he returned to Gabriel's third period English class, though he sat in the back not participating, but not interrupting either. Several other errant students over the next few days crept back in as well and they too set themselves aside allowing those who had been there to continue with their engagement with what the teacher was offering.

"I think 'circumvent' would be a great vocabulary word," Nathan said two classes later and out-of-nowhere.

From there his energy grew prominent. He added to class discussions, did all his work, and rarely interrupted. In fact, he led many discussions. Gabriel didn't know what caused Nathan to hand in his *Theme Steinbeck* paper, but whatever happened outside of Gabriel's sphere and in conjunction with his encounter with the Poets' Circle influenced Nathan to try as hard as he could to show his best side in English class and to Mr. Abrams.

Everyone sat inside the Poets' Circle, waiting.

The school building had cleared. The halls were empty and it must have been at least five minutes after when the meetings usually started, yet no one began, for Nathan was not there. He had not returned despite the Circle's apparent magnitude.

Sammy started smiling, brandishing his gleaming white teeth.

"You got your braces off."

"Yup," Sammy said.

"Looks good, dude."

"Yup," Sammy said.

Commotion rose up, and Drew sprang to the door. Nathan stood in the hall watching his buddy in the red Starter jacket hurry down the corridor and vanish out the door.

Nathan stepped into the room, and everyone was scrutinizing him. Referring to his friend, Nathan said, "He almost came."

Nathan trudged to the front of the room. He turned and faced everyone. With the tips of his fingers, he pulled from his jeans pocket a crumpled piece of paper. He unfurled it. He held it in both his fists, and he started to read:

"'We're really sorry to have—'" he looked away from the page. "This was what Michael was gonna say. But I mean it too, I mean, I wrote it." He glanced back down to the paper. "'We're really sorry to have hurt Peter. We know that what we did …'" He paused again. "'We know that what we did was wrong. And we …'" Now he stopped reading completely. "I'm really sorry, I'm really sorry Peter. I wrote this and, I don't know, I know it was stupid and not just throwing the rock. … Anyways—I brought this." From his back pocket he pulled out an ancient iPhone. "It was Michael's sister's old one and we put a bunch of music on it. It's not connected or anything and I know you can listen to whatever you want and I don't know what you like, but … I thought you might like these songs. Michael insisted on some of the rap—I like it, maybe you will too."

Nathan handed the iPhone to Peter and Peter held it in his hands, looking it over.

"It works and everything," Nathan said now glancing back at the class, peeking at Gabriel. Nathan shrugged his shoulders. What else?

Isabel stood up to fill the void.

"Uhm," she said. "Maybe you can step into the hall and give us a second."

"Okay," he said. "I'm really sorry."

Once Nathan left and the door closed, no one spoke.

And then Lori said, "It took a lot of guts to come back."

Many agreed.

"He seems sorry."

"He does."

"Maybe he's just acting."

"How do we know?"

"We don't."

"Sometimes we need to trust our intuition," Gabriel said.

"I think so too," Isabel said.

"Though the Man doesn't want us to," Sammy said exhibiting his fresh white teeth.

"The Man doesn't trust his own intuition," Ned said.

"If it makes a difference," Gabriel said, "this week in my class Nathan's been more respectful, more humble, and more active than he's ever been before."

They all nodded, lending the observation its weight. The group seemed satisfied, and not just with Nathan's apology, but with themselves.

"Let's give him one good caning," Drew said, laughing.

"Come on—this is serious," Isabel said. "What do you think Peter?"

"I think a caning sounds good."

They all laughed.

And then they refocused on Peter as a metamorphosis played across his face. His tight skin softened, and everyone in the room grew solemn looking into his receding intensity.

After a moment he allowed—"It was nice of him." And then after another dramatic pause—"I think I wanna talk to him alone. I want everyone to leave."

They all kind of glanced at each other.

"Okay," Isabel said, peering around, and many were nodding their heads. "Okay."

Thus the meeting adjourned. They collected their things and headed for the door.

Lori held up her hand to Ned, "High five," and reluctantly Ned lifted his hand for her.

Nathan watched them all move through the door and file past, not engaging with him at all. Their work was done.

Nathan peeked into the room. Gabriel and Isabel stood at the front while Peter sat at his desk.

"Isabel, do you mind?" Peter said.

"Sure ... sure," she said, trying not to seem hurt.

Before she left the room she shook Gabriel's hand.

"Mr. Abrams, do you mind waiting in the hall?" Peter asked.

Gabriel wasn't sure.

"Please."

Gabriel stepped out into the hall, looking back in at Peter who gave him an assured smile. Gabriel looked at Nathan who was standing just inside the door and who was obviously nervous, but he too tried to smile for Gabriel.

Leaving Nathan and Peter alone in the room, Gabriel stood in the hall. For a long time he heard nothing, and the moments were full of tension. Gabriel was pacing. He heard commotion in the room so he flung open the door to see Peter still sitting and Nathan ten paces away still standing. Gabriel stepped back out, this time leaving the door ajar.

He could now hear them talking but he couldn't make out what they were saying and then after a few more minutes Nathan walked out, gave Gabriel a slight smile, and wandered down the hallway and out the door.

Gabriel stepped back into the classroom to see Peter putting his journal into his shoulder bag.

"Are you alright?"

"I am."

"What happened?" Gabriel asked.

"Nothing."

"Nothing?"

"Nothing."

"Okay."

Peter slid his bag up onto his shoulder, thought for a moment, and then said: "If I could hide ... I would, you know?"

Write out all your complaints.
Cross out those that don't matter.
Which is the most valid? Why?

In his bedroom after dinner Gabriel graded papers. A light knock on his door and Holly entered with his ringing cellphone that he had left on the kitchen table.

"It says 'City Pages.'"

"Who?"

She handed him his phone.

"Hello," Gabriel said, pressing his phone to his ear.

"Mr. Abrams?"

"Yes."

"Gabriel Abrams?"

"Yeah, who's this?"

"My name is Hillary Valdez. I'm a writer for the *Santa Fe City Pages*. You might have seen my column: 'The Valdez Account?'"

"I guess. I'm not that familiar though."

"Well that's alright. I wanted to ask you a few questions about Los Pinos High School."

"Questions? What kind of questions?"

"Basic questions. Actually I want to ask you specifically about ... well ... you."

"Me?"

"I understand you gave your students the option to either come or not come to your English classes. Is that true?"

"Uhm ... why do you want to know?"

"Because I believe it has relevance for our community."

"How so?"

"Let me ask you this: how many students have continued to attend your classes?"

"I'm sorry—I don't mean to be rude, but I don't see why this matters to—"

"Oh but it does. I was actually contacted by another teacher."

"You're kidding me."

"Mr. Abrams, this is an ongoing—"

"Ms. Valdez, I'm sorry but—thanks for your call—I have no comment. Have a good evening. I'm sorry. And thank you."

Gabriel hung up. His hands were trembling.

"She was from the *City Pages*."

"I got that much," Holly said with a comforting smirk.

"A reporter."

Gabriel didn't want anyone to speak in the halls of what he had done, and now it might shout up off the pages of the local weekly.

He looked at Holly and with a bit of unease he let out a laugh.

"What have I done?" he said. "People still read that paper."

Sammy boomed a poem.

The classroom door drifted open and Robertson slipped in. Because Gabriel's attention had abandoned the poets, the others looked which caused Sammy to look and the thread of his poem snapped.

Two weeks ago a new member had arrived for the Poets' Circle and last week another and two more today, though Robertson at the door constituted a different sort of invasion. People had heard that Robertson had claimed that Mr. Abrams had called him a 'bitch,' but of course Gabriel hadn't addressed the issue with his classes, even though he had wanted to shout from the tip-top of the clock tower that it was vacuous slander, but to waste class time in reference to it would be perpetuating it. Best to ignore it. Anyway, soon after the incident Robertson was transferred out of Gabriel's class.

But the Poets' Circle was something altogether different. They shared heartfelt and heart-wrenching poetry. They were curious about each other. They liked each other. So when the members had heard what their sponsor had supposedly said, they asked, and when Gabriel told them it was a lie they wanted to write a letter, sign a petition, make signs and protest in front of the principals' offices, chanting Mr. Abrams' innocence and demanding an immediate apology from Robertson, from his mother, from the principals, and from the school. Their vigor was too infectious and circumstances demanded attention. And besides they liked to get irate. When Nathan had entered the Poets' Circle and been accused by Peter, Isabel could do nothing but respond. And the group was growing. It was unmistakable: the circle was expanding, and the core members acted as if they had always expected success. They were in command and everybody wanted more—and not just Isabel. This blaze had been ignited.

When Robertson slipped in and the poets' turned to see, they didn't know who he was by looking at his face, but Lori knew and she whispered to Drew and Drew to Sammy and Sammy to Perry and soon everyone's expression dropped into a shade of hostility.

Robertson did have some nerve coming in here—especially after school when Gabriel was surrounded by allies. Under their glare, Robertson could do nothing but stammer.

"I ..."

They waited for him to say something, or for Gabriel to say something, or for a mass rush to pile on top of him.

Gabriel inched in under the tension, forcing a benevolent tone, "Can I help you?"

Robertson's chin wobbled. "I ... can I ..."

Robertson flexed all his muscles and shuddered. Over his hands he was wearing his tight gray gloves.

"I ..."

He was trying so hard. He squished his eyes shut, and then—

"I didn't make the bomb."

Heads swiveled and shoulders raised; the poets queried each other with their expressions. When their attention returned it lacked aggression—now they wanted Robertson to speak.

But he wasn't.

Not anymore.

He glanced over his shoulder; with his fingers, he squeezed his thighs.

"What bomb?" Gabriel asked.

"The one ... the one they found in the science building. Last semester."

"That wasn't a bomb," Ned said. "It was a box of broken computers—"

"—And cords—"

"—That someone wrote 'Boom!' on."

They all laughed.

"I know," Robertson said, "but Dr. Fitzpatrick says I did it."

"Did what?"

"Wrote 'boom.'"

"What're you doing here? What do we care?" Ned said.

"We know who you are," Perry said.

"Yeah, *bitch*," Lori said.

"Hey!" Gabriel admonished.

"I ..." Robertson tried to speak again and they gave him the space. "I didn't do it."

"So?"

"So, I ... I didn't do it."

"So?"

"You guys helped Nathan."

"So?"

"So ..."

"So why would we even care about you?"

"I don't know."

"Why would we even consider?"

"I don't know."

"What could we even do?"

Robertson was looking down—he peeked up but looked back down again. And then, slower, he said, "I don't know."

"Well then what're you doing here?"

"You're like the last person we wanna help."

"Or even be around."

"At least Mr. A feels that way."

They shifted around to look at Gabriel.

And Gabriel said, "I think we should hear him out."

"What?"

Gabriel looked at Isabel who was looking at him.

"Yeah," Isabel started. She stood up. "Why don't you come in?"

Robertson made no motion to step forward.

"Come in," Isabel repeated.

Having put himself in this position, Robertson had to take those few anguished steps forward. The room was quiet and Robertson's sneakers squished over the floor until he stood at the front—granted off to the side, like a dead branch having fallen from a tree.

"Why should we believe that you didn't do it?" Isabel asked.

"We already know he's a liar," Sammy said.

"Because I didn't," Robertson said.

"That hardly sways us," Perry said.

"He is such a schemer," Ned said. "Look at him—guilty as hell—he's trying to play us."

"What do you want us to do?"

"I don't know," Robertson said. "Talk to Dr. Fitzpatrick."

"She hates us."

"And you're a liar."

"I'm not lying." Robertson was rubbing the tops of his thighs.

"Look, Robertson," Isabel said, "that's your name, right?"

"Yeah."

"Well, Robertson, no one here believes you. And no one's gonna help you ... unless somehow we believe you. How's that gonna happen?"

"I don't know."

"How are we gonna help—" everything Drew said was funny "—we're a goddamn poetry club."

"Yeah we're a poetry club," Lori said.

"Really? Are we?" Isabel said.

"He should write a poem," Perry said.

"A poem?"

"He should write a poem to convince us he's not a liar."

"He is a liar, what's a poem gonna do?" Lori said.

"It sounds like a good idea."

"I can't write a—I don't know anything about poems."

"Then leave," Sammy said.

"Yeah, this is the Poets' Circle."

They sent Robertson out into the hall to write a poem into his big phone. Once he left and the door shut a silence overtook the room.

"Anybody wanna write something?"

There was more silence. And then everyone cracked up laughing.

"What's so funny?" Lori asked.

Once the laughter subsided, Ned said: "What's a poem gonna do?"

"The kid's a liar."

"Let's give him a chance," Gabriel said.

"Yeah, see what he comes up with," Isabel said.

They sat in silence—until they all started laughing again. Lori too.

"Come on let's write something," Isabel said.

After they all finished writing and after they were all finished waiting, Drew threw open the door, but Robertson was gone.

Isabel cut across the arroyo behind the school. On the afternoons of the Poets' Circle she had to walk home for all the school buses had already left. A city bus could get her close but she liked to walk. It took her longer and that was okay. Her home life was weird but bearable. Matthew was wrapped up in his basketball season.

When Isabel scooted down into another arroyo, gaining speed to make it up the opposite embankment, someone was behind her running. Isabel jerked around.

"It's okay," he said. It was Robertson. He was panting, out of breath.

"What do you want?"

"I wanna talk."

"You followed me?"

"I wanted to talk to you alone."

"For what?"

"I don't know, I just did."

"You left—you didn't write a poem."

"I couldn't."

"You should've tried."

"I did—I couldn't.'

"Such a copout."

"It's not."

"What do you want—why'd you follow me?"

"I want you to help me." He had caught his breath now. "Or get the poetry people to help."

"Help you what?"

"I already said."

"What are we supposed to do?"

"Kids get raped in juvie!" Robertson jerked his head, turned away.

"Well what am I supposed to do?"

"I don't know. Convince Dr. Fitzpatrick."

"Convince her what?"

"That I didn't do it."

"Did you?"

"No."

"Why should I believe you?"

"Because."

"Because you're a liar?"

"I'm not."

Isabel brushed him off with a snicker.

She stared off at the distant mountains, and Robertson sucked back into himself.

And then, renewed, and with fierce eyes, he pronounced these words: "I know where you've slept."

"What?" Confused by his cryptic assertion, Isabel glared. "What are you talking about?"

Robertson squeezed his lips together giving Isabel an all-knowing look, his head nodding as his meaning crystallized in Isabel's brain.

Dread shivered up her spine. Embarrassment. She didn't know how he knew, but she knew exactly what he was talking about—her secretly sleeping in Mr. Abrams' classroom. How could he know? Without another word or glance, she hurried away, and Robertson didn't follow.

*

"Everybody should have a choice—even when we're young."

"Especially when we're young."

Gabriel's creative writing students usually ignored the buzz emerging from Gabriel's freshmen classes, for creative writing was a different world, occupying—maybe the same space—but a very different corner of the cosmos separated by a whole chunk of the day and leagues upon leagues of maturity.

"I might choose the same things I've already been forced into."

"But at least it'll have been our decision. Right?"

"Can we choose too, Mr. Abrams?"

The question came almost two weeks after Gabriel had given the option to his third period class, and, ironically, the question came from Perry who wouldn't leave creative writing class even if the room were on fire.

"Yeah can we, can we choose to come to this class or not?"

At this point, inside his freshmen classes, Gabriel had already suffered the immediate consequences, yet the issue seemed to grow out of the cracks of his room, circle through the principal's lair, and weave in and out of other teachers' classrooms on its way back to Gabriel's. He would have liked to have said, simply, no. You're required to attend. And been done with it. But he knew that would have been the wrong answer. He wanted his students to be in his classroom and not wandering the halls and the malls realizing that, yes, they did in fact want to be in Mr. Abrams' class. Couldn't they skip the gestation interlude and get right to the eager-to-learn phase—which his creative writing students were already in?

"In my French class the students were all demanding the choice and Ms. LeBrauch freaked and kids just walked out."

"You're kidding me?" Gabriel said.

"No, like twenty students just walked."

Gabriel wanted nothing to do with what went on outside his classroom. He didn't want teachers or principals to burst through his door and he certainly didn't want what he did in his room to corrupt another teacher's class.

"They asked nicely if they could decide, but Ms. LeBrauch got upset *at that*. She kept saying 'you can't leave, you can't leave,' as the students walked out."

"Did you walk out?" Perry asked.

"No, heavens, I need an 'A' in French."

Gabriel tried to ignore the commotion boiling outside his classroom, but it's hard to disregard a tempest after having set it off.

And it wasn't all hearsay. In the halls students Gabriel did not know pointed him out to other students he did not know. This sort of recognition dogged him. As he passed a teacher in the quad, he heard her mumble in some snotty way beneath her breath, "Can't we choose too?" And at the end of the last faculty meeting he attended, an older teacher raised her hand and asked if it were true that students were now allowed to *choose* whether they attended *required* classes. She was being flippant.

Again, Perry asked, "So can we?"

"Can you what?" Gabriel cringed.

"Can we choose?"

Gabriel paused and glanced around the room at all his creative writing students who were now silent as they waited for an answer. He looked at Isabel.

"Can we?" she asked.

"Can we choose?"

"Can we?"

"Can we choose?"

"And what will you choose?" Gabriel asked. "To walk out today? To take a free day tomorrow? I mean what are you asking me?"

"We're asking if we also get to come or not."

"Yeah it's only fair."

Gabriel couldn't hold a shield up against his creative writing students. There was no tactic or trick he could implement in order to control the situation. He had to open himself and see what would happen.

"You guys can do whatever you want," he said. "This is your life. Most of you are over sixteen and don't even have to come to school. But at the same time there are consequences to all our actions—both good and bad. Not many of us are buffered from those consequences; we don't get too many chances to make glaringly wrong decisions. And just like an experienced birddog you guys are all mature enough to know what's at the other end of a gun. So yes of course it applies to all of you. It does every day. It always has."

"So can we?"

"You've all already made your decision," Gabriel said, opening his palms in surrender. "You don't have to ask me to give you the power you already have. But if you want the specific space to make that decision than here it is: if you don't want to be here, leave."

With his left palm now held aloft, aimed towards the door, Gabriel paused for all of ten seconds.

And nobody made a move.

"Okay," Gabriel said, his tone shifting to business-as-usual. "Here's an article from the *Associated Press* telling of a man who washed up on a beach and wandered aimlessly and waterlogged along the shore until he was taken to a hospital by the police. They kept him there for a month. Nobody knew who he was and he didn't know who he was or even what language he spoke. In fact he didn't speak at all. But it turned out he was an incredible pianist. This stranger spent hours in the hospital chapel playing masterpieces that no one had ever heard. Crowds gathered. Here's the article. I want you guys to use your imagination and write who this man was—or is. How did he end up there, what was wrong with him, how will it end? Be inspired by the article and take it where your invention leads."

As Gabriel passed out the article and the students bent their heads to read, Gabriel noticed a teacher standing in his doorway. He didn't know for how long she had been there, and, when Gabriel spotted her, she left.

"Is this the poetry club?"

"It is. Come in."

New members arriving every meeting became almost annoying. Some wanted to be poets, some didn't. Maybe they knew Nathan. Maybe they'd heard about Mr. Abrams. As if seeking refuge, the core members started showing up for lunch in Gabriel's classroom for impromptu poetry gatherings, and they kept very quiet about it. Let the afterschool meetings expand, but keep their lunches sacred.

As if for the benefit of the new members for the afterschool sessions, Isabel had returned to her formal introductions. "Welcome to the Poets' Circle. We're here to share ourselves as well as to ..."

One by one they turned to see what the others had turned to see until everyone's shoulders and necks and heads and eyes had cranked around to Robertson slouched in the doorway. He pushed himself into the room and took the closest chair—the one in the way back. Everyone stayed twisted in their seats, looking. For a specific effect Gabriel cleared his throat. Some turned back to the front. Gabriel had to fake-cough a little louder.

"Shall we? Begin?" Gabriel said.

Isabel, still strained, kept glaring at Robertson.

"Isabel," Gabriel had to say.

With great effort she composed herself. "Okay, well, where were we? Does anyone have a poem?"

"I got one."

The force of Ned's delivery coupled with the wrath of his words launched the group headlong into the meeting. After Ned, several other students read their poems as Robertson slouched in the back.

Isabel couldn't contain herself. Although other hands were raised, to Robertson she said: "Do you have something you want?"

As she said this, Robertson pushed his palm into the air as if raising his hand had been his intention the whole time even before Isabel had assailed him.

"I do—I, I have something."

Robertson had only one glove on. The group watched him pull out his big phone and swipe over the screen until he found what he was looking for. He read his poem and it was a very short poem and he mumbled it and Isabel glanced around to see if anyone had understood what he had read.

She had no patience for Robertson. "Can you read it again, but enunciate—please—so we can hear you?"

Robertson's nostrils flared; he was nervous. He read:

I don't want to be where I can't say things
I don't want to be embarrassed
or abused
I want to be liked but also for what I am

No one looked up. Robertson's poem was almost nothing, but it paused the group. He had laid himself out there in the open.

Before anyone could say anything, Robertson raised his hand again; his palm went up and then he pulled it down before raising it a little higher.

"I have another one," he said.

Longer, his next poem attempted to rhyme. It wasn't like his first, but the fact that he had a second spoke of his effort.

The circle opened.

Robertson looked around at everyone. "So?" he said.

"'So' ... what?" Perry asked.

"So." Robertson struggled to communicate. "Will you help me?"

"Help you what?"

"Help me tell Dr. Fitzpatrick that I didn't write 'boom' on a bunch of busted computers."

"You come in here for two seconds and expect us to help you."

"His first poem was good," Peter said.

"What are we supposed to do anyways?" Lori's tone was not aggressive.

Robertson seemed both pathetic and determined and it was obvious that some of the poets were considering his plea. They looked to Ned to say something brash, yet his shoulders rose as if admitting he had nothing to say.

"We could do something probably," Perry said.

"I have a Disciplinary Committee meeting next week. My mom's gonna be there. And Dr. Fitzpatrick, my counselor, a police officer I think."

"We could show up."

"We could also—"

"Are you crazy!" Isabel broke off what was building. "This is the guy who tried to nail Mr. Abrams to the cross—remember? This is the guy who lied and every one of us knows it but he says nothing of that and we consider none of that. And now we want to go and pronounce him an honest moral upstanding student in good stead. Vouch for him? I don't. He's a liar. Can't you see that? Come on Robertson I dare you to tell me you're not, tell us all, tell Mr. Abrams."

Everyone turned to Robertson.

Gabriel didn't want to be amused—but what great theater! Yes, Gabriel had been swayed by Robertson's poem and by the group's reaction to it. Gabriel had, amidst all the excitement, forgotten—not forgotten but momentarily dismissed—the fact that Robertson had claimed he had called him a 'bitch.' Gabriel had been plucked up in the flow of the group's emotions and sympathies, but now he too glanced over at Robertson anticipating some sort of rebuttal.

Robertson's pale face gave off that dull, stumped look. He kept glancing down into his phone as if for support. His expression tightened and then tightened more. His chair scrapped back as he found his feet, standing up though still hunched over.

He peeked up at everyone in the room. Tried to look at them. And then he looked back down at nothing as he started to speak:

"Maybe half of inmates are raped. Annually. More than forty percent go back. Spend their lives in jail. It's called recidivism." Robertson tried again to peek up at the poets though they seemed confused. Robertson cleared his throat, struggled to say more, "I'm, I … " He glanced up through the students at Gabriel. "Mr. Abrams, I, I'm uhm … I'm sorry. I don't know why I, I … I liked you, you were my favorite teacher. I felt like I wanted, like I wanted … We just keep going back and forth, me and my mom, we … just froze, freeze. Our Chevy motel." He laughed to himself. "But my dad's worse. You're right—I don't know how you can help. Just forget it okay."

With that he left the room, dragging himself away, shutting the door behind him.

"I'm inspired," Perry said. "Let's write something."

"You have a prompt?"

"How 'bout a group poem?"

Perry ripped a page from his journal and wrote the first line of the poem and passed it to Sammy who wrote the next line who then slid it over to Isabel. The page made its way around the circle each member adding a line until it was done. Sammy read it and it was goofy, but they liked it.

As they left the classroom they stalled just outside the door. Gabriel moved towards them to see. When he arrived, the logjam had cleared as the poets moved down the hall towards the exit. Gabriel glanced down at what they had been looking: Robertson sitting on the ground against the wall just outside the door. He had his phone out and was ferociously tapping into it. Gabriel leaned in for a peek and saw on the screen what must have been an emerging poem.

Gabriel had to hurry to the bathroom so as not to be late for class, but before he could get there a teacher stepped into his path.

"Mr. Abrams, can I have a moment of your time?"

"No well I gotta—sure. What's up?"

Leading Gabriel to a corner of the hallway as if to grab a small slice of privacy, she whispered, "I just wanted to ask how your classes were going. Or, actually: Are your classes going? Are students attending, I mean, after ... you know?"

Gabriel shrugged, compelled to answer, "Some."

Another teacher had asked a similar question on a separate occasion. Even though it seemed a legitimate inquiry, and they were nice about it, Gabriel felt uncomfortable talking about it with people he didn't know and who would judge him. Even as the circumstances in his classroom improved, Gabriel felt disinclined to answer.

After the first couple days during which almost no one showed up for Gabriel's freshmen classes, one by one, as if they had grown cold, crept back in towards the fire, and having made that decision they were respectful and active, and the small circles of that first week began to grow in all of Gabriel's classes, but this did not alter the character, only the shape of the group. The students who had been there showed the others by example how to act, and the returning students, now being the newbies, were modest and polite and accepting of the civil environment. As they became comfortable with the new atmosphere, they sat up in their seats, listening, becoming familiar, and in time participating.

But not all of the students returned under their own volition. One morning during a heated debate, the classroom door creaked open. Staying outside, Jorge's mother watched as Jorge crept across the room to a seat. After he dragged out his notebook, his mother closed the door behind her.

All of Gabriel's classes threatened to grow back to their original sizes—even hinting at expansion. More than once an unfamiliar student arrived at his door requesting to be transferred into Gabriel's class. Gabriel would explain that he didn't know how that officially worked, but he was welcome to take a seat.

When Isabel, Tiffany, and I pulled into the parking lot of the caves, this big lumpy kid with greasy black hair greeted us. Isabel gave him a slow genuine hug, and then turned to me.

"This is Robertson. Robertson, this is Mark, Mr. Abrams' brother."

Robertson held out his gloved hand and with a faint grasp shook mine.

I was curious. While driving out to the caves I had asked Isabel why—because she had so much animosity towards Robertson—in the end she defended him against Dr. Fitzpatrick and the Disciplinary Committee.

"All Robertson's problems shoot two feet out in front of him like these invisible swinging fists," Isabel had said. "That's who you meet if you don't know him. One time in the Poets' Circle I looked up while we were all writing and he was ripping away at his page with his pencil as if he was carving holes in the desk through his paper. And everything he offered, every poem he read whether on paper or from his phone had resonance in some personal part of me. He always read right to me, facing me, looking at me. There was something... we shared an experience that was a quiet difficult part of each of us but totally separate."

Robertson's meeting with the Disciplinary Committee had been twice postponed, and in the meantime he continued to attend the Poets' Circle, becoming a dedicated member. It was as if he had been searching for a welcoming environment and then, once found, it was as if he had discovered something valuable inside himself that others valued as well. Though never invited, he started coming to the lunchtime gatherings, and one day only Isabel and Robertson arrived, and Mr. Abrams was occupied at his desk. Robertson suggested that they just forget it, but Isabel insisted as if to challenge him. They pushed the fronts of two desks together, facing each other.

"Let's do a group poem."

"Okay."

Isabel tore a piece of paper from her binder and on it she wrote, "The wind left the trees to their stillness," and pushed the paper over the desktops to Robertson who wrote, "Branches breaking into my heart."

"Mending the tear," Isabel wrote.

"Shattering the calm," Robertson wrote.

"The wind picks up and it brushes across my face," she wrote.

"Like razorblades," he wrote.

"And rising up off into a cloud."

"Sucked into a tornado."

"And finding its eye and observing its all."

"Sleeping in a gutter," Robertson wrote.

"Lazarus," Isabel wrote.

"Homelessness," Robertson wrote.

"Hope," Isabel wrote.

"Hopelessness," Robertson wrote.

Isabel looked down at the last word Robertson had written. Then she wrote, "Joy," and passed the page back to Robertson.

"Loss," he wrote.

"Found," she wrote.

"Lost," he wrote.

"Love," she wrote.

"Hopelessness," he wrote.

"Again?" she wrote.

"Yup," he wrote.

Isabel peeked up.

In almost a whisper, she said, "How did you know where I slept?"

"What?"

"That time in the arroyo, you said, 'I know where you've slept.'"

"I just did."

"No you didn't."

Robertson squeezed the pen in his fist. "I'm like you, you know."

"Like what?"

"My mom and I looking every night for somewhere to sleep."

"I'm not."

"You were," Robertson said.

"I was," Isabel said.

Steady eyes, they peered into each other's faces.

"Sometimes I have nowhere," he said.

"What do you do?"

"I don't know. At least, I'll have somewhere when Fitzpatrick sends me to juvie."

"She's not gonna send you to juvie."

"How do you know?"

"I just do."

"Maybe it's better the way it is."

"The way it is?"

"Yup," Robertson said, "the way it is."

Isabel opened the cover of her three-ring binder. From beneath the plastic pocket she slipped out the key to Mr. Abrams' classroom door. She placed it flat on the desktop, peeked over at Mr. Abrams who was absorbed grading papers at his desk, and then, with her index finger pressed to the top of the key, she slid it over her desktop to Robertson's desktop. The key sat between them, neither talking, neither touching, both looking at it. Then Robertson plucked it up and shoved it in his pocket.

*What statement do you want your
life to make? Write a Last Will and
Testament that will be broadcast
after you're done.*

𝒜 mess of teenagers, Search and Rescue officials, state troopers, and park rangers gathered in the parking lot where they had found (and since towed) Gabriel's car. After I met Robertson, Isabel led me around introducing me to many of Gabriel's students. Though a somberness inside every interaction, they greeted me with an energy as if they knew me. Perry took me in his big arms and hugged me.

One of the police car's sirens lit up for a split second to help assemble us together. On the way towards the caves a woman came up behind me and introduced herself.

"Mark, right? I'm Holly. Gabriel's ... roommate. We spoke on the phone."

"Right, hi. Hi. How are you?"

"Alright, considering."

On the short hike to the entrance of the caves, Holly and I walked together in silence. We could see no opening, no way in—just rough brown desert with its thin spreading of pine trees. The rich blue sky inspired intensity, and the kids ahead of us seemed to vanish into the dirt and scrub. We came upon a giant hole in the earth that was as vast as a cathedral. We slopped down through the mouth of the cave ringed with its black rock teeth. Just beyond this opening, the beginnings of three caves—the lava tubes—narrowed and darkened, leaving the atrium filled with light. On a rock in the kindness of the morning sun, Holly and I paused, staring towards the darkness, seeing bodies and voices and zigzagging shafts of light from flashlights and headlamps and cellphones.

"I can't believe I'm meeting you and you're not eight feet tall."
I glanced at her. "What?"
"Gabriel talked a lot about you. And in glowing terms."
I tried to smile.
"He claimed you could be happy in a bare room with a paper ball." She paused, and then—"He said when you were young and had to take care of him, on the spot you'd make up complete games to play like some sort of creative genius. He told me that more than once."
"He's being generous."
"He wouldn't agree."
"My mom would go to work and Gabriel'd get all rambunctious and if I didn't do something quick he'd be throwing things out the window—and I'd get in trouble."
We searched each other's faces as if for a hint of Gabriel.
Before we ducked into one of the caves, she handed me an extra flashlight. I hadn't even thought to bring one.

Gabriel was not graced with the benefit of teaching in a different century when students were respectful, teachers admired, and society supportive, and Gabriel was not used to having his best efforts wrecked at every turn. Nor was he familiar with being treated with such contempt. In order to succeed he had to adjust to the reality in his classroom. Often teenagers oppose all they encounter, rejecting everything sacred in their anguished act of growth. So many times Gabriel had mistaken a cry for help as a swipe from a battle-ax. Gabriel didn't have to become numb to be effective, but he couldn't be offended by every student's misplaced comment and then allow his wounded emotions to respond with the same amount of animosity.

Once Gabriel grew accustomed to smaller more focused classes—once he got used to having order in his room—he began to expect it, even as more students returned and even as some of the formally disruptive students returned. So when Gabriel prompted his students to write their lists that would become poems, and Nathan, who had since become a model student, groaned at the task, Gabriel paused, surprised and irked. Gabriel thought his lesson was a good one. This week during their poetry unit most of his freshmen didn't know what to write, so today they were making lists of anything and everything in order to turn those lists into poems—lists of the things hanging on the wall, lists of the stuffed animals on their beds, lists of what they could see out the window, lists of what was in their pockets, lists of what was on their mothers' shrines.

"This is stupid," Nathan said.

Gabriel felt his emotion well up in his chest, and that *feeling of it* made all the difference, for he knew that his anger was there and he knew he didn't want that emotion to command his action.

Instead of wrenching himself up and diving into a battle with Nathan, Gabriel didn't respond. As he stood there in the middle of his classroom experiencing his anger yet not projecting any bad feelings, not giving off any emotion at all, a strange thing happened: in the void, Nathan picked up his pencil and started writing.

As Gabriel paused there, motionless and emotionless, Nathan responded by easing forward in his chair and starting his work.

Later that same class as a student read his list-poem of the different components that make up the engine of a Dodge Challenger, Clarissa began whispering to Jorge. Gabriel asked her to stop and Jorge said, "Why?"

Gabriel stood there, not necessarily glaring, but waiting for Clarissa to stop talking. Gabriel refused to give it any energy. Not pouting or sulking or grumbling beneath his breath, Gabriel waited, and the class waited with him. Soon the whispering stopped, and Gabriel motioned for Rodney to continue reading his poem.

The next day in his first period, Gabriel was giving his greatest performance. Poised in the middle of the classroom, his arms stretched, fingers flexed in gesture, he pronounced, "'Each separate dying ember wrought its ghost upon the floor.'" Not just reciting Edgar Allen Poe, Gabriel embodied him. A tangled scratch in his throat, he crept through the desks with a limp. Through Gabriel, Poe's poem, "The Raven," draped a melancholic wing over his students, who crouched hushed in their seats, eyes following their teacher—when disengaged laughter seeped up into the air. Gabriel paused. Despite the rapture in the room, despite the performance unfolding before them, two girls were giggling.

Practicing what he had learned the day before, Gabriel emulated himself. He stopped and waited, giving no energy to the moment. And it didn't take long. The girls noticed that Mr. Abrams had stopped and then they stopped—even apologized.

In the next class, second period, as the momentum of "The Raven" barreled forth, Gabriel sputtering, "'the ebony bird beguiling my sad fancy into smiling—'" Amanda and Lissa started talking trying to be heard by each other over Gabriel's roaring presentation. Gabriel paused, but they kept on yapping, not having noticed that their teacher was waiting. It was like magic: other students, wanting

Mr. Abrams to continue, shushed them. And they stopped. Gabriel didn't have to engage them at all—he expended no energy. The students, taking on the chore of disciplining, brought the class back into focus.

He got it. In that moment Gabriel felt as if he could prosper as a teacher; he felt as if he had finally gotten it. Things began to coalesce, they began to make sense—it got easier. Teaching became possible.

Of course there was more to it than simply stopping and waiting. Gabriel had gained poise at the head of a classroom. Those few weeks of smaller more manageable classes gave Gabriel a taste of how his classes could thrive, so now he demanded it, though it was less a thought and more a feeling that he could preside over an orderly environment. He expected it. He saw himself in that role, he played that role, and he believed it—and thus his students did too.

He stepped through the void: On one side—floundering futility, and on the other—Confidence. And that confidence lent him the gravity to lead a class, to command a class.

Riding his bike home that night, he said aloud to himself, "I got it, forevermore, quoth the Raven."

Usually when something bizarre or thrilling or something extra malicious happened at school everyone was talking about it. Yet for some reason nobody knew what Matthew had done. Isabel found out around their dinner table.

Alone in a classroom between periods, Matthew, Isabel's stepbrother, had charged his Chemistry teacher, Mr. Hart, and knocked him down. Supposedly. That's what Mr. Hart claimed, though Matthew denied it. But that wasn't the issue. Matthew was failing Chemistry and a student/athlete had to pass his core classes to remain eligible to play. The LPHS basketball team was on a championship run, and nobody wanted Matthew to miss a single game, especially Dr. Fitzpatrick, for the team brought the school much needed positive attention.

At the dinner table Matthew played with his fork in his strong, stubby fingers. He admitted nothing and nobody pressured him. They accepted the notion that he had toppled his Chemistry teacher. Not one person seemed concerned to punish him; everybody was focused on how to keep him on the basketball court, and this didn't make Isabel feel any safer, it couldn't remove the lump from her throat, it wouldn't ease her disturbed heartbeat.

"Dr. Fitzpatrick said if you write an apology to Mr. Hart and pass a makeup test ..."

Matthew's mother didn't have to finish her sentence. The gist was that everyone involved, including Mr. Hart, would let it pass, press no punishment, accept the apology, and allow Matthew to play in the state tournament.

But Isabel—Isabel was just about to freak right out of her chair. Matthew deserved punishment, expulsion, imprisonment—anything to check his rage. Above all else she wanted him admonished, she wanted him castigated, she wanted him not to be a part of her day, to no longer hold sway over her life, she wanted him sent to juvie jail until he was fifty. How could they consider ruining Robertson's life for writing a word on a box while conspiring to conceal a true menace's transgression so he can play basketball? It made Isabel sick. By being feckless with real issues, Dr. Fitzpatrick was endangering her.

Isabel didn't want to but everyone expected her to—she even expected herself to do it.

Before school she went to make an appointment with Dr. Fitzpatrick, and as she spoke to her secretary Dr. Fitzpatrick walked up. Isabel stuttered, not having anticipated to be standing in front of her.

"Robertson Sandoval has a meeting in front of the Disciplinary Committee and we want to come in and, well—be character witnesses."

"And when is this meeting?" Dr. Fitzpatrick asked.

"Well it's been cancelled but now it's supposed to be next Monday."

"Here, Darlene, give me that." Dr. Fitzpatrick's secretary handed her an appointment book, and Dr. Fitzpatrick leafed through it.

"Oh yes, Robertson Sandoval. And what do you want to say?"

"Well, he's sometimes hard to know, and we want to give those who sit in judgment of him a fuller picture."

"Hmm. There will be some luminaries there whose time I don't want to waste. I'll give you a minute or two at the beginning. Try to be precise."

Dr. Fitzpatrick was writing in the appointment book.

"And what's your name?"

"Well, it's not just me. We're the—Poets' Circle."

"The what?"

"The poetry club."

Dr. Fitzpatrick glanced up. "The poetry club?"

"Yeah."

"Mr. Abrams' club?"

"Yes."

She rested the pencil back in her knuckles. "I will not allow you or Mr. Abrams to disrupt this meeting. What Mr. Sandoval did is not of little consequence. So, no, thank you for coming, but I am going to have to deny your request."

"We don't plan to do any—"

"This is not the place for—"

"—We just want to defend—"

"Excuse me, please don't over-talk me ..." She glared at Isabel. "This is not the place for you to try to stand up for something that may very well have little relevance to the issues at hand."

"If we don't stand up," Isabel said, "you'll never know how what you do affects us."

"We are very aware."

"It doesn't seem that way."

"What is your name?"

"Isabel Vasquez."

Dr. Fitzpatrick wrote Isabel's name in her book. "Ms. Vasquez, you may not be aware of the many reasons we do things."

"And you may not be aware of how the things you do affect us ... " Isabel paused; she wasn't used to being disrespectful.

"Yes, that may be a wise place for you to stop, Ms. Vasquez."

Gabriel locked up his bike and headed towards the school building. A strange energy hung in the air and Gabriel felt it as a ghostly shiver in the back of his neck. A few early students gathered outside before school and watched Gabriel trudge past. Gabriel pulled open the door and entered. Down the hall two custodians on ladders were scrubbing a large dark smudge from the wall. In black spray-paint and in big sloppy letters someone had graffitied something and as Gabriel approached he tried to read it but the custodians had already washed away enough to make it unintelligible. Gabriel shuffled around the corner towards his classroom. His attention, drifting away from the custodians, began to focus on a similar marking on the wall at the end of the next hall. He could read this one and it stopped him midstride. In big black capital letters done with large wide lines someone had sprayed: ¡ABRAMS! Slowly Gabriel's head shifted to his right to see on the wall across from his classroom another big black sprayed ¡ABRAMS!

"Oh shit," Gabriel said.

He entered his classroom and eased the door shut. He crept through the desks and sunk down into his chair. The smell of spray-paint had followed him into the room; in fact the stinging stench of fresh paint crawled into all the nooks and crannies—palpable everywhere in the school building. The night before someone with a can of black paint had sprayed ¡ABRAMS! on the walls and in the bathrooms. It took all day for the two custodians to do a bad job scrubbing the walls, leaving huge smeared paint splotches and swirls of black chaos throughout the building.

Many of Gabriel's freshmen entered his classroom smirking at him as if Gabriel were somehow involved, and Gabriel in turn tried to move right past it, pressing forward with his lesson without a mention. What else could he do? It was so much more than guilt by association—the act in itself implicated him.

During the lunch period on this day Isabel, Lori, Sammy, and Ned were eating in Gabriel's classroom as the poets often did whether they had a poetry meeting or not. Ned sat off by himself scrolling through his phone while the others together whispered about the defaced school walls, yet they were kind to Gabriel—they left him alone. Gabriel stayed at his desk, for he often had teacherly things to do during lunch. As he picked at his food he was trying not to think about it, but in truth the graffiti was just about all that filled his head, and how could it not—the persistent reek of paint permeated like diesel.

His classroom door opened, bounced against the wall and then swept back to a close. Everyone looked up.

Standing inside the room, Robertson glanced around with his chin held out, a smile tight in his lips. He was slowly nodding his head with assurance as his eyes settled on Isabel. And then he gazed at Lori and Sammy and Ned. And finally at Gabriel. He pulled his bag in front of him and dug into it—out from which he yanked a black speckled can of spray-paint. Robertson wiggled it and the ball inside clanked with a thin jingle, demonstrating that the can was empty. Then, casually, he tossed it across the floor and it bounced and spun and rolled to a stop near Gabriel's desk. They all glared at it—this used up can of spray-paint motionless on the dull tile floor in the middle of Mr. Abrams' classroom. A troubling quiver trembled up Gabriel's spine.

Ned climbed out of his seat, plucked up the spray can, and fell back into his chair, concealing the can in his own backpack.

Everyone had watched Ned and now they were all staring at him. He had to say something.

"Let's keep this on the down-low," Ned said and then he was eyeballing each of them—even Gabriel—as if securing their compliance. "Robertson?"

With his wide smile barely contained, Robertson nodded his head, agreeing.

Roberson was not the most likable individual. His many problems often hindered his social potential at Los Pinos High, yet his covert nighttime action spoke in an eloquent manner to the likes of Ned and Sammy and even to Isabel. But to Gabriel? Gabriel was very much distraught over his name being tagged all over the school, though he figured his best course of action was to follow Ned's insistence—to keep quiet. At least for the moment. Robertson was soon to go in front of the Disciplinary Committee. He was toying with fire.

After school the smell of paint continued to bother Gabriel. On a whim he opened the closet in his classroom—and sure enough there was the source of his room's lingering paint smell. A black dripping ¡ABRAMS! had been sprayed on the inside back wall of the closet.

Throughout the whole next day Gabriel continued to smell paint, even after school when his room felt tight with bodies. Two more students bumped in through the door, which just about doubled the size of the Poets' Circle to almost a full class. Gabriel climbed out from behind his desk and sat next to Perry. Isabel lumbered a small circle to the front and stewed in the center as the general uproar refused to yield.

"Hello!" Isabel yelled. "Does anyone have a poem?"

"What's the matter?" Perry glanced across at Isabel.

"I do," Robertson said.

"Does everybody want to come in and sit down?" Gabriel said.

Robertson stood at the front and read a long poem, steeped with a defiant tenor that referenced the accusations against him.

"'As a lie alone in a corner I sit'—I love that," Perry was complementing Robertson's poem. "It's just like that—people look at me and right away think ten things that aren't true."

"Isn't this supposed to be some sort of insurrection?" a new guy asked.

"It's a poetry group."

"Is it?" Ned said.

"Aren't we gonna bombard Fitzpatrick or something?" another new kid said.

"What's your name?" Isabel asked.

"Christopher."

"Do you even know who Robertson is?" Isabel asked.

"Who?"

"He wrote 'boom' on the bomb."

"Or they say he did."

"How many in here know Robertson?" Isabel asked.

The core group of poets raised their hands.

"So what?" Christopher said.

"This is Robertson. We're going to the Disciplina—ah ..." Isabel paused; she hadn't told anybody yet. "Well, actually ... yesterday Dr. Fitzpatrick denied our request to defend Robertson at the Disciplinary Committee meeting."

"What?"

"You're kidding."

"Lame."

"So lame," Sammy said. "They won't let us do anything."

"I didn't wanna go anyways," Tiffany said.

"Everybody should just die," Lori said.

"They'd like that," Peter said.

"Well what are we supposed to do?"

"Blow shit up, of course," Ned said.

"Yeah," laughed Christopher.

"I don't wanna hurt anybody."

"Collateral damage," Ned said.

"That's awful."

"Is it?" Ned said. "It's what's done—read the news."

"That doesn't make it right," Isabel said.

"It doesn't make it wrong either."

"You are such a nihilist."

"Thank you, Isabel," Ned said, "but I'm not a nihilist. If anybody—Lori's the nihilist."

"What's a nihilist?" Lori asked.

"Then what are you?" Isabel asked.

"Practical," Ned said.

"A nihilist is someone who cares about nothing," Perry said.

"You think hurting people is practical?" Isabel asked.

"I never said anything about hurting people," Ned said.

"But you're advocating blowing things up."

"And what would you do?" Ned said to Isabel. "Write a poem?"

"You write poems."

"For very different reasons."

"Like what?"

Ned paused. "To organize my emotions."

"And that's not the same thing?"

"There's always an excuse to do nothing," Ned said. "And as we sit and wait they defile us. Fuck I wanna blow shit up now. And so does everyone in this room—including you."

Everyone looked at Isabel.

And then to Isabel Ned said, "Am I wrong? Perry wants to. Lori does. All these people do."

"I do," Sammy said.

"Yeah, me too."

"Yeah."

"Fuck yeah."

"That's why all these new people are here," Ned said. "They're not poets."

"It's just not right," Isabel said.

"I don't care what's right. I want results. ... Drew got kicked out today."

"Kicked out of what?"

"School," Ned said.

"For what?"

"He failed out."

"You can't fail out of public school."

"Tell that to Dr. Fitzpatrick."

"Drew's not here?"

"That's awful."

"Still," Isabel said, "you can't randomly blow up wha—"

"I never said 'randomly.'"

"Isabel, he's joking," Sammy said.

"Why not focus on what we're doing now," Isabel said. "This is still about Robertson."

"No it's not."

"What about you Robertson?"

"Me? I don't know, I only know my father's gonna be at the Disciplinary Committee meeting even though he's been asked not to."

"By who?"

"If he gets custody of me, it's, that's why all this …"

"All what?"

"What's the point?" Ned said. "They're gonna do what they're gonna do. They're gonna send him to juvie or make him live with his prick father who does what? Beat you up? Writing a poem's not gonna help—it's all bullshit unless there's some repercussion, something to jar them, let them know we're also to be feared."

"That feels good," Sammy said. "Right?"

"Right."

"Remember," Gabriel said, rising up, gathering their attention, "we have to live with the consequences. People die and sometimes for the greater good, but none of us want to kill someone. In the end you may be perpetuating more wickedness than any amount of good you had hoped to accomplish. And what if in ten years you regret it? The person's still dead. You're still in prison. Yes, I definitely want the spectacle of an explosion and the immediacy of those results, but also … don't we want to be effective? Blowing stuff up seems a little unwieldy and there is no way any of us is going to do anything like that because if you were—someone in here would report you. And I'm not saying who. But I do understand your rage. I've done some pretty stupid things in my life."

"Like what?"

Gabriel chuckled.

"Yeah, Mr. A—like what?"

"Come on."

"Come on, Mr. A."

"Well," Gabriel said, finally, "once, dressed as Santa Claus on Christmas Eve, I threw a brick through a cop's windshield."

"Really?"

"You're kidding."

"Did you get caught?"

"No, but I made the ten o'clock news."

"Do you regret it?"

"Well—no. But nobody got hurt."

Gabriel was riding home after school when a young woman on a bicycle rode up next to him.

"Hi," she said, peddling.

"Hello."

They rode along together.

"I'm Hillary."

"Hi Hillary."

"Do you remember me?"

"Should I?"

"Not really. I'm Hillary Valdez. The repor—"

"—Reporter."

"Yeah."

Gabriel stopped his bike and so did she.

"Look Ms. Valdez—"

"Hillary."

"Hillary. What I did, I did for my students. And they have impressed me, so—please—don't make things harder. I just want my students to be involved, to care. And not too many people outside my classroom act as if they want that same thing."

"I definitely want what's best for our children. And our community. Can I buy you a cup of coffee?"

"I don't think so."

"A cup of tea?"

"No, no thank you."

"Have you read any of my articles?"

"No."

"I brought some." She started to dig into her shoulder bag. "Read them. You'll see I'm fair and that—"

"I'm sorry. I need to focus on my students. That's it. Any sort of attention, positive or negative, won't help."

"You're not getting this. You're a new teacher; you're not tenured. You could get fired, and it won't be any big hassle full of lawyers like it would be for a bitter, burnt-out teacher who is tenured and who shouldn't be teaching anymore. They say it takes five years for a new teacher to get it. We as a community need to support new teachers—especially ones as promising as you."

"I don't want to draw any attention to myself."

"You're already drawing attention. You're not the first person I've talked to. Did you know Dr. Fitzpatrick's getting calls from parents whose students aren't in your classes, don't even know who you are? Asking if their children get to decide to go to school or not. Dr. Fitzpatrick is hanging by a thread, she's being evaluated, she's desperate. Let me buy you a beer?"

"No thank you."

Prints of modern art crowded the walls. Above Dr. Fitzpatrick's desk the painting of *The Scream* seemed way too appropriate to Gabriel. He would have preferred to avoid Dr. Fitzpatrick, especially with his name having been sprayed all over the school, but he couldn't let it stop him from doing what he needed to do. From across her desk, Dr. Fitzpatrick glared at him, yet she allowed him to state his purpose.

"Robertson Sandoval is a member of our poetry group and the other members want to give the Disciplinary Committee a full picture of who he is, specifically because of the gravity of what he is being accused. And I agree. This will offer them a chance to be heard and may help to lend them more confidence in themselves."

"Mr. Abrams, one of your students already came to me with this same request."

"I know, but she feels you turned her down because she's my student."

"These Disciplinary Committee meetings follow a strict structure and some of the people who will be at this specific meeting don't have time for the whims of students who really have nothing to do with the issues at hand."

"I believe this is a perfect opportunity for my students to be involved in issues that do affect them."

"And how does this issue affect them?"

"It will affect one of the members of the Poets' Circle—"

"Is that what you call it?"

"Yes," Gabriel said gaining traction, "I believe if a student wants to be involved, we should encourage him. Students think they have no power and therefore drift into the background. Or worse."

"Are you threatening me?"

"No! Of course not."

"Mr. Abrams, how many years have you been teaching?"

"Well, no years really—this is my first."

"I've been in education for more than twenty. I think I may have gleaned a lesson or two that you haven't."

"I'm not saying I'm an expert, I'm just talking about my students."

"But you're also talking about the Disciplinary Committee, you're also talking about my job."

"I'm not meaning too."

"But you are."

"Well, I'm sorry, I just think my students would benefit from having a voice. I mean I think this is a metered and appropriate way for them to protest—"

"Protest?"

"Not protest, but have their voices heard."

"Mr. Abrams, do you know how busy I am? Do you know how much of my time you've consumed? Do you realize that your English classes are required, and that a student can't graduate from high school unless he passes freshmen English? Do you realize what you did is illegal? Not even mentioning the defacing of our walls, mind you."

"I'm sorry. I didn't mean to take up your time."

"That's what you're sorry for?"

"That seems appropriate."

"I could have you fired ..." She paused, waiting. "No comment? Mr. Abrams?"

"It seemed like the right thing to do at the time. And then I regretted it—but now I don't. Most every single one of my students has returned. And my classes are far more constructive because they chose to be there."

"*Most* of the students have returned?"

"All but one. Or maybe two."

"That's a failing, Mr. Abrams. You owe each and every one of your students your best. And if even one falls through the cracks—"

"I'm doing the best I can with—"

"And does that include doing my job?"

"Of course not."

"Then why do you insist?"

"I'm not insisting."

"Then stop."

"Stop what?"

"You're a troublemaker, Mr. Abrams. And that has been made oh-so clear. You're a disruption to the learning process."

"Kids can have all the geometry skills in the world and amount to nothing unless they believe in themselves."

"You have no idea how close you are."

"Close to what?"

"This close, Mr. Abrams, this close." She held her pinched fingers aloft.

Their exchange had froze into a stare-down, and Gabriel felt fire burning up inside of him.

Gabriel pulled his glare away. There was no room for a fistfight in his boss' office. Sometimes no matter how much you reason, no matter how much you protest, no matter how right and rational and clear you are you still can't change someone's mind. Gabriel's rage begged to take control and he knew it, but like the many battles in his classroom this one wasn't worth fighting. Sure, it could have been gratifying to start kicking and scratching and screaming, but this was a moment to acquiesce, and he didn't feel as if he were selling himself out or betraying his ideals for any flimsy trinket. He was doing it for his students. Gabriel didn't need to have an argument with Dr. Fitzpatrick. This was his students'—the Poets' Circle's—confrontation. They needed it and Gabriel would help them get there and in a prudent and effective manner. Gabriel didn't require permission from Dr. Fitzpatrick or any governing body to do what he believed was right. His students too. They didn't need Dr. Fitzpatrick's consent to express themselves. If we wait around for permission we'll end up delaying our lives and find ourselves old and worn-out having done nothing we set out to do.

I am mouse
 I am dust
 I am mildew
 I am letter
 In word
 On page
 In book ...

As Perry delivered the latest version of his *Tiny* poem, everyone stared at Sammy—well, not at Sammy, but at the tinfoil ball nestling next to him on his desktop. A tense smirk in his lips, Sammy sat satisfied, admiring his grapefruit-sized tinfoil orb as if it were a trophy.

Robertson, imitating a plump gangster, peeked out from beneath a black felt fedora. "What is it?" he asked, for Sammy's mysterious tinfoil bewitched them all.

And poor Perry—"That's all I got so far," he said concluding his poem, never really having their attention.

"Sammy?" Lori said.

"What?"

"What is it?"

Sammy released a giant grin: "It's an explosive-inducing endeavor."

"A what?"

"A bomb," Ned said.

"A tinfoil bomb?"

"And what are you going to do with it?" Isabel asked.

"Nothing," Sammy said.

"Nothing?"

"Then what's the use?" Ned said.

"Well, maybe."

"Maybe what?"

"Maybe I'll do something."

"A ball of tinfoil is not a bomb," Lori said.

"It's not just tinfoil."

"Then what is it?"

"Inside here," Sammy said, "are four thousand ... tightly packed ... strike-anywhere Ohio Blue Tip match heads." At the top of his fingers, he displayed the tinfoil ball. "If I throw this against anything—anything—it'll burst into flames."

Gabriel had heard enough. "Give it to me," he said standing, "give it here, right now" but—

Robertson grabbed for the tinfoil and it bounced to the floor but did not explode. It rolled up to Ned who picked it up as Sammy leapt for it. They scuffled, Ned holding it away from Sammy who was thrashing and reaching when, from behind, Robertson snatched it. Ned jerked around with Sammy on his back and Ned, Sammy, and Robertson, struggling for the tinfoil ball, spun to the floor, their force shoving desks aside and displacing poets.

In the midst of the fray an arm (Robertson's?) swung forward flinging the tinfoil ball towards the wall where it smashed, bursting into a field of flames.

Slow rippling flames. Fragile flames. Yellow flames.

The whole room stared, transfixed, the bouncing light of the fire reflected in their dry faces.

With stunned stiff joints Gabriel stared as well, shocked into paralysis as the flames began to ripen.

He had to crack himself forward as if emerging from a papier-mâché mold.

And then—all at once—Gabriel was in motion, grabbing his jacket, on his tiptoes swiping the jacket over the flames again and again until he was on his knees snuffing the last of the fire into nothing.

For a moment on his hands and knees he didn't move, except for his eyes, dazed, darting from left to right but not looking at anything at all. He was disoriented. On the ground scattered out from the baseboard were what looked like a mess of dead black bugs—the four thousand spent match heads, and off to the side the ripped apart silver shell of the tinfoil ball, its edges singed and brown. And next to it, upside down—Robertson's fedora.

Gabriel stood up, stood back. He looked at his jacket which besides a little smoke residue seemed unharmed. He didn't know what to do or what to say—in fact, he wasn't thinking about what to do or say. He was alone, looking at his wall, studying it, but there was no scathe, no burn, no nothing. Peeking closer, he did find some evidence: some singe marks at the bottom of the Wonderful World posters hanging on the wall that his students had made. Other than that—only the match heads and the tinfoil on the floor.

And the smell of sulfur.

At the sound of the applause Gabriel jerked around—the poets were clapping, shouting, but Gabriel was not about to smile, not about to accept their ovation.

"Open the window," he commanded, "open the door."

Tiffany opened the door and Perry the window and the cross breeze sent a cold chill into the room, but Gabriel's heart thumped hot in his chest, and he didn't pause for their laughter or their agitation, their exhilaration, their jostling—he tumbled right over their din—

"Do you want to kill us? Do you think that's funny, do you think that's going to change something? Why would you bring that to school?"

"I don't know," Sammy said.

"There's no time not to know. Everyone. Sit. Now. Find a seat."

They pushed and shoved for the few seats in front, and Gabriel dragged a chair right up against them, facing them. The students in back lurched over the others, pressed themselves against them—almost climbed the backs of those in front in order to get closer, to tighten the circle, and from his seat Gabriel gazed up at the dome of students above him, a seething waterfall set to crash down into a cacophony of angst and desire and fire—yes fire! Their combustible energy pierced through Gabriel, spiraling into an unruliness. He couldn't help it—he admired them, he admired the immensity of the force propelling them.

Even so Gabriel felt compelled to scold them, yet he couldn't muster his inner shrew. But still—he had to say something.

"You don't want to ruin your lives before you even get out of high school."

This felt awkward leaving Gabriel's mouth, but it was true. He didn't want their difficult high school years to plague their whole lives. They were all so anxious to become what they were figuring out they could be. Gabriel felt their vitality bouncing off the walls and banging into him. Ceasing to try to say something appropriate or wise or teacherly, he peeked up to witnessed them bustle with potential, a small smile sneaking across his lips.

List three things you do every day.
List three things you never do.
List three things you hope to do.

The first morning of spring Isabel woke up at 12:31, 2:15, 3:02, 4:32, and 5:04.

Finally, she crawled out of bed. Even felt refreshed. She couldn't wait the several hours for her bus, so she grabbed a banana and headed for the door. She walked with determination, each step encompassing a spring of excitement like little explosions throwing her feet forward. She took detours down different blocks, around the plaza, past the Indian School, knowing if she hadn't she would have been way too early for school. As she crossed Aspen, in the middle of the block between passing cars, she had to dodge a bicyclist. At first she thought it was Mr. Abrams and skipped to start to run after, but stopped. It wasn't him.

As she headed up the hill towards the campus a slow yellow school bus passed below. Out the window a voice sailed: "Poets rule!"

Isabel didn't know who it was—maybe Sammy. Her look didn't linger long. The connection was made. Anticipation reared up above the school like a tattered, determined flag, and Isabel marched into the building feeling self-possessed. This was their moment. And it wasn't just a poem. Robertson's life teetered on the precipice. The Disciplinary Committee meeting was to happen right after school.

When she looked down the hall to see if she could glance Mr. Abrams, Matthew rose up out of the morning haze. He stomped up in an instant and pushed her, pushed her hard, his right elbow pressing into her breast as he shoved her into a set of lockers. Filled with anger and imprecision, he tried to pin her there, bending his forearm into her windpipe, and Isabel battled to keep him off. She shook and twisted and lashed out.

"What do you want?" she screamed.

"Don't you dare say anything to Dr. Fitzpatrick?"

"Why would I?"

"You would."

"I have nothing to say about you."

"I should tie you in a knot and stuff you in a locker."

"What is your problem, what did I do, what have I ever done to you?"

Matthew released her, took a step back, and Isabel's fingers crawled up her body to clutch at her throat.

"Carlos told me about your meeting with Dr. Fitzpatrick."

"Lori's brother?" Isabel said. "It has nothing to do with you."

"Don't lie."

"I'm not."

"Fuck you—"

His shoulders charging again, he came at her with his fingers grabbing at her cheeks and her eyes, his elbow jabbing into her torso, his face contorted and for a split-second so close to hers.

On instinct Isabel swung away, pushing on his shoulders, and in so doing Matthew crashed against the lockers and tumbled to the floor, but he sprang right back onto his feet—now glancing down the hall in both directions to see who saw. He jerked at Isabel as if to scare her, as if to attack again, but Isabel refused to flinch.

"You think you're so special," he said.

"I know I am."

He laughed. "You're pathetic."

"*You're* pathetic."

Isabel glared at him. And then without fear she turned away, turned her back on him, and walked down the hall.

"What a loser," Isabel thought, or maybe she said it.

In her first period French class she peeked at the students beside her. She was finished with Matthew, she no longer feared him—or maybe she did, but she no longer cared. If he were to beat her bloody—fine—she would take it, she would die if need be, but she would fight back—she would never again stutter around afraid of him. In fact, she would stop thinking about him entirely, and she would start right now.

Isabel loved Gabriel's response to the Poets' Circle after Dr. Fitzpatrick denied their request to attend Robertson's Disciplinary Committee meeting:

"We go anyway," he had said.

Like a band of misfits, like a circle of insurgents, like outlaws, like a bunch of brawlers punching their way to the front, they—this tiny but growing force of nothing—were up against all the power. They would march forward into the cannonballs of their adversary's overwhelming might even if they were to be cut down to the last one of them. Ned knew the truth—this wasn't just about Robertson: this was precedence, this was the beginning of momentum; a punch into the tyrants' brick wall—this was about making that wall buckle.

In the halls between periods Isabel kept her eyes open for Mr. Abrams, but she didn't see him. Between third and fourth she strolled past his classroom and peeked in, yet she didn't see him there either—another teacher was sitting at his desk. This was curious; where was he? At lunch she sat with Lori and when she asked Lori if she had seen Mr. Abrams, Lori freaked:

"What! He's not here? We can't go without him."

When finally the last period of the day rolled around—creative writing—Isabel marched through the halls right to Mr. Abrams' classroom anxious to mingle with his encouraging energy in anticipation of their after-school encounter. But all the hope in her heart crumbled upon seeing at the front of his classroom—not Mr. Abrams, but Mrs. Callow, a math teacher. Perry told Isabel that Mr. Abrams hadn't been there all day and hadn't arranged for a substitute. Mr. Abrams' first period class, for half the period, had roughhoused outside his locked door until security arrived. Administration was informed and regular teachers were coerced into babysitting Gabriel's classes during their prep periods.

Mrs. Callow had no assignment for the creative writing class nor a desire to teach or interact at all. She asked the students what they were working on and then without waiting for an answer she told them to do it. Behind her laptop she sunk down into Gabriel's chair. The students pulled out their cellphones and notebooks and homework.

Isabel opened her journal to one of her final blank pages. Where was Mr. Abrams? Isabel glanced around the classroom and caught Perry's eye. He shrugged his big shoulders. He had nothing on his desk. He dipped down into his bag and drew out a notebook.

Where was Mr. Abrams?

Isabel felt deserted, she felt angry, she needed Mr. Abrams to be there now. His absence felt like a sin, an abandonment, an affront. Where was he? How could they go to the Disciplinary Committee meeting without him? They weren't invited; in fact, they had been denied ... twice. And once to Isabel's face. No way could Isabel lead the expanded Poets' Circle to the Student Services building without Mr. Abrams. A shudder fired up through her body. She was overheating.

Maybe Mr. Abrams had something pressing he had to do during the day and will appear after school. The bell will ring, the poets will gather, and Mr. Abrams will arrive on horseback. Isabel exhaled a gust from her chest. Pen in hand she leaned forward to write and drew a tiny black circle on the last page of her journal.

After the final bell rang Mrs. Callow made everybody leave the room. As the multitude of Los Pinos High School students marched to the exits, the poets outside Gabriel's classroom gathered in a mess around Isabel, who smiled even as her eyes reached out over their heads hoping to spot Mr. Abrams.

"Where's Mr. Abrams?"
"I don't know."
"Isn't he here?"
"He hasn't been here all day."
"That's what I heard."
"Where is he?"
"Isn't he coming?"
"I don't know."
"Isabel?"

She heard her name like a distant echo. Suddenly she felt fiery. She thought maybe Mr. Abrams was absent on purpose. That this was his ultimate lesson. Opening the cage door and giving his students the freedom to fly out and conduct themselves without supervision, without prodding—all the lessons having been imparted, now they must be put into action without a professional telling them what to do and how to do it and giving them a good grade for it. If Mr. Abrams were secretly watching, how would Isabel want to act in order to impress him? How would her very best self proceed in this ungoverned moment?

To the others it must have seemed as if Isabel were a prophet: taller than the rest, self-possessed, staring out over their heads into the haze of the ether world as if coming into the grips of some higher force, some expressed knowledge, an inspired purpose.

"Maybe he's not supposed to be here," she said in answer to their worries, still staring out over their heads.

In the hallway they were not a mob. They looked smaller, dwarfed by the now empty corridor even though they were all there, all the core members and many of the new ones and several stragglers.

Following Isabel they treaded down the hall towards the light.

No secretary at the front desk, so the group pushed up to the entrance of the conference room. Isabel paused against the closed door collecting herself as she would before performing a poem. And then she shoved open the door revealing Dr. Fitzpatrick, her face like a flicked-on light of pure panic. She sprung stiff up straight at the head of a long oval table that was surrounded by high-backed leather chairs in which sat Mr. Sheldon (a school counselor), Mrs. Sheffield (a Math teacher), a man in a suit with a badge clipped to his breast pocket (a cop), another man in a gray suit (a trustee from the Board of Education), Mr. Reade (the freshmen principal), Ms. Sandoval (Robertson's mother), and slunk down in the big chair in a corner—Robertson, whose face lit up at the poets' appearance.

Dr. Fitzpatrick's frenzied expression dimmed into irritation. "Can we—help you?" she said.

"Yes," Isabel said, feeling the agitated mob on her back. "We're here to defend Robertson."

"I, ah, this is a closed meeting—did not Mr. Abrams tell you? Is he here?" Dr. Fitzpatrick bent around to see.

"He's not," Isabel said.

"And did I not say as much to you?"

"You did, but we think it's important for our point-of-view to be heard."

"This is not the time nor the place for your antics. I'm going to have to ask you to leave."

The crowd pressed at Isabel's back, forcing her to take a step into the room as they spilt in after her.

"They're all adults in here," Ned said.

"That ain't fair," Sammy said.

"This is not a basketball game," Dr. Fitzpatrick said. "This is a Disciplinary Committee meeting."

"Still—" Isabel said.

"This is your chance—right now—to leave without further consequence." Dr. Fitzpatrick waited, the sound of the trustee scratching notes on a yellow legal pad behind her. And then—"No? ... Okay." Dr. Fitzpatrick marched to a side table and plucked up the phone. "Darlene, get security in here. Why wasn't this stopped? ... You should have, yes. Now."

"We're not trying to make trouble," Isabel said. "We just, well, we want the members of this committee to know about Robertson."

"This committee does not have the time to be wasted by your—"

"We're not wasting anybody's time," Ned said. "And if we are—*good*."

"This is a Disciplinary Committee meeting revolving around sensitive issues regarding, yes, Robertson Sandoval, but also the running of this entire institution which hosts almost two thousand students not to mention the faculty, administrators, and all the other hard-working members of our staff. This isn't exclusively about one student, and all of you crowding in here demanding we address minute grievances is not only unhelpful, but hurtful and counterproductive and I cannot stand for it—not for myself, not for the members of this committee, not for Mr. Sandoval, and not for each and every one of you—"

"No thank you."

"—whose safety is my main concern. Mr. Sandoval's schedule of dishonesty is not up for debate—your Mr. Abrams can attest to that. So if we can clear the room that would be very much appreciated."

"What is that, a speech to the superintendent?"

"Out! All of you. Now."

"We're not here to cause trouble," Isabel said.

"Your presence alone satisfies that."

"We deserve to be here," Peter said.

A security guard arrived and Dr. Fitzpatrick said, "Please escort them out." She rolled her chair on its wheels back towards the table.

"Okay, let's go," the security guard said, "come on, that's it, come on, let's go, everyone out."

But nobody moved.

The security guard seized Sammy's arm—"Don't touch me!"

The man with the badge sprang to his feet, but the trustee held his fountain pen aloft—

"Excuse me," the trustee said, placing his pen down on his pad. "I wouldn't mind hearing what they have to say."

"Oh, okay. Okay," Dr. Fitzpatrick said. "Uhm ..."

"I wanna say something," Perry said. "And I don't mean any disrespect, but this place, this place you call an institution, is still a school, and a school is supposed to be for kids, yet you've labeled Robertson and that's it and he deserves more."

"Robertson feels things deeply," Isabel said. "You experience his struggle through his words."

"Make no mistake," the trustee said, "what Robertson is accused of is serious."

"But he didn't do it," Sammy said.

"Yeah he's being railroaded."

"For all of you to accuse him," Lori said, "is just awful. Especially 'cause of what's happened to him."

"What's happened to him?"

"Let him speak."

"Yeah, speak."

"Robertson?"

"What?"

"Speak."

Robertson peeked around.

"What?"

"You have to say something."

"Now?"

With a prodding expression, Robertson's mother looked at him, her palm and fingers motioning upward to get her son to stand.

Expecting something, everyone waited, and Robertson pushed himself up from the depths of his chair. Beads of sweat like a mustache appeared under his nose. He was wearing a shirt and a tie which hung askew from his neck. The room was quiet, giving him the space to speak.

"I, uhm ..."

Robertson squeezed his fists, rubbed the tops of his thighs.

"I, uhm, uhm ..."

But that was all he seemed able to muster. His mother glared at him, but now he refused to look at her.

His mother stood up, her eyes pressed through space towards her son. "You're rubbing your thighs, Robertson—you're lying? It's a lie? You lied?"

"Mom."

"You lied?" She said, "To *me*?"

"No."

"You're still rubbing your thighs."

"Ma."

"You've been lying—to *me*."

"Fine okay but God whatever. I just wrote 'boom' on a box. I didn't mean anything by it. It was funny at the time. I didn't know she'd lockdown the whole school and call the bomb squad."

"You're lucky your so-called father's not here. He'd—"

"I'm sorry."

"You lied?" Lori said.

"I'm sorry."

"You're sorry?"

"You're sorry?"

"What?"

"What the fuck!"

"Sammy!"

"Are you serious?"

"You're kidding," Perry said. "We came in here—vouched for you."

A dark wet stain appeared in Robertson's pants below his belt, growing down his leg.

"Well that settles it." Dr. Fitzpatrick stepped forward.

"It does?"

"Does it?

"I can't believe this—we defended you."

"It's alright," Dr. Fitzpatrick said. "If we can now clear the room." To the security guard— "Sir, can you please …"

The security man spread his arms and tried to coral the students towards the door. The man with the badge tried to help, but Ned ducked under his arm.

"I don't care if he lied," Ned said. "It sucks he did, but why shouldn't he of. I would of. People like you should be mopping floors—not holding sway over our lives."

"Ned!" Mr. Reade said, standing, bumping Dr. Fitzpatrick's chair.

"That's enough," the man with the badge said.

"Enough of what?"

"Enough of this."

"I don't care if he lied either," Sammy said. "I would have."

"Me too."

"You know better than that Sammy," Mrs. Sheffield said.

"*Do I?*"

"This is completely inappropriate."

"*Is it?*"

"Please," Isabel said. "This is not meant to be rude."

"You've been given everything," Mrs. Sheffield continued, "and still—ingrates all of you—ingrates."

"Mrs. Sheffield!"

"What Mr. Reade?"

"Is *that* appropriate?"

"Is any of this?"

"We all go through this and grow up," Dr. Fitzpatrick said. "Whether it's me or the members of this committee or your parents. Growing up is not supposed to be easy."

"You act as if, as if," Lori said, "if you don't put us down you're not doing your job."

"I'm simply saying," Dr. Fitzpatrick said, "that the world is filled with ambiguity. You can't live an adult life with what you believe in as a child."

"That's stupid," Sammy said.

A student, one of the new members, was making rhythmic sounds with his mouth.

"As we are young and ready," Ned said, "you're old and invested."

"Please do not speak to me like that," Dr. Fitzpatrick said.

"Easy Ned," Mr. Sheldon said.

"Why not?" Ned said.

"Because it's disrespectful," Dr. Fitzpatrick said.

"It's the truth."

"Who told you these things?"

"I told myself."

"Did Mr. Abrams?"

"I used to love school," Sammy said, "until I met Mr. Abrams. And that's a compliment."

"I have tried to succeed," Isabel said, "and in a way you would approve of. But when we need you to be fair—more than fair but decent and understanding—you've failed us. So Robertson lied, so he wrote 'boom' on a box. Look at his life, his struggles—they mean something. Look at who he's becoming. You don't—"

"This has to stop."

"—have to extract a pound of his flesh, not for some stupid thing he did without thinking. That's what we do—we're teenagers."

"If there were a revolution tomorrow—"

"Easy Ned."

"If there were a revolution tomorrow, your life'd be over 'cause you've invested in this mess."

"At this point you are all trespassing." Dr. Fitzpatrick yanked out her cellphone and into it—"I need everybody in here, right now. ... I don't care, get them back."

Sammy stuck a finger in Dr. Fitzpatrick's face. "You should be listening a lot harder to us."

"You should be following us."

"At least acting as if you cared about us."

"'Cause you don't."

Christopher, one of the newbies, pushed a student who stumbled into another who tripped, sending a ripple like a ruckus through the horde.

"I wish I could express what Robertson does in his poetry," Isabel said, "and you want him to rot in some juvie dungeon while you let the bad ones run free because they score baskets and make you look good."

"I know you, Isabel Vasquez," Dr. Fitzpatrick said. "I know how well you've done, but I worry how a teacher like Mr. Abrams influences—"

"How can you possibly blame Mr. Abrams?"

"I'm not blaming anyone," Dr. Fitzpatrick said.

"Mr. Abrams should be principle," Sammy said.

A smiling Christopher pushed Sammy and Sammy turned around and pushed him back.

"You have no idea what kind of danger you put me in," Isabel said.

"Me?"

"Yes you."

"What possibly could you mean?" Dr. Fitzpatrick said.

"Matthew Romero."

"The basketball player?"

Two students were shoving each other and laughing and the man with the badge grappled with them. The security guard grabbed at his walkie-talkie and was shouting into it when a launched student crashed into him, sending papers off the table flying.

"You've let it start again," Isabel shouted at Dr. Fitzpatrick.

The trustee was furiously writing, Mr. Sheldon swung at the papers spiraling through the air, a bulletin board fell off the wall, and another pushed student tripped past Robertson's mother.

One of Isabel's long legs rose up then slammed down, kicking over Dr. Fitzpatrick's empty chair with such force it tumbled half across the room ramming up into Perry's shins and silencing the room.

Everybody stared at Isabel as the floating papers settled to the floor.

Glaring at Dr. Fitzpatrick, Isabel righted her frame, took a breath and then launched into her poem:

I know the feel of his fist
round my throat like a rape
I know the aimlessness
of homelessness
my feet my bed
like open sores
bleeding
and I'm running

and you
Dr. Fitzpatrick extracting
heroes as lepers
from my life

I know a rage in my bloodstream
I know broken glass coursing through my veins
and I know to get it out I cut myself

Dr. Fitzpatrick's hand rose to cover her mouth, and Isabel just kept glaring at her. Lori leaned up against Isabel, wrapped her arm around her, and in the aghast silence the stomping of many feet rushing up the stairs could be heard rupturing through the walls.

Three security guards, half in their street clothes and half in their untucked uniforms, burst into the room as Ned grabbed Christopher, who was laughing, and flung him into Perry and the security guards, upon seeing Perry clutching the twisted chair in his monstrous paws, leapt on him and his huge body collapsed over the chair and he yelped.

The man in the suit with the badge, trying to pull him off, grabbed at one of the security guards, but the force of the pile tugged him into the scrum, which knocked over Robertson and two other students. The sound of snapping wood, the chair broke beneath the weight.

Mr. Mark Abrams

The only sound in my classroom was the scratching of pencils. Bending over their desks, the students squeezed their writing utensils in their fists, scribbling into their notebooks. I crept around the room, peeking over their shoulders, a smile a hint on my lips. I love to see my students engaged. I rounded a corner of desks and a boy drew backwards in his chair and, as if a rogue wave exploded over me, he delivered a violent sneeze.

Disgusted and soaked, I froze there, holding my elbows away from my body.

My mind scurried through all the diseases with which I might have just been sprayed. I could have been angry, maybe I should have been angry, but I wasn't about to scream at this kid, though Gabriel might have, and probably more than, "Cover your mouth!" If he were here, he'd know now that the student didn't mean to sneeze. Sometimes a grossness can exit a perfectly decent teenager.

Even though my head understands that Gabriel's gone, without a body, my heart will always hope. Not a day passes that I don't imagine my classroom door swinging open, my students turning to see, and Gabriel, as alluring as he was back then, striding in with a smile as big as his head. Give Gabriel another year in the classroom and he'd have become a master.

Though my worst days as a teacher can be grueling, my best are transcendent. I feel like a blessed soul when I get to witness the bright glow of comprehension seep across a struggling student's face. That's the moment that makes all the turmoil worthwhile.

Gabriel was born on the hottest day in the middle of August, and baking hot to me is like being in Gabriel's presence. I can feel the intensity of August even in winter. It's always August to me. A touch of heat—a sweltering day, an overheated room, even a warm gush from a vent on a cold December night—brings Gabriel's spirit settling all the way down into my bones as if I were a sponge and he the warm water of the Mediterranean. I am immersed.

So emotional with all his might, Gabriel charged into that which he thought was right. He poured his full energies into his passions. But, as he came to realize, sometimes in this life sweating as much as possible won't help us accomplish the most important tasks. We need a bit of grace. We need to balance what is inside of us with what is outside of us. We need to flow down with the current of our lives, we need to be aware and smart with our energy. Because he so much wanted to succeed in the classroom, Gabriel became more metered with his effort and his emotion. And for that short time, the winds gathered behind him, but it is not a single person—even someone as wonderful as Gabriel—who can lift up a sinking continent.

It was a somber search that chilly spring day in the caves and out in the desert with the numerous students and park rangers. All the poets were there and many of Gabriel's freshmen, including Jorge,

Alejandro, and Nathan, as well as other students who weren't in any of Gabriel's classes.

It was so dark inside those caves—even with all the different flashlights darting every which way. I sat on a rock and watched the lights and listened to the voices echoing through the chambers. It wasn't peaceful, for there were too many people in these confined caverns. A high-pitched voice called out to someone, and then someone called back. And then another called out and another repeated it until voices were calling back and forth, crescendoing into a cacophony of barks and screeches and howls.

And then the sounds died down into silence and despite all the people below the earth, it was quiet. Headlamps and flashlights and cellphone lights in the distance seemed to steady as if a prayer rose up around us all.

Without Gabriel in my life, every year on his birthday—it's like, brother, I love you so much. I just want everything good I do to do for you. Or because of you. Inspired by you. Any energy in the world I feel as if it's yours. I want to do good things, I want to succeed. I want when I think of you the wind to be at my back or in my sails or puffing me up bigger than I could possibly be by myself. And every day of my life without you it is as if it is your birthday and I don't get to spend it with you, yet I think of you all day trying to send you good feelings, trying to wish you 'happy birthdays' with my thoughts. I can't even call you.

Because you're no more, there's a sense that I don't have to feel your pain any longer, that I never again have to worry that you're alright. I'll always hold close your heavenly spirit. That's helpful, I guess. I just want to know where your students go and how they have been affected by you. I want to track them through their lives, but that's just not the nature of teaching. With hope we send our students off into the world, and that hope is the knowledge of what the future holds. But I just want to see your energy in them. I guess

I sense that energy inside of me. I feel like one of your students who will never see you again yet will always be inspired by you.

In the afternoon, all the groups came out of the caves and spanned out across the desert. The search and rescue teams had us walking at a specified distance from each other. From the air we must have looked like ducks walking south in formation, and the afternoon wore on as if our webbed feet were losing strength and because of that our sense of purpose as well.

The sun sunk into the grasp of haze lingering on the horizon. A helicopter chopped through the air just above our heads. As it grew dark, our bodies staggered along, empty water bottles clenched in our fingers, a clump of eager students stumbling forward over the jagged, barren landscape.

A visual artist, Muller Davis lives in Santa Fe, NM, where he taught language arts in the public schools for five years. His two previous books—*Drag Her Out Into the Light: Art and Poems and Always Us Embracing: Poems & Drawings* are filled with weirdness and available on his website: monkeymonkeylove.com.